MURDER IN BLOOM

LIZ FIELDING

A Maybridge Murder Mystery Book 3

JOFFE
BOOKS

Joffe Books, London
www.joffebooks.com

First published in Great Britain in 2024

Cover art by Dee Dee Book Covers

ISBN: 978-1-83526-706-6

CHAPTER ONE

The rose-pink Tudor bricks of Beaumont Court glowed in the light of a sun that had not long risen over the ridge of hills to the east of Maybridge. A faint mist curled along the river, creeping over the long meadow, dewing the gleaming traction engines of the steam fair, and, on the bank, the sleeping ducks had their heads tucked under their wings.

Yesterday evening the place had been packed with workmen making last-minute tweaks to the showing rings and gymkhana arena where four days of events would take place.

Local plantsmen and flower arrangers had been putting the finishing touches to their stands. Gardeners, bakers and makers of wine, beers, cordials and every kind of preserve had arrived to lay out their produce for judging. Photographers had been hanging their pictures and parents had brought along children proudly carrying miniature gardens, flower posies, painted stones and vegetable animals to place on the display tables for the children's competition.

There were all the trappings of a classic country show, but this year, piggybacking on the success of Malvern and Tatton Park Flower Shows, the organising committee had decided to take the Maybridge Show upmarket and include several classes of show gardens.

Designers from all over the country had been working to the eleventh hour making final amendments to a whole variety of classes, from balcony gardens to the largest of the show gardens, which had a 'Back to Nature' theme. All of them were hoping to create the standard of perfection that would command a gold medal.

To add to the excitement, the show organisers had persuaded Maybridge-born celebrity gardener, Daisy Dashwood, to film her weekly show, *The Potting Shed*, in the central marquee.

It might not be Chelsea, but after the turmoil of the previous year it felt like a fresh start for local garden designer Abby Finch.

Her vision had been clear, her design accepted, and she and her Earthly Designs team had spent the last three weeks creating an abandoned quarry that looked as if it had been gradually reclaimed by nature.

She hadn't had time to worry about what the judges — or Daisy Dashwood — would make of it. When the bell had signalled that time was up the previous afternoon she had been too tired to think of anything beyond sinking her aching limbs into a warm, lavender-scented bath.

Now, though, all was quiet as she approached her garden and saw the envelope pinned to the board that said, *Abby Finch, Earthly Designs, The Old Quarry*.

Her heart was beating so hard it was making her ears ring. She reached for the envelope, then drew back.

While it was closed, it could be anything. Schrodinger's Award . . .

"What is it?" Lucy, her oldest daughter, who'd dropped her at the gate and had clearly run all the way from the car park, demanded. "What have you got?"

Abby shook her head. "I can't look. You open it."

"Mum! This is your big moment."

"Or not . . ."

Lucy rolled her eyes but took the envelope, flipped open the flap, pulled the card out halfway and held it against her chest. "You'd better sit down, Mum."

Abby swallowed.

She'd told herself that it didn't matter. She'd created the garden that was in her head. She'd poured her heart and soul into the project, shutting out everything else, and she'd told herself that she was happy with it. Nothing else mattered.

Except, of course, it did.

It was why she couldn't open the envelope. Why her heart was pounding, her mouth dry.

She ignored her daughter's suggestion and remained standing. "It's silver, isn't it?" There was a wide range of awards for the various classes at the show, from every colour of rosette to a gold medal, but a silver medal was the lowest award for a show garden.

"Would that be so bad?"

"No, no . . . It's my first show garden. I didn't expect anything else." She might have hoped for an award but she didn't have to work too hard for a smile. "I've achieved a lifetime ambition, created a garden that I'm proud of and it's been a wonderful experience."

"It's taken months of your life. You could have had a baby in the amount of time you've spent creating this," Lucy pointed out, the card still clutched to her chest as her sweeping gesture took in her mother's creation.

There was just a hint of a question in her intonation.

Now that she and Jake were living together it was a question that had been hovering at the back of her own mind — and presumably everyone else's, too.

Would he want a child of his own?

With her youngest about to move up to high school did she want to start again? The big Four-O was looming and she had a business to run.

"Mum?" Lucy prompted.

"Very nearly." Her design had been submitted the previous October — eight months ago. "But without the morning sickness and hours in labour," she joked. "Well, maybe the labour," she added, although a team of masons from Finch Properties, the company she'd inherited from her late

3

husband, had been the ones who'd extracted the stone from a long-disused part of the quarry.

And Eric Braithwaite, who'd worked on the restoration of the Victorian walled garden that was now the headquarters of Earthly Designs, had supervised the hard landscaping.

But she hadn't been idle. Sourcing the perfect trees, growing dozens of each plant and creating mats of wild meadow grass so that she could choose the one that was 'just right' on the day had consumed all of Abby's available time.

Everyone assumed that growing 'weeds' was easy. They grew well enough where you didn't want them, it was true. Getting them to perform on cue and planting them to look as if they'd been there for ever took considerably more time and skill.

She still bore the scratches from the brambles. Keeping the dandelions from spreading everywhere had required constant vigilance. Keeping their delicate seedheads perfect had required hairspray.

"So, a silver would do, but how would you feel about silver gilt?" Lucy asked.

"What?"

"I asked how you'd feel—"

Abby made a grab for the card, but Lucy whisked it out of her reach. "Now we're getting the truth."

"Lucy!" She had to be winding her up.

"Ta-da!" She whipped the card around, displaying at its centre an embossed gold medal.

"What? No . . ."

Before Abby could take in what she was seeing, Lucy had flung her arms around her, enveloping her in a hug.

"Sorry, sorry, sorry, I shouldn't have teased. We all knew you could do it. Hold up the card and I'll take a photograph to send to everyone. Jake is going to be so mad he isn't here."

"Sophie and Tom won't have their phones."

Her two younger children were away during the summer half-term break. Sophie was at Guide camp and Tom at a cricket academy, and they'd both had to surrender their phones on arrival. Lucy would be leaving almost immediately to spend the weekend with her boyfriend — and Abby's apprentice — Cal Henderson, at a music festival. The two of them had been close for almost a year. He was a lovely lad, but they were very young to be so serious.

And Jake, the high-school lover who'd dropped back into her life at the worst moment in her life and refused to drop back out again despite every encouragement, was on a business trip in Ireland. He'd wanted to put it off so that he could be with her this morning, but she'd urged him to go, knowing that she'd be working every hour until the last moment.

As it was, she'd barely had time to take out her phone and send him a photograph of her medal card before the show committee arrived with their celebrity guest, Daisy Dashwood.

Lady Hamilton, the chair of the committee, introduced her. "Daisy, this is Abby Finch, our local entry. It's her first show garden and it seems that, remarkably, she's won gold."

Daisy, wearing a flowing, pale green ankle-length dress embroidered with flowers and her famously warm smile, shook her hand. "Congratulations, Abby."

"Thank you, Miss Dashwood."

"Daisy, please," she urged. "I had a look at the show gardens yesterday evening while the judges were about their business and was completely blown away by your design. The way you've shown nature reclaiming an abandoned quarry is masterful. The water-stained stone—"

Her praise was interrupted by a series of explosive sneezes.

"I'm so sorry, the grass pollen is dreadful this year . . ." Daisy put out a hand. "My hay fever has never been—" she was caught by another sneeze — "so bad. Fay!"

The summons was peremptory and a woman who'd been standing a little apart from the group, presumably Daisy's PA, stepped forward and handed her a nasal spray.

Famously affected by hay fever, Daisy Dashwood had turned the affliction to lucrative advantage by sneezing in the television adverts of a popular over-the-counter nasal remedy, before using that winning smile to indicate her relief after a quick squirt of the bottle.

She used it now, blinking repeatedly, to clear her eyes. Fay retrieved it and handed Daisy a tissue and they all waited until she'd composed herself and turned to face the camera of the regional TV news team who were following her.

There was a moment of hesitation as she swayed slightly, putting her hand to her head as if she couldn't remember what she'd been saying. "Where was I?"

"The water-stained stone," Fay prompted.

"Oh, yes." She waved an apologetic hand. "I swear I sneeze the words right out of my brain."

Everyone laughed politely as she turned to look at the garden, inviting the camera to follow her gaze as she so often did on her television programme.

"The pioneer trees, the way the buddleia is growing out of the rock, the bramble and clematis vitalba winding around the rusting machinery and over the abandoned workman's hut, which inside is a cosy reading refuge — charming!" she added. "I love how the run-off from the wild-flower meadow at the top of the quarry has formed a pool, the use of a fallen slab of rock as a seat . . ." She turned to face the camera. "Abby has captured the 'Back to Nature' theme in a way that's both enchanting and utterly believable."

"It should be," Lady Hamilton muttered in what she imagined was *sotto voce* to the mayor. "She does own a quarry."

Not *sotto* enough.

Daisy raised an eyebrow. "I'm sorry, Katherine . . . I didn't quite catch that."

Lady Hamilton, grand dame of a dozen charitable committees, wasn't the kind of woman to blush. "The Finch family moved into property development a long time ago," she explained, "but they started quarrying stone on their farm on the far side of Hunter's Hill back in the nineteenth century. Abby inherited it all when Howard Finch died last year."

It was a bit of a sore point with Her Ladyship.

If Howard hadn't behaved so badly over the divorce settlement, dragging things out as he fought every penny, he'd have been safely married to Izzy Hamilton, Her Ladyship's glamorous daughter, and they would now be living on the Finch estate with their little baby girl.

Instead, he was entombed in the family vault beneath St Michael's church, and it had been Abby, still officially Mrs Finch when he'd been killed, who, along with his four children, had inherited the bulk of his estate.

Daisy's eyebrow's rose a touch at the introduction of such an off-note to the moment. "Of course. My father worked for Finch Developments for most of his life. I should have made the connection."

And then, belatedly, she did.

Howard Finch had been the parliamentary candidate for one of the safest seats in the country and his death had been national news. Daisy might not have been spending much time in Maybridge these days, but she couldn't have missed it.

There followed the kind of awkward moment when no one knows quite what to say but then Lucy, with her heart set on a career in PR and marketing and who until that moment had been filming the exchange on her phone, seized her moment.

"Actually, Miss Dashwood, this is not the first time you've met my mother. She's always telling us about the day you presented her with an essay prize when she was at Maybridge High."

Once! Abby had mentioned it once when it had been announced that Daisy Dashwood would be at the show, but Daisy's attention was instantly engaged.

"What was it?" she asked. "The prize."

"It was a book token, Miss Dashwood."

"Of course. Aren't they always?" She pulled a sympathetic face. "So boring."

"Not in this case," Lucy said, and Abby knew exactly what was coming. "She used it to buy a copy of your book,

First Steps in Gardening. She's brought it with her for you to sign."

What?! Abby stared open-mouthed as Lucy, a picture of innocence, produced the book from the bag slung across her body and held it out.

Daisy, no doubt thrilled at an opportunity to promote her book, took it and ignoring the rest of the committee party, who were anxious to move on to the next garden, where Quentin Latimer-Blythe would be waiting for his turn in the spotlight, waved it aloft as she smiled into the television camera.

"Isn't that just wonderful? Abby bought my book, *First Steps in Gardening*, as a child and today she's been awarded a gold medal. You must join me on *The Potting Shed* this lunchtime, Abby, and we can have a lovely chat about how you got from *First Steps in Gardening* to this."

Her gesture took in the garden behind and, not waiting for confirmation — presumably no one had ever declined such an invitation — said, "Fay darling, let Kevin know that Abby will be joining us."

"Kevin has already arranged with the show committee to have Mr Latimer-Blythe as your guest," Fay reminded her.

"Quentin?" She glanced briefly in his direction. "But Kevin knows how much I—"

"They wanted someone well known," Fay cut in quickly. "To help raise the profile of the Maybridge Show."

Daisy gave her assistant a chilling look. "A new star, inspired by me, will make a much more interesting story than trotting out someone whose garden is twenty years out of date," she said, quite loud enough for Quentin to hear. "But finding another basket chair for the set will give Kevin something more useful to do than drool over that blonde bimbo he's managed to shoehorn into my potting shed." Then, smile back in place, she waved the book at Quentin. "You won't mind if Abby joins us on the set this afternoon, will you, Quentin darling? She has such a great story . . ."

Quentin didn't look especially thrilled at the prospect but before he could speak, Daisy was again caught by a series of sneezes.

Fay relieved Daisy of the book, which she tucked in her tote bag while she searched for a pack of fresh tissues.

"Give me the spray."

"You've reached the limit," Fay said, then, with a sigh, handed it over.

Daisy used it. "Nothing seems to be working this morning." Eyes still streaming, she lifted her hand and then let it drop. "Water. I need some water. And my sunglasses. It's so bright . . . Where's my hat?"

"You said you didn't want it," Fay said.

Abby, who'd stowed her aged, scruffy but much-loved hat in the hut as part of the set dressing and was instead wearing the elegant Panama hat her close friend Megan West had given her as a gift, was concerned that Daisy didn't look well.

"Maybe you'd like to see how we've transformed the workman's hut?" Abby stood back to invite her in and give her a moment to get out of the sun, sit down and recover.

Daisy clearly relieved, said, "I'd love to."

She stepped a little unsteadily into the shade and sank into one of the chairs. Beneath her make-up she looked pale, and Abby offered her a bottle of water from the pack tucked away out of sight of anyone passing.

Fay produced Daisy's own water bottle, pale green with a daisy motif and her name. Waving it away, she accepted the one Abby was holding out to her and took a long drink.

"It's so comfortable in here," she said, "with a copy of my autobiography within reach. And a hat! Just what I need." Without waiting for an invitation, she took the aged straw hat off the table and put it on her head. "Perfect."

She remained where she was for a moment, before getting to her feet and, still a little unsteady, batted away Fay's anxious offer of her arm.

"Don't fuss. Just give me my glasses."

Fay handed them over and made to take the bottle of water, but Daisy hung on to it. "Now where was I?"

"You had just invited Abby to join you on *The Potting Shed* at lunchtime," Fay, whose expression had not changed, reminded her.

"Yes, yes. Sort it out," she said airily, before stepping back out into the sun and walking towards Quentin with the cameraman in tow. "So pretty," she gushed, barely glancing at Quentin's show garden. "Beautifully presented as always, darling, but nature tamed and put in a cage. Did you actually read the brief?"

"Oh, God . . ." Fay grabbed one of Abby's flyers from the stand, presumably to fill Daisy in on her background. "Come to the marquee about ten minutes before the show starts," she called as she raced after Daisy, apparently less concerned about her health than what she might say in front of the cameras.

CHAPTER TWO

Lady Hamilton watched Daisy's unsteady path towards the next garden. "I *know* it's early," she murmured, "but I'd say that our celebrity might have had a bracer before she joined us this morning."

"I don't think so, Katherine," Abby said. Daisy wouldn't have been the first celebrity driven by the stress of performing to reach for the bottle, but that hadn't looked like the effect of alcohol. "The grass pollen is very high. She shouldn't be out here."

"No, but I'm sure they'll edit out the wobbles when they use the footage on the local news this morning." She turned back to regard the quarry garden and, making a belated effort to be gracious after her somewhat back-handed compliment, said, "Congratulations on your medal, Abby. As you know, a well-stocked herbaceous border is more to my taste — Quentin will be staying with us this weekend. He's going to create a white border for me. In the style of Sissinghurst," she added, in case Abby didn't get the reference to Vita Sackville-West's famous garden. "We will see you at May's birthday party on Sunday?"

Her Ladyship's granddaughter, May, was Abby's god-daughter as well as half-sibling to her own children. "Yes, of course."

But Katherine Hamilton was already headed towards Quentin, arms extended. "So lovely to see you gracing our small show with your presence, Quentin. And with such an enchanting garden."

Quentin Latimer-Blythe was a well-known designer who had won gold medals with gardens at Chelsea and Hampton Court. He had made a point of telling Abby that he'd only agreed to design a garden for Maybridge as a favour to his dear friend, Lady Hamilton. *'It's a new show and they needed a name to raise the profile, my dear . . .'*

Abby hadn't bothered to tell him that the show had been a fixture since Tudor times. It was the show gardens that were new and they were all Quentin cared about.

He and Her Ladyship were clearly well acquainted and Abby wondered if the commission of the new white border had been a sweetener to get him on board.

On the other hand, places at Chelsea were limited and sponsors wanted exciting new designers, those who'd fully embraced biodiversity and whose designs would create a talking point. Daisy's comment about Quentin's garden had been barbed — no love lost there — but she was right. He had ignored the 'Back to Nature' theme by a mile.

Maybe he'd assumed that, in a small, unknown show, he didn't have to kowtow to what he considered to be a modern fad for weeds. Abby was surprised his design had been accepted, but then again, his good friend Lady Hamilton was the chair of the committee. It was a brave man or woman who could look her in the eye and say no.

However, while he clearly thought himself a cut above the other designers at the show, he'd been nothing but charming to her, a fountain of industry gossip and quick to offer the shelter of his umbrella in a sudden downpour.

He joined her once the committee had moved on, although on this occasion his smile didn't quite meet his eyes.

"Daisy was on form this morning," he said. "The drying-out session doesn't appear to have taken."

Daisy's alleged problem with alcohol had been one of his favourite items of gossip, but having witnessed their evident dislike of each other she realised that it was more than gossip. It was deeply personal.

When Abby made no comment, he shrugged. "She's looking good, considering. She's obviously had quite a bit of work done since I last saw her . . ." Then, as if catching himself, "Congratulations on your gold, Abby. Your design was certainly original and these days, if you haven't got a patch of nettles and a privy . . ." He was staring somewhat pointedly at the clump of nettles growing at the side of the workmen's hut. "And hometown advantage always helps." He didn't wait for Abby to respond but raised his Panama hat. "Time to find some breakfast before the gates open, I think. There's no day that can't be improved by a bacon sandwich, although whether I can find any coffee worth drinking . . ."

On her phone, Lucy paused her flying thumbs to watch him walk away. "That was a bit rude."

"About the coffee?"

"About Daisy. And that dig about hometown advantage. The RHS judges don't give a fig where you're born."

"He was disappointed." Abby watched him head across the showground to where the scent of bacon sizzling on the griddle at the Buttery's pop-up café was attracting a crowd.

And rude. If Quentin had assumed that because the Maybridge Show was attached to a small, if ancient, market town he would be facing a judging panel of Lady Hamilton's charity committee cronies, he'd misjudged her. Katherine Hamilton was far more ambitious than that and the RHS judges worked to strict criteria. Following the brief was on the list.

"He might be having a bad day," Lucy said, returning to her texting, "but you've got a gold medal and Daisy Dashwood has invited you to chat with her on *The Potting Shed*!"

"Nicely done, Lucy, but I'll pass."

She admired Daisy. She'd bought her autobiography for her own Christmas stocking — not that she'd had time to read it — but designing and building a show garden had been all about fulfilling a personal ambition. A silver gilt was as much as she'd hoped for. The gold medal had been the icing, the sprinkles and the candles on the cake.

Lucy looked up. "What do you mean, you'll pass?"

"I have no interest in being on television."

"Mum! Have you any idea . . . ?" Her daughter was momentarily lost for words. But only momentarily. "The legend that is Daisy Dashwood is going to tell all her devoted fans that she's the reason you won a gold medal. I can use that to promote the heck out of Earthly Designs—"

"I'm sure you can, but if I get more work, I'll have to take on more staff."

"So?"

"That's a responsibility, Lucy. More people relying on me." She'd taken on Cal as an accredited apprentice, supported by the local authority, who was now attending college one day a week, and Kate Brooks, who'd joined her part-time after Christmas, was already doing a lot more hours to cover for her in the run-up to the show. "People are struggling and if the work dries up—"

"I'm not talking about bread-and-butter garden maintenance. This is your chance to make your name as a designer. You might even get a chance at Chelsea."

"Highly unlikely. The competition is fierce." As was the cost.

"With the right publicity you might get a sponsor. And Daisy's gone off with your book," Lucy pointed out. "You could ask her to sign it for you on the show. She'd love that."

"Oh, please! I can't imagine anything more embarrassing."

"Are you sure about that?" Lucy had a stubborn look that Abby knew of old. "Her autobiography was on top of the pile of the books in the hut. I'll bet she clocked that when she was cruising the show yesterday evening."

"Don't even think about suggesting I ask her to autograph that, too."

"I already have," she replied. "It didn't get to the top by accident." Then, going in for the kill, "You'd be helpful to Daisy, too. There's been a lot of negative stuff on social media recently."

"What kind of negative stuff?"

"About her age and her drinking. James Clifton, the new guy who won gold at Chelsea last year, has taken her television presentation spot this year and there's a glamorous young gardener on her show now. The rumour is that she's being lined up to step into Daisy's shoes."

Abby stared at her daughter in astonishment. "How do you know all this?"

"Because I've been following anything and everything being said about Daisy Dashwood in the media. You don't think it was an accident that I had your book with me? All I needed was an opening and I knew she'd grab it. Her agent will be breaking their neck to get the story into the garden pages of the nationals."

Abby shook her head, but she was laughing. "My daughter, the media queen!"

"I'll be able to get you a feature in one of the gardening magazines off the back of this and don't worry about being on television. Daisy will do all the talking — just sit up straight and make sure the Earthly Designs logo is clearly visible. You can't buy this kind of publicity."

"My daughter, the media queen who isn't listening to me. I'm going to find Fay and tell her to count me out."

"What? No! She'll think you're crazy. You *are* crazy!"

"Probably," she agreed, but she could do without the media digging around to fill in her background. The most cursory online search would bring up the innuendo-laden newspaper story about the Finch family that had appeared in the *Maybridge Observer* the previous year and she could do without a re-run of it in the nationals.

"She'll tell the story whether you're there or not. After all the work you've put into your show garden are you going to let her grab all the headlines?" Lucy's frustration bubbled over. "I could spin a dozen stories out of this. You might even get Daisy to come and do a feature on the restoration of the walled garden."

Lucy knew exactly which buttons to press, Abby thought. The restoration of the walled garden had been a project from her heart and she was intensely proud of it.

"It's important, Mum."

"It's important to Daisy. I can see the headline in the gardening pages now. '*Housewife, 39, Credits Daisy Dashwood with her Success*'." If she was lucky. They could easily replace 'Housewife' with 'Tragic Widow of Murder Victim' . . . And that was just the headline. Once they started digging, they wouldn't stop — and the story wouldn't be about gardening. Lucy was eighteen now. An adult. She would have no protection from the press badgering her for her 'story'.

"Please, Mum. It's not just Daisy. This is important to me. For my career."

"Really? You're taking a gap year and then you'll have three years at Bath Spa—"

"I'm not going to waste my gap year," Lucy cut her off mid-sentence. "I've applied for an internship with a marketing company in Bath."

Abby took a breath. "You didn't think to mention it?"

"You were busy with this." She gestured towards the garden. "The competition is horrendous, Mum, and there didn't seem any point in saying anything until—"

"Until?"

"Until there was a chance. But they've looked at the stuff I've been doing for Earthly Designs on social media and the sales material I designed for Penny's home baking business and they called me yesterday. They want to see me on Tuesday at three."

"Lucy . . . That's amazing!"

"It won't just be me," she said, quickly. "They'll have had hundreds of applications. Some of them from graduates. But I've made some sort of shortlist."

"And the stunt you just pulled to get your mother on television won't hurt your chances?"

Lucy didn't have to say any more. All her hopes were written in her face.

"And if, as a result, the story about what happened to Daddy is a headline in the Sunday dreadfuls this weekend?" Abby cautioned.

"Oh, please! You think they didn't Google me? That they haven't checked out my socials? It's what everyone does. Prospective employers, flatmates, banks, boyfriends . . ."

With Lucy handling her PR, Abby didn't have to get involved with social media, but she knew how the world worked. *Was that why Cal was so easy for Lucy to be with?* she wondered. He'd been there on that awful day. He knew the whole story. More than had ever been made public. With him, Lucy would never have to explain.

"What happened to Daddy is never going to go away," Lucy said, furiously blinking back tears, "but I'm not going to let it control what I do for the rest of my life, and neither should you." She threw up her hands in the kind of dramatic gesture that Abby would have expected from Sophie, her youngest, who'd been born a drama queen. "If you can't take the publicity that goes with winning a gold medal, why did you do this?"

It was something Abby had asked herself more than once when nature seemed determined to thwart her. But from the first time she'd seen the Chelsea Flower Show on television, the glorious show gardens, she'd wanted that.

At school, at horticultural college working on her degree, it had been her dream, something to aim for — right up until the day she'd come home after graduating and realised that her mother had become too fragile to be left on her own. And there was no one else.

She'd let the job at a famous estate go, parked her dreams and gone to work for a local plant-breeding nursery and garden centre. It was there that she'd bumped into

Howard — the date she'd run out on at the school prom — and when he'd been careless with the condom, they'd set up home with her mother and she'd settled down to marriage and motherhood.

Once Howard's indiscretions had reduced their marriage to something to be maintained solely for the sake of the children, she'd started her garden design business as a way of grabbing back a little of her own identity. When the chance to enter a design for the Maybridge Show had cropped up, she hadn't hesitated.

It wasn't the colour of the medal that had driven her to seek perfection, it was her own frustrated ambition.

"I never expected to win gold, Lucy," she said. "I thought I'd be a footnote in the local paper's coverage."

"No one works as hard as you did to come second, Mum."

"It's not a contest. At least, only against yourself. There'll be more than one gold medal winner today."

"But none of them have been invited on to *The Potting Shed*," Lucy pointed out. "I did that."

"Yes, you did, and it was a brilliant wheeze," Abby conceded, just as her phone began to ring.

"That'll be Jake," Lucy said.

"No, it's Megan."

"Abby! I've just got Lucy's text. Congratulations, that's the best news. And you're going to be on *The Potting Shed* with Daisy Dashwood! You must be over the moon! Is it too late to get a ticket?"

"You can have mine." Abby looked across at her daughter. "If I'm on stage, I won't be needing it."

CHAPTER THREE

The next hour or so was crazy. Abby's build team had arrived, along with Cal and Kate Brooks who was carrying a very welcome tray of coffee cups and box of doughnuts. She was a great addition to the team.

They'd save the real celebration until they could do it properly, when Jake was home. If the weather held they'd have a barbecue in the garden with all their families and friends.

He'd texted her a load of emojis — medals, trophy cups, flowers, champagne, hearts — and a note to say that he was just going into a meeting but would call her later.

She was still grinning when Gary Jackson from the *Maybridge Observer* turned up with his camera.

"It will be great to have you on the front page with such a good news story for the town," he said.

She and Gary had crossed swords in the past, but both he and his editor knew that the increased profile of the show was important in promoting Maybridge as a great place to visit and to do business. It was all going to be good news.

"The front page?" She mock-groaned. "What'll it cost to have a few inches photoshopped off my thighs?"

He grinned. "Well, since you're offering, I've got a couple of hanging baskets that the wife's been nagging me to plant up."

"I walked right into that one," she said. "Drop them off when you're passing and Kate will sort them out for you."

"Will I need to bring the plants?"

"You will if your wife has strong ideas about what she wants in them." He looked blank. "Colour?" she prompted. Then, because she was in an incredibly good mood and it was never a bad idea to keep on the right side of the local press, "Tell her to give me a call."

Once Gary had his photographs, she saw Lucy checking her phone. She and Cal were going to a music festival where his band was playing over the weekend and it was time they were leaving.

"Are you all set?" Abby asked. "Water and food in the car in case of hold-ups?" She'd vetoed them going on Cal's elderly motorbike and loaned them her not quite so elderly Volvo estate. Not as cool as arriving on a bike, but safe and with bags of room should the heavens open and the site get flooded. "Full tank?"

"I should stay," Lucy said.

"You think I need someone to hold my hand?"

Her daughter gave an awkward little shrug. "I dropped you in it."

"Cal has a rehearsal this afternoon and you need to get away before the traffic builds up. I promise I won't let you down."

"You'll be brilliant. I've texted Megan. She's going to take pictures for me. We can all watch it on catch-up when we get home but I've sent Jake a link. He might be able to pick it up on his phone."

"He'll be in meetings."

"Yeah, yeah, yeah . . ."

"Go!"

Lucy checked an incoming message, grinned and then gave her a hug. "I love you, Mum."

* * *

Megan, Abby's best friend, and partner in the estate agency Marshall and West, arrived within minutes of the gates opening. "This is so damn exciting." She looked around. "Where's Jake?"

"He's still in Dublin," Abby said. "He wanted to put it off, but it's a big contract."

"Oh . . ." She seemed surprised, but shrugged. "And of course you told him not to be so stupid."

Abby shrugged. "He has responsibilities to his staff and I don't need anyone to hold my hand."

"Of course you don't. How long before the show starts?"

"Long enough for a cup of coffee and a look around."

Having left Kate to man the show garden, they took their time walking across the showground, looking at the stands, pausing to chat with stallholders they knew and to admire a line-up of vintage tractors.

Abby had just taken a photograph of a locally made Cretan-style pot with an eye-watering price tag to send to a client who wanted a Mediterranean-style garden, when an announcement warned *The Potting Shed* ticket holders that they had to be seated in the central marquee within five minutes.

"No one will be admitted once filming begins . . ."

"This is it," Abby said as they made their way to the huge marquee in the centre of the showground where all the major events were taking place. "I should have checked my hair."

"You look great. Just relax and imagine you're chatting to a friend."

Megan gave her a hug then headed for the entrance, while Abby walked around to the rear of the marquee, where Fay was getting the sharp edge of some man's tongue.

Tall, thin, his grey-streaked hair caught back in a ponytail, presumably this was the Kevin who'd had to find a chair for an unexpected third party.

"What do you mean, Daisy's lying down?" he demanded. "She should have been here five minutes ago."

"The sun gave her a blistering headache, Kevin. And her hay fever—"

"Hangover more likely. Poppy will have to cover for her." He looked around. "Damn it, where's she disappeared to?"

"Oh, I thought you knew. Poppy's gone to A&E."

"A&E?" It took him a moment. "She's gone to the hospital? Why?"

"It was about twenty minutes ago. I'd just come to check everything was in place on the set. She was on her phone, carrying a cup of coffee and not looking where she was going. I called out a warning but she tripped over one of the cables. The lid came off the coffee and it went all over her. I'm surprised you didn't hear her scream."

"Is she badly hurt?" he demanded.

"Well, you know how hot—"

"I have to go." He raised his voice. "Ross!" He thrust the clipboard he was holding at the man who materialised at his shoulder. "Where were you? Why the hell didn't you tell me about Poppy?"

"Your phone went to voicemail—"

"Never mind," he said, cutting him off. "Take over until I get back. As for Daisy . . ." He pointed at Fay. "There's a tent full of people who've paid good money to sit in on the recording of *The Potting Shed*. Tell her that if she isn't on stage when the titles roll, she's finished."

With that Kevin strode off towards the car park, clearly more concerned about the stand-in than his ailing star or the show he was supposed to be directing.

Fay glared after him. *If looks could kill,* Abby thought, *he'd be lying flat on the grass with a knife in his back.*

She swiftly backed out of sight before anyone realised that she had witnessed this unpleasant scene, counted to ten and walked around the corner of the marquee as if she had just arrived.

"Mrs Finch! Perfect timing," Fay exclaimed. "Ross is the assistant director — he'll sort you out with a mike while I give Daisy a call."

Ross, tall and good-looking with an untidy mop of fair curls, gave Fay a look that suggested that there was no love lost. Holding the mike, he turned to Abby. "I need to fix this to your collar."

"Oh, right."

She tilted her head to give him access to the collar of her dark green Earthly Designs polo shirt. "Daisy's not here yet?" she asked Fay, all innocence.

"Not yet." Fay said, phone to her ear. "Her hay fever makes this kind of appearance very difficult. It's why she dropped out of Chelsea this year. She didn't know about this—" a wave of her free hand took in the showground — "until the deal was done."

"The pollen count is very high. It would have been wise to stay inside until she was needed here," Abby suggested.

"I did warn her, but she does love seeing the gardens, talking to the designers and growers, and she stayed out far too long. It was really affecting her eyes and throat by the time she went back to the house. I've never seen her like that before. And then she had a nosebleed."

"Really? Is that normal? I noticed that she was having trouble with the light."

"The nosebleeds happen if she overuses the spray. I wanted to call the doctor, but she insisted that she just needed to put her feet up. Lying down did seem to help but she must have dropped off . . . Come on, Daisy, pick up . . ."

She looked calm, but Abby could see that the hand holding the phone was shaking.

"She's been under a lot of pressure lately," Fay admitted, dropping her voice. "Poppy Jensen, the one with the low-cut dresses and sultry looks who fancies herself as the Nigella Lawson of gardening has been getting a lot more screen time on the show lately and she has her eyes on the top spot."

"That's never going to happen," Abby said. "Daisy Dashwood is *The Potting Shed*."

"No one is indispensable and there have been . . ." She hesitated, glancing warily at Ross.

Curious, Abby lifted her eyebrows.

Fay shook her head. "Nothing. She's been working very hard on a number of projects and it's given Poppy the chance to push herself forward. She's got the director wrapped around her little finger. Well, you saw his reaction." Her mouth flattened into a thin line. "There's no fool like an old fool."

Abby knew how tough it was for older women on television. The temptation to have a nip and tuck to keep the lines at bay and the chin taut must be overwhelming.

Fay gave up on the phone. "I'll have to go and fetch her. Ross, tell Nadia that she'll have to stay and chat with Abby until Daisy gets here." Then to her, "Tell her about meeting Daisy for the first time and the school prize," she urged. "Show them your book. That'll hold them until Daisy arrives."

"You took it," Abby said. "My book."

"Did I?"

"You put it in your tote bag."

Fay glanced inside it. "It's not here . . . Daisy must have taken it. Seeing it today made her realise that it's time to update it. I'll make sure she brings it with her. Five minutes. Ten at the most—"

"No, wait. What about Quentin? Shouldn't he be here by now?"

He was used to appearing on television, while her only public appearances had been to give talks to local WI groups and gardening clubs.

"He's apparently been called away on an urgent family matter." She gave a huff of annoyance. "He and Daisy have never got on and she wasn't exactly tactful this morning. You were just the last straw."

Oh, cheers, Abby thought as Fay hurried across the meadow towards the house. She was sorely tempted to do the same in the opposite direction, but she'd promised Lucy.

Ross was glaring after Fay — presumably assistant directors didn't take orders from the star's PA.

It was a nightmare. No Daisy, no Poppy, no Quentin and an irritable assistant, but she was stuck with it and telling herself that Nadia Stewart, presenter of the regional lunchtime magazine programme, would do the heavy lifting, she smiled.

"It looks like it's just us, Ross."

"Yes." He found a smile in return. "Yes, of course." He fixed the battery pack to her waistband. "Have you turned off your phone?"

"No . . ." She checked for messages — mostly congratulations from clients — then turned it off just as Nadia arrived.

"Where's Daisy?" she asked.

"Delayed," Ross said. "And Quentin has been called away. This is Abby Finch, a local garden designer who won a gold medal this morning. You'll have to stay and talk with her until Daisy gets here. You'll have seen her with Daisy on the local news this morning," he prompted.

"Will I?" She called up the earlier news bulletin up on her tablet, scrolled through it, took a minute then nodded. "Oh, right, the school prize. We're just coming out of the midday news headlines and weather. Wait at the side for me to introduce you, Abby."

Having fixed a smile to her face, she went into the marquee and stepped up onto the stage to a huge round of applause.

From the side entrance Abby could see that it had been dressed to look like the set of *The Potting Shed* with a bench, garden tools, and everything that Daisy would need if she was going to do a demonstration that involved taking cuttings or dividing plants.

There were some rather splendid troughs of hydrangeas in front of the stage — maybe not that wise in view of Daisy's hay fever — and a couple of basket chairs.

"Good afternoon!" Nadia began. "Welcome to *The Potting Shed*, which is coming to you live from the Maybridge Show this lunchtime. I know you're all excited to see Daisy Dashwood and get her answers to some of the questions you've submitted in advance. She'll be with us in just a few moments. First, though, we have with us Maybridge garden designer Abby Finch, whose debut show garden was awarded a gold medal this morning. An incredible achievement, I'm sure you'll all agree, but she's been quick to credit Daisy with her success and we definitely want to hear about that, so please, give a big welcome to your own Abby Finch."

Nadia extended a hand to invite her up to the stage.

The audience, aware that a television camera was panning the marquee, took their cue from Nadia and applauded Abby as she stepped onto the stage and was waved into a seat.

"Congratulations, Abby, and thank you for taking time out to join us on *The Potting Shed* on what must be a very busy day. How does it feel to have won gold for your first show garden?"

"It's a bit of a shock, to be honest," Abby said. "I haven't quite taken it in."

Nadia smiled. "Those of us who saw Daisy on the news earlier know that she was hugely impressed with your design, Abby, but you were quick to credit her with your success. How old were you when you first met her?"

Given her cue, she trotted out the story of the school prize, doing her best to follow Lucy's instructions to sit up straight and smile.

With Nadia asking the right questions, the story emerged, but when Daisy still hadn't appeared Nadia must have had some "Keep going" instruction in her earpiece. She asked a few questions about how Abby had got from Daisy's book to a gold medal, skilfully drew out the story of her early work in the school garden and, presumably getting prompts from a researcher, went on to ask about the sensory garden Abby had designed many years ago for the local park.

"Having seen your garden," Nadia wrapped up, "I'm stunned at the way you managed to construct a mini quarry in three weeks so that it looks as if it had been there for ever. Don't miss it," she advised the audience, before picking up a card from a pile in front of her.

"Abby, while we wait for Daisy, maybe you can answer some of the many questions sent in by our audience." She looked around. "Elizabeth Carpenter from Maybridge Allotment Association?"

A woman who Abby recognised from a gardening club talk stood up.

"Good afternoon, Nadia. Good afternoon, Abby. Congratulations on your gold medal. I was going to ask Daisy how she would deal with blackfly on her runner beans. How to control them without using chemicals?"

"Good afternoon, Elizabeth," Abby said. "Did you manage to take cuttings from that beautiful Begonia Rex that you brought along to the garden club?"

"I did!" she said. "Thanks to your on-the-spot demonstration. I'm amazed that you remembered."

"I'm not great at putting names to faces," Abby said, "but I never forget a plant."

That earned her a ripple of laughter and, safe on her own ground, she said, "Let's see if I can do the job with the blackfly. I usually find a good sharp squirt from a hose pipe will shift them, or you could dilute a few drops of peppermint essential oil in water and spray the plants."

She paused, and glanced behind her at the sound of a disturbance outside the marquee.

"Is there anything else you can do?" Nadia, a professional who was evidently used to ignoring disruptions, urged her to continue.

"Removing them by hand is effective. If you can't bear squishing them with your bare fingers, wear a pair of those thin latex gloves we all bought by the hundred during the pandemic."

"Let me go!" Daisy's croaky voice reached those at the front of the audience and heads turned in the direction of the side entrance.

Something was clearly wrong and, in an attempt to keep the audience focused on her, Abby raised her voice. "Companion planting with nasturtiums, which the blackfly love, can help alleviate the problem. They distract cabbage white butterflies from your brassicas, too. They also add colour to the veg patch and you can pickle—"

"Fay! Where are you? I can't see!"

The cry was nearer now and there was a rustle as several hundred people turned in their seats to watch Daisy Dashwood stagger through the side opening that led to the stage.

She managed a few steps, reaching out her right hand, blindly searching for something or someone to support her. In her left, she was clutching a water bottle that clattered to the floor and bounced away as she pitched forward, landing face down in the grass.

CHAPTER FOUR

Abby froze. It wasn't the first time she'd been confronted with such a scene. Assailed by a nightmare rush of flashbacks, she clung to the arms of the chair, anchoring herself to the spot.

It felt like an eternity but could only have been seconds before the crash of a falling chair as audience members further back stood up, jostling to see what had happened, jerked her back to reality.

Nadia was fully occupied in cutting the live feed while the cameraman's instincts were to carry on filming and members of the audience were holding their phones aloft trying to catch footage for social media.

No one was helping Daisy and, appalled, Abby yelled at them. "Show some respect!" She pointed at the cameraman. "Call an ambulance!"

He stared at her for a moment then, coming to his senses, grabbed his phone while Abby jumped down from the stage.

"Miss Dashwood? Daisy . . . ?"

"They want to know if she's breathing," the cameraman said.

"Yes." Just about. "Tell them it looks like a heart attack." She had no idea what had happened, but she knew that would make it a priority.

Abby moved her into the recovery position while one of the stewards arrived and covered her with his jacket.

"You need to get everyone out of here," Abby told him, using her body to shield Daisy from the intrusive cameras, although it was far too late for that.

The audience would have had their phones in their hands eager to film Daisy's arrival. It would take just one person to have caught her desperate cry for help and dramatic collapse for it to be all over social media within minutes.

She didn't know if Daisy had a family, but if she did, that was not the way they should hear about what happened. And where the hell was Fay?

Abby was stroking Daisy's hair back from her forehead, murmuring reassurance about help coming when she realised that her lips were moving. She was trying to say something.

Abby bent closer. "What is it, Daisy?"

Her lips were moving but her voice was very faint. *Trick? Rick?*

Abby breathed a sigh of relief as a couple of St John's Ambulance first-aiders, on duty at the show, arrived to take charge.

"An ambulance is on its way," one said, as the other bent to check her vital signs. "What happened?"

"She was white, sweaty, having trouble seeing and unsteady on her feet. She made it into the marquee and then just keeled over."

"Was she in pain?" the first-aider asked. "Clutching at her arm or chest?"

"No, but I'm sure someone in the crowd will have it on their phone. Nadia," she called, "can you ask if anyone caught what happened on their phone? For the paramedics."

Nadia, who was apologising to the audience and assuring them of a refund, nodded, but before she could make an appeal a woman came forward to show what she'd caught on her phone.

One of the first-aiders glanced at it while the other moved Abby to one side. "Do you know if she was on any medication?"

"She uses an over-the-counter spray for hay fever. Her PA did warn her that she'd already had the maximum dose but she took some more. Would that be dangerous?"

He shook his head. "Unwise to keep using it, but it wouldn't cause this kind of collapse."

"Well, you'll need to speak to her assistant for anything else. Her name is Fay." She realised she didn't know her surname.

"Is she here?"

"No, she went back to Beaumont Court to look for Daisy. She must have missed her."

"Maybe someone could find her?"

Abby nodded.

Ross was standing outside the marquee, clearly shaken. "I tried to stop her . . . How is she?"

"Not well." Abby stepped out of the way as an ambulance drew up alongside the marquee and a couple of green-clad paramedics grabbed their bags and headed inside. "Have you seen Fay?"

Nadia appeared. "Abby . . . Thank you so much for holding the fort. You were brilliant."

"You made it easy," Abby assured her. "And the audience was very kind considering they had to make do with me wittering on instead of Daisy, who they'd paid good money to see."

"Yes, well, I heard she has a drink problem."

One of the paramedics returned for a stretcher trolley and hurried back inside.

"She's not drunk, she's ill," Abby insisted, peering past her, trying to see what was happening. "Do you have Fay's number?"

"Somewhere, but can you ask Ross? I've got ten minutes before I have to go and talk to a knitting and crochet group who've been making post box toppers for Pride Month — heaven help me — and the make-up girl has disappeared."

"All heart, that one," the cameraman muttered as he shouldered his gear and followed her.

Abby turned to Ross. "You have to find Fay. She needs to know what's happened."

"I've got to see the set cleared before the next show . . ."

"You can't do anything until they've moved Daisy," Abby said, exasperated. What on earth was the matter with the man?

"I can't leave. There's no one else here and I'm responsible for the gear. I'll give you her number."

Who did he think was going to run off with *The Potting Shed* set? Unimpressed, Abby switched on her phone, tapped in the number and let him go.

"How's Daisy?" Megan asked, the minute she caught up with her. "There's a rumour going around that she's dead."

"Sssh . . . No, she was still just about breathing when I left her."

"Then she's in good hands, but you're shaking and I'm prescribing hot, sweet tea."

"Not now. I've got to find—" Before Abby could finish, her phone pinged. "It's Lucy," she said. "I need to check."

"Are they okay?"

"Yes. She was watching the programme on her phone and saw what happened."

She quickly texted back.

I'm fine. An ambulance has arrived. Daisy's in good hands. Concentrate on having a good time. xxx

Her phone pinged again. It was Gary Jackson.

Can we talk?

Abby, realising that she would be the one the press would be desperate to talk to, muted her phone.

"Tea," Megan repeated, firmly, but the paramedics had wasted no time wheeling Daisy out of the marquee.

"Daisy!" Fay cried out, pushing her way through the crowds that were beginning to mill around, wanting to know what had happened.

"Let me through! I have to go to her—"

"Stop! Calm down!" Abby caught her before she threw herself on the stretcher. A hysterical woman was the last thing the paramedics needed right now.

Abby's sharpness seemed to get through and Fay stared at her for a moment, her expression blank. "Oh, it's you. Someone said they'd seen Daisy collapse. Were you there? Did you see what happened?"

"Daisy seemed to be in some distress," Abby said, as calmly as she could. "What the paramedics need to know is if she's on any medication. Apart from the hay fever spray."

"She was prescribed something for high blood pressure." She wasn't looking at Abby but at Daisy as the ramp was slowly raised to horizontal so that they could wheel her inside the ambulance.

"Is there any chance she might have been drinking?" Abby persisted. "It's important to be honest, Fay."

"I know what people are saying but she hasn't had a drink in months. Not since she and Patrick Farrell became partners."

The paramedic nodded to show that he'd heard and began to close the doors.

"Wait!" Fay cried. "I need to stay with her."

"It would be better if you followed us," he said with a look at Abby and the slightest shake of his head.

"Yes, we'll do that." Abby took Fay's arm and urged her away from the ambulance. "You'll be in the way," she said, gently.

The ambulance pulled away with a blip on the siren to clear the way.

"But . . ." Fay turned on her. "You don't understand!"

"Is there anyone you need to call?" she asked. "Daisy's family? You mentioned Patrick Farrell?"

Was that what Daisy had been trying to say? Patrick?

"Yes. Daisy's bought an old manor house on the river in Lower Haughton. They're converting it into a restaurant and spa hotel."

It was *that* Patrick Farrell? The hot celebrity chef? And Daisy had bought Hartford Manor?

A stunning Jacobean manor house with its own trout stream, famous for glamorous parties attended by film stars, and where Edward VIII had spent weekends with Mrs Simpson, speculation had been rife about the mysterious new owner. A Russian oligarch had been favourite, closely followed by a sheikh or a footballer.

"I'd have thought that would have been a big news story," Abby said.

Realising what in her state of agitation she'd blurted out, Fay clapped her hand over her mouth. "Oh, God, you won't say anything, will you? Daisy will kill me." She swallowed. "If Patrick doesn't get there first."

Patrick Farrell was a brilliant, if famously hot-tempered, chef who'd had a very public falling out with his backer, culminating in a fist fight that had spilled out into the street. The police had been called and the press had a field day as the physical fight had been followed by insults and accusations flung in both directions all over social media. His restaurant hadn't survived the fallout.

"Honestly," Fay pleaded, when Abby, too stunned to speak, didn't respond. "It's been kept tight under wraps."

"Well, yes, but if they're going into business together it's going to be public knowledge soon enough . . ."

The look of desperation on Fay's face stopped her.

"They're not just business partners, are they?"

Fay groaned. "They're going to launch the hotel with their wedding reception. A lifestyle magazine has paid a fortune for the exclusive rights. They're the ones insisting on the secrecy. They don't want to give their rivals a chance to get undercover photographers on the staff."

That made sense. It had happened with other celebrity couples and a relationship between Daisy Dashwood, who had to be close to sixty, with a fiery and seriously good-looking chef twenty-five years her junior would be big news in the lifestyle magazine world.

A wedding in a new venue they'd created together would be a picture editor's dream.

"Shouldn't you let him know what's happened?" Abby asked.

"He'll blame me," Fay said, clearly not relishing the thought. "I should have stayed with her." She took a breath. "But you're right. Daisy will want him with her." She fumbled in her tote bag for her phone and called up her contacts.

"It's gone straight to voicemail," she said after a moment. "He was at the cottage last night and he's probably in the garden with his headphones on. I'll have to go and tell him. I'll call a taxi."

A taxi would take fifteen or twenty minutes to arrive. "It'll be quicker if I take you." Abby turned to Megan. "I'll take a rain check on the tea. Tell Kate I'll be back as soon as I can."

CHAPTER FIVE

Weir Cottage was situated in a secluded location on Longbourne Reach, not too far from the spot where Jake's houseboat was moored.

Built from the local buff-coloured stone it was picture-book pretty with a porch covered in the first flush of pink-and-cream roses, although the rest of the front garden was neat but dull. There was no suggestion that a nationally famous gardener lived there and maybe that was the point — to maintain her privacy.

Abby had intended to simply drop Fay off, assuming that Patrick would drive her to the hospital. But when she pulled up, Fay clutched her arm. "Come in with me. Please. Patrick can be . . . unpredictable."

"He's bound to be upset," Abby said, "but this isn't your fault."

"He'll say I should have been with Daisy, and he's right. I shouldn't have left her. And he can fly off the handle at the least thing."

Fay was on edge and appeared to be frightened of Farrell's legendary temper, so, much as she welcomed the chance to see Daisy's garden, it was with mixed feelings that Abby climbed out of the van and followed Fay through the gate.

The one bright spot among the otherwise unremarkable front garden was a sleek silver sports coupé, top down, parked in front of the garage.

"Nice car," Abby said as they walked up the path.

"It was Patrick's birthday present from Daisy," Fay said, voice flat.

She unlocked the door. There was no sign of him inside and in the living room the French windows were wide open, sheer linen curtains lifting in the slight breeze.

"He'll be outside," Fay said, and Abby followed her into the garden.

On the left, screening a large vegetable garden that lay to the side of the property, a thick hedge of Rosa rugosa in full bloom ran down towards the river. At the end nearest the cottage, a gate was set into it and beyond it she caught a glimpse of the raised beds, familiar from visits by *The Potting Shed* cameras.

She would have loved to linger but Fay was hurrying down the slope of the garden to where Patrick Farrell was stretched out on a lounger, in a shady spot screened from the river by a large willow tree.

Fay had been right about the headphones, and he had his eyes closed. When he didn't hear her call his name she touched his arm to get his attention. He sat up, startled, instantly alert before he realised who it was.

"Damn it, woman . . . ! What are you doing here? Shouldn't you be with Daisy?" Catching a glimpse of Abby, he stood up, tossed the headphones on the lounger, still emitting the sound of a heavy metal track being hammered out, and said, "Who the hell are you?"

Patrick Farrell, she thought, *was a man who lived down to his reputation.*

"Abby Finch," she returned mildly. "Fay thought you'd want to know that Daisy's been taken to hospital. When you didn't answer your phone, I offered to give her a lift so that she could tell you in person."

"Hospital?" Patrick Farrell looked from her to Fay. "She was fine this morning. What happened?" he demanded, as if Daisy's collapse was somehow her fault.

He towered over Fay and she took a nervous step back. "I wasn't there but Abby saw it all."

"Where were you?"

"Ch-checking the set. To make sure there were no more nasty tricks."

He made some sort of non-committal grunt and turned to Abby, eyebrows raised, inviting an explanation. "Well?"

Abby didn't take kindly to bullying and, not far short of six feet herself, she stood her ground. "She collapsed during the filming of *The Potting Shed*, Mr Farrell. That's all I can tell you."

He let an expletive slip then turned on Fay. "You stay here."

"But I have to be—"

"The press will be on to it. There'll be all kind of rumours flying around. The least you can do for Daisy is to keep a lid on it."

He flicked open the sunglasses hooked in his breast pocket and, with them in place, strode across the garden and into the house. Neither of them spoke until they heard the throaty roar of his birthday present as he accelerated down the lane.

Fay, white-faced, blinked back tears. "God, I hate that man. Whatever Daisy sees in him . . ."

Abby might be turned off by that kind of overpowering macho posturing, but she hadn't missed the broad shoulders, the vivid blue eyes that were such a contrast to his thick mop of dark hair, the sheer physical presence of the man, and knew she was in a minority.

What Daisy saw in Patrick Farrell was pretty obvious. Attention from a fit young man would have given her a new lease of life. It would have made her feel young again, desirable. The more interesting question was what Patrick Farrell saw in a woman old enough to be his mother. She might be a national treasure with a warm smile and a natural prettiness, but she was no Joan Collins.

What she did have was the means to indulge him with a stylish sports car for his birthday and a manor house from which he could relaunch his career.

None of which, she told herself very firmly, was her business but if he went racing up to the hospital demanding to see Daisy their relationship was going be to all over the redtops by morning.

Maybe he didn't care. Maybe he thought it was time to put himself out there, declare his interest, just in case. He could be right. That shake of the head from the paramedic did not bode well.

It had been a private ambulance, hired by the show organisers to cover the health and safety requirements of their insurance. A cynic might think that Daisy's swift removal was so that she wasn't certified dead in the marquee, which would have caused all kinds of problems.

She gave herself a mental slap and told herself that Daisy was in the best possible hands. "Come on, Fay. I'll make you a cup of tea while you work out what you're going to say when the phone starts ringing."

"I just want to go to the hospital. To be near her."

"They'll be assessing her. It will be some time before they'll let you or Patrick see her. And he's right," she added. "Things are bound to get a bit hectic once the news breaks." The news cameras would be at the hospital, but the phone would be ringing off the hook. "You should take a little time to gather yourself. Have you had anything to eat today?"

Fay stared at her as if she was crazy. Clearly the idea of eating while Daisy was sick was unthinkable. She shook her head. "Just a piece of toast."

"Well, you're not going to be any use to Daisy, or Patrick for that matter, if you pass out from hunger. Let's see what we can find." Ignoring the lure of the garden, she urged Fay back inside the cottage, found her way to the kitchen and looked around for the fridge.

"The larder is through here." Fay opened a door and switched on the light.

"Wow . . ."

Abby's larder at home was little more than a walk-in cupboard but Weir Cottage had a larder at least three metres square. There were shelves filled with homemade preserves, pickles, chutneys, as well as syrups and cordials, all best kept in the dark to preserve their colour. Below them was a range of cupboards, the marble top creating a wide shelf on which lay several trays of eggs, white, brown and pale blue.

The far wall was home to a tall refrigerator and a large chest freezer and the third was taken up by a long work-top with a butler sink set into it and a dishwasher beneath. Tucked in the corner behind the door was a desk with a little MacBook Air, presumably to make notes on her recipes.

"I have larder envy," she said.

Fay smiled. "Daisy had this purpose built when the cottage was extended."

"Has she lived here long?"

"It was her family home. She moved in when her father and then her mother had to go into a care home. Dementia," she added. "Daisy was terrified that she'd get it."

"It's not hereditary," Abby said.

"No, but it's understandable . . ." Fay took a deep breath. "She was so excited about this. It was more than a larder. It was her workroom. Where she prepared and stored her preserves and pickles. All the basic raw ingredients come from the garden. Her book — *From the Garden to the Table* — is being published in the autumn. Patrick has added a few recipes to get his name on the cover." She pulled a face. "And a share of the royalties. Well, he's broke . . ."

"Just in time to coincide with the glut of vegetables in the garden," Abby said, choosing to ignore the implication that his only reason for romancing Daisy was financial. "Very smart." But with the best will in the world, there was more here than one person could possibly use. "What will she do with them all?"

"They'll be used for displays at book signings. She has the personalised blank labels printed and then writes the name of the preserve in by hand."

Fay took a jar from the shelf and handed it to Abby so that she could see.

"Daisy Dashwood's Rhubarb and Ginger Chutney . . . Not one I've come across before."

"She's very into the health-giving property of plants. Her latest project is a book about the garden as a source of medicine and skin care through the ages," Fay said. "She takes the rose hip and elderflower berry syrups in the winter to stave off colds and she makes teas from a lot of the herbs and roots. She's working with the company who are going to produce some of them commercially to sell in the spa."

"All this and the hotel, too. Where on earth does she get the energy?"

"She's leaving the renovations at the Manor to Patrick." Fay replaced the chutney on the shelf. "But Daisy has a lot of faith in organic vegetables and her herbs. She does have lovely skin."

"Yes, she does." Although it had been pale and clammy when she'd collapsed. Abby looked up. "Do you help her with this?"

"Oh, yes." It was the first time Abby had seen Fay smile. "I help with the picking and preparation."

"Not Patrick?"

"He's too grand to be her sous chef," Fay replied, her expression a mix of disgust with Patrick and pride that she was the one helping Daisy. "Although he is interested in her rose hip syrup."

"Made from Rosa rugosa hips," Abby said. "Did you know that during the Second World War, when they couldn't import citrus fruit, the government used them to provide the children with vitamin C?"

"Yes, Daisy told me about it. She swears by it to keep colds at bay. Patrick's been experimenting with it and with her elderflower and elderberry syrups for desserts. For the new restaurant."

The syrups were lined up in small glass bottles on the far shelf alongside jewel-coloured jellies and jams.

"She dries her own herbs?" Abby dried a few culinary herbs for her own use, but there were many more here. Some were in small, labelled tea caddies — lemon balm, several kinds of mint, chamomile — and some were presumably mixes that Daisy had created, labelled '*Sleep*', '*Vitality*', '*Memory*'. It would require a lot of space to produce that amount. "Where does she do it?"

Fay looked blank.

"Dry the herbs?"

"Oh, there's a drying shed in the kitchen garden. Can we get on?"

Abby, instantly remorseful, said, "I'm sorry, it's just so interesting, but you're worried about Daisy."

"Will she be all right?" Fay asked anxiously. "You were there . . ."

"Honestly, I don't know. Has she had attacks like this before?"

"Never. But it's the worst I've ever seen her with the hay fever."

"Was it just today?"

"The pollen count has been very high all this week, but today . . ." Fay wasn't actually wringing her hands, but she was close. "She shouldn't have stayed outside for so long."

"No. Let's get you something to eat so that you'll be strong for her." She didn't wait for an answer but opened the fridge and, unsurprisingly, with Patrick Farrell in the cottage, the contents were very different from what Abby kept stocked at home — the stuff required to fill a teenage boy who was always hungry and refused to stop growing.

There were some very fancy mushrooms, cheeses wrapped in waxed paper stamped with the name of a famous store in Covent Garden, and a large pack of the best quality Scottish smoked salmon.

She turned to Fay. "Do you fancy a smoked salmon sandwich?"

Fay let out a squeak of alarm. "Patrick has that flown down from Scotland. It's not for—" She stopped before she finished the sentence.

While Fay thought of herself as Daisy's friend and companion, it would appear that Patrick Farrell saw her as someone not worth his notice. Staff, a lower order of being . . . Abby wondered what it was like working in his kitchen. She hadn't much taken to Patrick Farrell on first sight and her impression of him hadn't improved.

"He's living here, then?"

"Oh, no, just weekends and the occasional night. He's spending all his time at Hartford Manor supervising the alterations and the installation of the new kitchen."

"They must be close to completion if he can spend the day sunbathing. Have you been there?"

"No. As I said, Daisy went early by herself to look at the gardens. She's prepared a design for the kitchen garden — they're planning on using as much of their own produce as possible. They're going to do gardening weekends with workshops." Fay paused, no doubt thinking about Daisy, wondering how she was. "She hasn't been there since. Because of the magazine."

"I understand that, but I thought you might have gone over there so that you could give her a progress report?"

"I did suggest it." She shrugged. "Patrick wouldn't have it. He said I'd be in the way."

And in the way at the hospital?

"He does want you to take care of things here now, but you won't last long if you're faint from hunger. Since there's a distinct lack of supermarket own-label stuff in here, I'm making an executive decision to scramble some of those pretty blue eggs to go with the smoked salmon."

"God no!" Fay was genuinely horrified. "He'll kill anyone who touches his pans."

"His pans?"

"The first weekend he stayed, he took one look at Daisy's kitchen and insisted that everything be replaced." She sighed. "He might have had a point. Some of the stuff had been here since her parents got married, although when I saw the invoice for the knives he chose . . ."

"Hundreds?"

"And the rest."

Which presumably Daisy had paid for. Which, again, was absolutely none of her business.

"Don't worry, his pans are safe from me. I spotted a microwave so all I need is a heatproof bowl and a whisk."

"Only if you'll stay and have some, too," Fay said.

"So that if Patrick makes a fuss about the salmon, you can blame me?"

"No! I wouldn't—" she began, clearly panicked.

Abby grasped her hand. "I was just joking, Fay."

"Oh . . ." Then again, "Oh . . . Of course."

Her laugh wasn't convincing and Abby gave herself another mental slap. Fay was anxious about Daisy and nervous around Farrell, who undoubtedly found her awkward twittering irritating.

"Don't worry. He'll be far too worried about Daisy to make a fuss and if he does you really can blame me. Do you want to cut some bread and lay out the salmon?" she suggested, in an effort to keep her occupied.

Leaving Fay to lay a couple of places on the breakfast bar, open the salmon and cut the bread, Abby set about whisking the eggs in between short bursts in the microwave until they were soft and creamy. At that point, since she might as well be hanged for a sheep as a lamb, she added a dollop of some double cream she'd spotted in the fridge before adding it to the plates containing the smoked salmon.

The landline hadn't rung, but Fay's mobile was lying on the breakfast bar and when it rang, Kevin Tarr's name appeared on the screen.

"*Now* he's concerned about Daisy," Fay said. "I'm letting it go to voicemail."

"He may still have been at the hospital when Daisy was brought in," Abby replied. "He might have some news."

Fay, stricken, grabbed the phone, quickly dialled up the missed call and listened for a few moments.

"Bastard!" she exclaimed and tossed the phone back on the breakfast bar. "Not so much as a sorry for leaving us all in the lurch, just 'What the hell happened? Call me.' No doubt he's worried about what the production company will say about him leaving the set to fuss over Poppy when Daisy was sick and the programme was about to go on air."

"Was it a very bad scald?"

Fay shrugged. "Bad enough. She was so busy checking her phone that she didn't notice a cable. She tripped, the lid came off her coffee and she flung it all over her neck and chest. Maybe if she'd been wearing a bit more..." She forked up some egg but paused with it halfway to her mouth. "I'm sure the prospect of getting the show to herself next week will ease the pain."

Fay was smiling, Abby realised. Not much sympathy there...

"You're not going return Kevin's call?"

"No. Let him stew."

None of her business, Abby reminded herself once again. She wasn't even sure why she was still here except that Fay didn't look as if she should be on her own. And maybe, if she was honest, there was the temptation of Daisy's kitchen garden.

The Potting Shed was sometimes filmed from there. It was packed with fruit and vegetables and an extensive collection of herbs, which Daisy would often use to prepare a tea for a guest.

They had just finished eating when the landline rang.

"That might be the press," Abby warned.

Fay shook her head. "No. This is an unlisted number. It has to be the hospital."

She was too late. The answering machine had already clicked in and an impersonal voice was inviting the caller to leave a message.

Before Fay could intercept, the beep cut in and a muffled voice said, 'Is the old witch really dead?'

CHAPTER SIX

Fay snatched up the phone. "Who are you?"

There was a moment of silence but then whoever it was hung up.

For a moment she just stood there, the receiver in her hand, her face white. "How could anyone be so vile?"

Abby put a calming hand on her arm, took the phone from her and replaced it on its stand. "Did you recognise the voice?"

Fay shook her head. "I'm not even sure if it was a man or a woman."

"It was muffled. Maybe if we listened again—"

"No!" Fay jabbed at a button. A pre-recorded voice asked if she wanted to delete the message but before she could jab at it again Abby caught her wrist.

"Let go!"

"Patrick might recognise the voice," Abby told her.

For a moment Fay resisted, then let her hand drop to her side. "Yes, of course. I wasn't thinking."

"Shall we try 1471?" Abby punched in the number but got the 'unlisted' response.

"It's always unlisted," Fay said. "What is it with people who have nothing better to do than abuse good people like Daisy?"

"That wasn't the first?"

"No, although I don't know how many recently." She lifted her shoulders in the suggestion of a shrug. "I don't stay here now." She left Abby to draw her own conclusions as to why that was.

"Has it been reported to the police? I'm pretty sure that the phone company can run an intercept."

"Daisy just brushed it off as a prank, but there's been quite a bit of abuse on social media recently. Fortunately, she leaves all that for me to deal with so she doesn't see it."

"What kind of abuse?" Abby asked, concerned. "Prank or not, you should report any threats to the police."

"There were no actual threats. It was all about her age, or that she was a drunk, or so senile that she couldn't tell a dandelion from a dahlia. Suggestions that the television people should put her on the compost heap, which I'm sure they thought was very clever. Unpleasant but not the kind of thing to bother the police with."

"Maybe not, but extremely distressing, and these things can escalate. You said earlier Daisy's number was unlisted too but whoever called knew what it was."

"A few of the television people know her number. It might even be from someone Patrick knows. He broke up with Susie Grainger, the supermodel, when he met Daisy."

"That must have stung." Abby took out her phone, did a search for the two of them.

Asked for a comment on the break-up, Susie had told a reporter that Patrick Farrell was a "mummy's boy" and that she was "only interested in grown men".

"Ouch," Abby said, holding it out for Fay to see.

"That suggests she knew."

"Yes, it does."

"So why didn't she sell the story?"

"How much money would it take to ease the humiliation of being dumped for someone who, lovely though she is, is very nearly old enough for a bus pass," Abby said. Vitriol, on the other hand, came cheap. "Maybe she confined herself to a little online trolling. Would she know this number?"

"There's no reason why she should but then the only reason she'd know about Daisy is if she'd been checking Patrick's phone. But surely it's him she's angry with?"

"Undoubtedly, but if she went after him, everyone would know it was her."

Fay thought about that, but then shook her head. "Honestly, why would she bother? She's already hooked up with that Brazilian footballer. It's more likely to be Poppy Jensen. And Kevin Tarr certainly has this number."

"That compost jibe does have the ring of a gardener about it," Abby agreed, "but surely Kevin wouldn't be stupid enough—"

"Sod this," Fay said, without warning. "I'm not hanging around here waiting for news. The press won't call here, they'll call Tessa Anderson to find out what's going on. Daisy's agent," she added, by way of explanation.

She took her mobile from her pocket, found the number in her contacts and hit the call icon. Thirty seconds later, she was rolling her eyes in annoyance before leaving a message to say that Daisy had collapsed on air and had been taken to Maybridge hospital.

That done, she looked up. "You can drop me off at the hospital on your way back to the show."

Slightly taken aback at this sudden show of assertiveness, Abby said, "Of course." She hadn't been about to leave Fay to make her own way there but cut off her dash to the front door by suggesting she shut the French windows before they left.

Fay's phone remained silent, but Abby's was pinging continuously with new messages on the drive to the hospital — no doubt the press and everyone she knew calling to find out what had happened.

She could do without any more drama in her life, so when she pulled up in the drop-off zone at the hospital entrance, fearing that Fay might lose her nerve and decide she needed a wingman to face Patrick Farrell, she said, "Give Daisy my best wishes."

She needn't have worried. Fay slipped her seat belt and clambered from the van the minute it came to a halt and, without a backward glance or a thank you, raced towards the entrance.

Abby watched as the automatic doors swished open and then closed behind her then realised that Gary Jackson was at her window.

"It's okay," he said, quickly. "I don't want anything from you."

Before she could tell him that was just as well because she didn't have anything to give him, he said, "I just wanted to give you the heads up. It hasn't been announced yet, but Daisy Dashwood died in the ambulance on the way to the hospital."

CHAPTER SEVEN

Abby said nothing.

"You don't look surprised," Gary said.

"No." There had been a number of occasions when she'd had to call an ambulance to her grandmother and then her mother, and she was familiar with the process. Temperature, oximeter, blood pressure, ECG . . . None of that had happened.

The paramedics had realised the urgency and had chosen to do all that once they had her in the ambulance and on the way to hospital. Abby wondered if they had used the defibrillator in a desperate effort to save her.

"I'm really sorry, Abby," Gary said. "She's knocked you off the front page again."

Back in December, the news that her design had been accepted by the show committee had been swept off the front page by the announcement that Daisy was going to bring *The Potting Shed* to the Maybridge Show.

She hadn't cared then and she didn't care now. The front page was the last place she wanted to be and, right at that moment, she was desperately wishing she'd followed her instincts and stayed well away from *The Potting Shed*.

"Was it her heart?" she asked.

"Is that what you thought? It's what you told the cameraman."

Bad news travels fast.

"I said that to make sure they made it a priority."

"Good thinking."

"It's just so sudden . . ." She stopped, aware that anything she said was likely to end up as a quote in the *Observer*.

"She may have had health problems that she's kept quiet about," Gary suggested. "We'll have to wait for the post-mortem. Did she say anything?" he asked, almost as an afterthought.

This time Abby gave him a hard stare and he held up his hands and backed off. "It won't just be me asking. You were there, Abby, and this is big news. There'll be a camera team here before you know it and you'll be the one every news hack will want to talk to."

She groaned. The first place they'd look for her would be at the show and Kate was standing in for her there.

Abby was on her way back to Beaumont Court, wishing she was driving something less 'look at me' than her flower-bedecked Earthly Designs van, when she realised that Gary Jackson hadn't mentioned Patrick Farrell.

No one could have missed him arriving in that sports car. Both she and Fay had assumed he was rushing to the hospital but maybe his first instinct wasn't to be with Daisy, but to leave her cottage before the press found him there.

* * *

"Thanks for holding the fort, Kate." Abby had half-expected to find her being bombarded with questions, but she was relieved that the visitors seemed to be only there for the gardens.

"I enjoyed myself," Kate said. "After this afternoon's drama there has been a lot of interest in your garden. A lot of disappointment that you weren't here," she added, wryly, "particularly from the gardening pages of the national press—" she bracketed the words 'gardening pages' with finger quotes — "who'd apparently turned out en masse to report on the show gardens."

"Plenty of digging going on?" Abby asked.

"I very nearly offered one a spade." She handed over a little pile of business cards. "I said I'd pass these on with their messages and impress on you the urgency of calling back since they all had deadlines and didn't want you to miss out on the publicity."

"How thoughtful of them."

"My words exactly, although I couldn't say when you'd have time to call them back. Not even the ones who swore they were only interested in talking to you about your gold medal."

"Stringers hotfooted here from Bath and Bristol, I imagine. I'm so sorry to have left you to deal with them."

"Don't be. It was thoroughly entertaining."

Clearly Kate had enjoyed playing the gullible assistant but Abby had no illusions about the press frenzy that would surely follow Daisy's death, especially once her relationship with Patrick Farrell became public property. Well, they weren't going to hear about it from her.

"Unfortunately, Kate, they won't be the only ones once the news breaks. I suggest we make a strategic withdrawal while the coast is clear."

"News? What happened at the hospital? How is Daisy?" she asked.

"I never made it to the hospital." Abby explained briefly what had happened. "There's been no official announcement but when I dropped off Fay, Gary Jackson told me that Daisy had died in the ambulance."

"Daisy's dead?" she said, shocked. "How would he know if it hasn't been formally announced?"

"I imagine he has a contact inside the hospital who phones him with any breaking news."

"I suppose," Kate said, "but there must be all sorts of rumours flying around in there. You know how it is when there's a celebrity involved."

"She looked terrible, Kate. She was barely breathing."

"That's awful. She was no age. Somewhere in her fifties? I suppose she must have had some underlying health issue. Heart, maybe?"

"It's possible, only . . ." She shook her head.

"What?"

"She wasn't well earlier," Abby said. "She sat in my hut for a couple of minutes to recover."

"Could it have been a stroke?" Kate suggested.

"Maybe." But Abby couldn't push the nagging doubt that had been growing ever since Fay had told her about the online trolling.

It had been quite specific. That she was too old, past it, drinking. It felt as if someone was trying to get her fired from *The Potting Shed* and there were a couple of prime candidates for that. But did they want her out of the way badly enough to do her real harm?

"Unless there's a known medical issue there'll need to be a post-mortem." Kate pointed out. "We'll have to wait for that."

As they walked towards the car park, several people they passed called out to Abby, some to congratulate her, some to ask how Daisy was doing. She either smiled and called back thanks or lifted her shoulders and shook her head. Whichever it was, she kept walking.

At last they reached Kate's car. "Do you want me to cover for you here tomorrow?" Kate asked. "It will be easier for me to fend off the press." She struck a sad pose. "I wasn't there," she said, with a dramatic sigh. "I don't know anything."

Abby laughed. "That's a kind offer but I'm expected to put in an appearance, and you need to get on with the hanging baskets. I've told Gary Jackson we'll do a couple for him, by the way. I suggested his wife get in touch about the colours."

"Ellen Jackson belongs to my book group. I'll give her a call this evening. I take it you won't be charging him?"

"One for the PR account," Abby said. "It might be a good idea to bolt the gates once you're inside to avoid being bothered. There's a message on the answering machine about the office being closed this week because of the show so feel free to ignore the phone. I'm going to grab a few clothes and stay at the houseboat for a couple of days."

"Will you be okay on your own out there?"

"The next houseboat is only a scream away and, honestly, I'm so tired I'll be lucky if I don't fall asleep with my face in a ready meal."

"Even so, it's good to have company, even if it's just for a comfort cuddle," Kate said, a little wistfully. Divorced, her children grown and flown, that had come from the heart.

* * *

Abby put the van away in her garage so that it was out of sight. Inside she tracked Patch and Princess down to where they were curled up together on Sophie's bed and gave both cats a cuddle.

"I'd take you with me, but you're both so stupid that you'd fall in the river," she told them. They stretched and followed her back down to the kitchen hoping for treats.

Not that stupid. She checked their food and water hoppers, but Lucy had filled them with enough kibble and water for a siege before she'd left.

Once sure that the animals were catered for and all the doors and windows safely locked, she filled a backpack with her laptop and enough food and clothes to keep her going for a couple of days. Jake wouldn't be back until Tuesday so she didn't bother to leave a note, just went across the road to warn her neighbours that she'd be away for a couple of days.

June had gone into town, but Beattie, who'd been watching *The Potting Shed*, greeted her with a hug. "Are you okay? I know Jake and the children are away so you can come and stay here if you need some company."

"That's very sweet of you, Beattie, but I was in the middle of it and I'm afraid there will be newsmen sniffing around so I'm going to the houseboat."

Beattie sniffed dismissively. "Reporters. Ghouls, the lot of them. How is Daisy?"

Bearing in mind Kate's warning about rumours, she said, "Not well, I'm afraid."

"No. That didn't look like a fall she was ever going to get up from, poor woman. But no busybody reporter is going to get anything from us. You cut along and don't you worry. We'll call Harry if they make a nuisance of themselves."

PC Harry Walcott had become a firm favourite with Beattie and would be welcomed with tea, cake and gossip. His only problem would be escaping.

She was halfway down the path when Beattie called, "Congratulations on the gold medal, by the way! *The Potting Shed* tickets sold out within minutes, but we managed to get some for a cooking demonstration tomorrow. We're looking forward to seeing your garden."

"Great. I'll see you then."

Cal had left his motorbike in the garage when he and Lucy took her car. It was the same one Howard had taught Abby to ride when they were dating. She put on Lucy's crash helmet and, after a couple of turns up and down the lane to get the feel of it, she discovered that it was indeed like riding a bike. You never forgot . . .

Once at the houseboat, she made the cup of tea that had been on hold for hours, then curled up on the sofa with her phone to catch up on her WhatsApp messages.

Her heart picked up a beat when she saw that there was one from Emmy Baker, the Guider running Sophie's camping trip. Canoeing and abseiling had been booked into the week and the only reason for a message was sure to be bad news . . .

Then, she laughed. It was a photograph of two rows of girls in T-shirts and shorts, each holding up a letter that read:

CONGRATULATIONS
TO SOPHIE'S MUM!

It was Sophie, with a mile-wide grin, who was holding the exclamation mark.

A message from Emmy said:

Lucy texted the news so that I could tell Sophie. Many, many congratulations from all of us. Maybe we could talk about doing something gardening related with the Guides when you have a moment?

Abby grinned. Emmy was not a woman to miss an opportunity.

Thank you, Emmy, and thank all the girls from me. I love it. I hope you're all having a great time. I'll call you next week about a project for the Day Care centre that the girls could help with. Enjoy the rest of your week.

There was no message from Tom, but Lucy probably didn't know how to get in touch with the leader of the cricket boot camp or, if she did, she'd chosen to save him the terminal embarrassment of being given the news in front of a group of lads he'd only just met.

They were all growing up.

As if to prove it, there was the promised text from Lucy confirming that they'd arrived safely and pitched their tent. She'd even sent a photograph of their handiwork.

There were a load of congratulatory texts from friends as well as one from her cousin Charlotte, who was taking a half-term break in France with her family. Lucy's texting thumb had been busy.

She sat for moment, looking out across the river, smiling as a great crested grebe swam by the window with her chicks perched on her back. And then, maybe because of Daisy's death, far too young, she found herself thinking about Sarah, Howard's mother, who'd apparently abandoned her infant son to run off with a lover nearly forty years earlier and never been heard of again.

Abby had never believed that story and she'd been so sure she'd caught a glimpse of Sarah at Howard's funeral, but despite strenuous efforts to find her, even using DNA volunteered by Lucy, there had been nothing.

Maybe it was time to accept what everyone had been telling her — that it had been her imagination filling a need for answers. Or a ghost, there to see her son laid to rest.

There was a lovely scented cream hybrid tea rose called 'Sarah', and she ordered a pot-grown one from her favourite online nursery. She'd plant it in her memory garden and leave her to rest in peace.

Meanwhile, there was no peace for her. Her phone was still pinging with disturbing rapidity. So far she'd had twenty-three missed calls and was trying to decide whether to listen or just delete the lot of them when she heard a thump on the deck above her, warning her that she had company.

It was a weekday, otherwise she'd have assumed the couple who lived in the houseboat moored alongside had heard a motorbike arriving and come out to check that it wasn't kids, bored during half-term and up to no good.

It was more likely to be an opportunist thief checking the houseboats in the hope of easy pickings. As she sprang from the sofa, intent on challenging the intruder, her eye was caught by a news app notification on her phone screen announcing the sudden death of celebrity gardener Daisy Dashwood.

Until that moment, she realised, she had longed for Kate to be right that news of her death was just a rumour circulating around the hospital.

CHAPTER EIGHT

Abby had only known Daisy Dashwood in the same way as the rest of the country, as a warm and friendly presence on the television screen, and through her books. She had always encouraged young gardeners and her enthusiasm for the quarry garden this morning had been genuine.

And she had spoken her last word right in front of her.

The click of the door sounded like a bullet through the silence of the cabin, bringing her back to the thump on the deck, and a shiver ran through her.

She was not alone.

"Abby?"

She looked up and thought she was seeing things as Jake ducked into the cabin. "Beattie saw me and told me where you were. I'm so sorry about Daisy." He took her into his arms to give her a hug and then pulled back. "Abby? You're shivering."

"You gave me a fright. What are you doing here?"

"Holding you?" he suggested and a shuddering sigh escaped her.

"I was the last person she spoke to."

He didn't speak, just gathered her up and held her until the shivering stopped, and then he leaned back and looked into her face. "I'm sorry," he repeated.

Abby frowned. "Sorry? What for?"

"For giving you a fright. I should have been there. The plan was to surprise you first thing this morning. Be there when you opened the card."

"Oh . . ."

Lucy's smile, Megan's surprise made sense. They knew.

And Abby realised that all morning, while she was celebrating, talking to Daisy, fretting about *The Potting Shed*, insisting that Jake was where he had to be, she'd been mentally holding her breath, expecting him to turn up. Because that's what he did. Appear just when he was needed most.

And he had. Not to celebrate her achievement but to be there with a hug when it was the one thing in the world that could comfort her.

"It's okay, Jake. Your timing, as always, is perfect."

"No thanks to the entire transport system."

"The plane was delayed?"

"My hire car got a flat and there was no spare. By the time I'd got that sorted and reached the airport my flight had gone and the next one was fully booked. The only seat I could get was on a much later flight to Heathrow."

"And your car is at Bristol."

"I let the train take the strain."

"Very sensible but why didn't you call me? I'd have come to Chippenham station to pick you up."

"Lucy sent me a text to let me know about your appearance on *The Potting Shed*. I was watching you on my phone and just about to discover how to deal with blackfly when my battery flashed a one per cent warning. Which was when I realised that I'd left my portable charger plugged in at the hotel."

"Idiot."

"You'll get no argument from me," he said, "but I'm here now and I have champagne, although I don't imagine you feel much like celebrating. Sit down and I'll get us both a tot of brandy and you can tell me everything."

A minute later, curled up on the sofa, the first sip of brandy warming her throat, Abby gave it to him, blow by blow. Everything from Daisy's arrival at her garden to the moment she'd collapsed, followed by her brief meeting with Patrick Farrell and, finally, Gary Jackson's warning.

"I get the impression you didn't take to Patrick Farrell."

"No, but I'm probably jumping to conclusions. He was rude and thoughtless, but he must have been worried about Daisy." Or more likely, since he didn't go to the hospital, the publicity.

"You're not getting involved?" Jake asked.

"Absolutely not." She shook her head. "Why would I?"

"Why indeed?" he replied, with just the faintest touch of irony. "It isn't as if you have a track record for poking around in unexplained deaths." The irony, no longer faint, was underlined by his raised eyebrow.

"No." She took his hand. "Honestly. There'll be a post-mortem and the coroner will decide that she had a heart attack or a stroke or an overdose of whatever was in that spray she uses or . . ."

"Ate a dodgy mushroom?" he completed for her when she stopped, realising she was doing exactly what she denied.

"Daisy wouldn't make that mistake." But then again, it might not have been a mistake. It could have been deliberate.

"But?"

"Damn it, Jake, stop reading my mind!"

"I don't need to be a mind-reader, my love, you can't help yourself. But who would want to kill Daisy Dashwood?"

"When you've been in the business for as long as she has there will be a queue of embittered people she'd stepped over on her way to the top harbouring a grudge."

"Are you saying that there's more to Daisy Dashwood than her skill with a trowel and a sweet smile? I'm shocked."

"No you're not." Abby dug her elbow into his ribs. "She was in a tough business where image is everything, although it slipped a little this morning. She was very cutting about Quentin Latimer-Blythe's garden. But then he was pretty unpleasant about her facelift."

"She's had a facelift?"

"It's tough for women on television. Lines give a man character but those close-ups are cruel on a sagging jawline. But he was pretty rude about my weeds, too."

"Really? Megan said that he'd taken something of a fancy to you."

"She was teasing. He was just being kind to a garden designer who'd clearly only got a place because she was a local woman. Or, at least, he was until his garden got a silver gilt and mine got gold."

"That must have stung."

"He implied my medal was down to an incomprehensible fad for weeds and, much nastier, home advantage. Have you had anything to eat?" she asked, desperate to forget about everything that happened after she'd opened the medal envelope. "I didn't bring much with me, but I could manage a cheese omelette."

"I'm sure it would be the best cheese omelette ever, but I'm in the mood for something more substantial. I'm going to take a shower, then I suggest we take a walk down to the Pike and Heron so that I can indulge in one of their fine steaks while you tell me what's really worrying you about Daisy Dashwood."

He didn't hang around for an argument, and while he was in the shower, Abby called Fay. Her call went straight to voicemail and she left a message offering her condolences and telling Fay — since Fay didn't appear to have any local friends she could call on — that she should get in touch if she needed anything. Or just to talk.

Ten minutes later she and Jake were walking along the towpath with a flotilla of ducks surrounded by their recently hatched ducklings, keeping pace with them in the hope of food.

"Greedy beggars," Jake said.

"You've got to make hay while the sun shines. It's what we all do," she said, thinking about Daisy's shelves stacked with herbs dried in fine weather and all the jars of preserves made from her summer fruit harvest, which would once, before supermarkets flew in fruit and vegetables year round, have been laid down for the lean months of winter.

And then there was the unseen bounty. The property, including Hartford Manor, and wealth stored in gilts and bonds for a rainy day. Daisy had no family, so who would benefit from her careful husbandry?

Jake didn't bring up her concerns about Daisy until later, when they were sitting in the garden of the Pike and Heron, surrounded by the peace and beauty of the river, sipping cold beer and waiting for their steaks to arrive.

"Okay, get it off your chest. What's worrying you about the death of Daisy Dashwood?"

"Honestly? I don't know." She shook her head as if to dislodge the unease that had settled there. "Maybe it was just the horror of it. I'd rather not talk about it. Tell me about Ireland," she urged. "I've never been. Where did you go? Did you visit a real Irish pub? There's a Japanese garden in Kildare I've always wanted to visit."

"It's green, beautiful, and yes I did go to an Irish pub. I even drank a pint of the black stuff. Sadly, I missed the Japanese garden, but we could visit it together if you come with me on my next visit."

"There's going to be a next time?"

"Contract signed," he said with a grin. "My next trip will be for business, but a visit to this garden will make it a research trip for you. I'm sure someone will ask you to create a Japanese garden for them sooner or later," he prompted, before she could make an excuse about not being able to get away because of the demands of Earthly Designs. "What we do when we're not talking business or looking at gardens is our affair."

She laughed, all thought of unexplained death forgotten. "How could a woman resist such an invitation?"

CHAPTER NINE

The *Maybridge Observer* was published every Friday, and looking at it online Abby saw that Daisy's death had come just in time to make the front page.

The story focused on her collapse in front of *The Potting Shed* audience, the dash to hospital and speculation about the reason for her death. There were expressions of shock and grief from her agent, and from Nadia Stewart.

Kevin Tarr, Poppy Jensen and the head of the production company that made *The Potting Shed* all said how wonderful she was, what a joy to work with and what a loss to everyone who loved gardening. Quentin Latimer-Blythe was apparently "deeply saddened" by the news.

There was no mention of Fay, who would be genuinely grieving. But she was one of those invisible women, eclipsed by the star she served.

There was no mention of Patrick Farrell either, so presumably he was keeping his head down. He must have had plenty of practice to have kept his relationship with Daisy under the social media radar.

The *Observer* had quotes from several people from the audience describing what happened but she was relieved to see that her own involvement has been curtailed to one brief sentence.

Local garden designer, Abby Finch, who was a guest on The Potting Shed *after her debut garden won a gold medal at the Maybridge Show yesterday, offered comfort to Daisy until medical aid arrived.*

Gary had kept her involvement to the minimum, which was generous of him, but he had a job to do. Her name was there and a quick search online would tell the press everything there was to know about her.

She could only hope that they found out about Patrick Farrell. Once that relationship was out in the open they'd lose all interest in her.

"Do you want a lift?" Jake asked, suited and booted — which in his case meant a vintage Led Zeppelin tour T-shirt, jeans and hi-tops. IT security men did not wear suits to the office.

"No thanks. I don't have to be there until the show opens at ten." Abby typed Patrick's name into the search engine to see if anything came up. "I'll take the bike."

"Don't do that. I'll send a car."

Catching the concern in his voice, she stopped focusing on the screen and looked up. "I'll be fine, Jake. Really."

He didn't look convinced. He looked as if he really wanted to tell her that he'd rather she didn't ride around on the ancient, if well-maintained and perfectly serviceable, motorbike that her late husband had once ridden to school more than twenty years ago.

Pretty much how she felt when she saw Lucy not only riding pillion behind Cal but taking the bike for a spin down the lane as he taught her to ride it. Exactly like back in the day when she and Howard had hung out in the summer-house on the Linton estate and she'd ridden the bike around the abandoned walled garden that was now the headquarters of Earthly Designs.

Maybe the answer was to buy Cal a truck. The business needed another vehicle and with some serious man-wheels he'd soon lose interest in a small motorbike.

"Abby?"

"Sorry, I was thinking. I'm going to stop on the way and check on Fay. After that I'm going home to check on the cats and pick up my van."

"Do you want to eat out tonight? We should do something, no matter how quiet, to celebrate your gold medal."

"We'll have a party for the whole team when it's all done and dusted." It wasn't just building the garden. Once the show was over it had to be dismantled and the grounds of Beaumont Court returned to their original state. "Let's open that bottle of champagne here," she suggested, "and I'll cook. What do you fancy?"

"I fancy you." He leaned in for a lingering kiss that, but for a toot from the waiting taxi, might have become something else. "Sadly, I have to go into the office and deal with the paperwork for the new contract."

He held her close for a moment, his hand tangled in her hair, looking deep into her eyes and with his lips a breath from hers said, "Don't forget the lifesavers when you're out on that bike." He kissed her again, leaving her too breathless to answer as he took a step back and headed up to the deck.

It was rare for her to be able to spend a night on the houseboat alone with Jake and she smiled at the creak on the little wooden bridge to the bank, at the "good morning" called out to his neighbours on the houseboat moored next to them, and the slam of the car door and sound of the engine getting fainter as it headed down the lane. Intimate morning sounds so different from the mornings at home that always seemed to teeter on the edge of chaos, although that was going to change.

Lucy would be done with school in a couple of weeks and once Sophie broke up for the summer, the morning school run would be history. Come September her little girl would be taking the school bus to Maybridge High. And

Tom was desperate to buy himself a motorbike and ride to school, just as his dad had done at sixteen.

The thought terrified her and, in that moment, she caught a glimpse of what Jake had felt when she'd insisted on riding that same bike this morning. It was the feeling she had whenever she waved him off to the airport, remembering the time he kissed her goodbye on the doorstep and hadn't come back for twenty years.

Mostly it was just part of the background hum of daily life but then, out of the blue, you were confronted with the fragility of life and a sharp pinprick of fear became focused on those most precious to you.

For a moment she thought about her children, all away doing something they loved, then made an effort to concentrate on what she should be doing. But, Fay, alone in the cottage, was on her mind.

She was surprised not to have heard from her. She'd been totally involved in Daisy's life, very protective of her, and now that was all gone.

Out of curiosity, she took a look at social media to see exactly what unpleasantness had been flung at Daisy. It was pretty much as Fay had said but was so clearly an orchestrated campaign to undermine her that anyone with half a brain cell should have been able to see through it. Maybe most people did, but with her death the hashtag #daisydeaddrunk had gone viral.

Nauseated, she closed her laptop and went to take a shower.

She was drying her hair when her phone rang.

"Fay . . . ?"

"Is it okay to call? You must be busy only you did say—" Her words came out all in rush. "And I wanted to thank you for your message last night. It made me feel less alone."

"You should have called if you needed someone to talk to," Abby said.

"That's kind of you but I didn't want to speak to anyone yesterday." Her voice broke on a sob.

"Fay, where are you now?"

"I called a taxi from the hospital and came back to the cottage."

"A taxi? Didn't someone from *The Potting Shed* offer you a lift?" Surely someone must have been there.

"I didn't see anyone," she said. "Patrick wasn't there, but that was a relief to be honest and he didn't come back here. This is the place Daisy loved most and I wanted to be surrounded by her. To feel her presence."

So, she'd been right about Farrell, but no matter what his true feelings were, Daisy's death must have thrown the whole Hartford Manor project into doubt, so would he have gone there? There must be ongoing work. He wouldn't turn to Fay; he must know what she thought of him. Not that he would care a fig about that.

No, Fay worked for Daisy and that begged the question, what was going to happen to her now?

What were your rights when your employer died? Did you get paid a month's salary in lieu of notice and that was that? Harsh but highly likely unless Daisy had made some provision for her.

She would have to talk to her own accountant and make sure there was something in place to protect her employees.

But first, Fay.

"You're on your own?" Abby asked. "Is there someone you could call to be with you?"

"I don't want anyone. I probably shouldn't be here. I always used to stay with Daisy when we were working down here, but of course, once Patrick came on the scene . . ."

Patrick Farrell's arrival in Daisy's life had obviously been Fay's worst nightmare but despite her own instinctive dislike of the man, she could understand why he wouldn't want Fay getting under his feet as she fussed around Daisy.

"It was a new relationship," she said, gently. "They would have wanted to be on their own."

"I understood that." There was another loud sniff. "Of course she was making the biggest mistake of her life. I tried

67

to tell her but she shut me down so fast that I didn't go there again."

There were moments when silence was the only response. This was one of them.

"It's not only men who get their head turned," Fay continued, no doubt referring to Kevin Tarr's obsession with Poppy. "Anyone with two brain cells to rub together could see that his only interest in Daisy was her money."

Pretty much her own thought, but Abby knew better than to say anything that could come back to bite her. "Where's your home, Fay?" she asked.

"What? Oh, right . . . I stay in an Airbnb now when Daisy needs me in Maybridge. It's very comfortable but I couldn't stay there last night. I picked up my things and came here."

"I understand, but I meant your actual home. Where do you live?"

"Oh, I see what you mean. I've got a flat in the basement of Daisy's London house. She had it converted for me so that I'd always be on hand when she needed me." There was a gulp that suggested tears were now flowing freely. "Daisy took out a mortgage on the house to help pay for the Manor. I suppose it will have to be sold now. And the cottage—" Another sob — "She always promised she would look after me, but I know she'd made a new will . . ."

Abby's heart went out to her. Fay had not only lost a woman she was strongly attached to, but her job, and almost certainly her home.

"Who will inherit, do you know? Did Daisy have family?"

"There was a cousin living in Spain. She was married to a local man, older than her with children from a previous marriage. Daisy was convinced he'd only married her because it was cheaper than employing a housekeeper and nanny. And there was always some excuse about why she couldn't come and visit Daisy over here. Daisy left her well provided for, but the money was hedged around in a trust so that her husband couldn't get at it."

"She really didn't trust him."

"No. But she died last year and I know Daisy changed her will then."

In favour of Patrick? How long had they been an item?

"Look, Fay, I have to go into the show," she said, "but I'm quite near you and I could call in on my way for a few minutes."

"No!"

Abby blinked at this instant refusal, but before she could respond, Fay said, "Sorry, that didn't come out right. I'd love to see you, but there's a television van parked outside."

"Are they bothering you?"

"They knocked, but I didn't answer. Maybe someone spotted Patrick at the hospital and they're sniffing for a story. If you come they'll know there's someone here," Fay said. "They'll be outside Daisy's London house, too. It was the same when someone started a wicked rumour that she was drying out in the Priory."

"That wasn't true? Why didn't she put in an appearance and deny it?"

"She was having some work done on her face."

"Oh . . . She'd rather people thought she was a drunk than vain?"

"No!" Fay swallowed. "No. She took the comments about her age to heart and Tessa Anderson suggested it. She's been Daisy's agent for the last fifteen years." She sighed. "Television can be so cruel."

"To women," Abby agreed. "No one seems to care if the men have grey hair and wrinkles."

"Tessa fixed it all up with a clinic in Switzerland and they went to stay in her cottage in France until all evidence of the surgery was gone. They're very good friends," she added.

"Did you go with her?" Abby asked. "To Switzerland? Or to France?"

"No. Daisy said I deserved a holiday from her cranky ways and she booked me on a cruise around the Greek islands."

"How kind of her."

"Yes, it was lovely, but that was when Daisy met Patrick Farrell," Fay continued. "Tessa is his agent, too, and she wanted to talk to him about what he was going to do next, so he drove down there. He was only supposed to be there for a couple of days but he stayed on and drove Daisy home. He was here when I got back."

That was interesting but, aware that it was a touchy subject, Abby didn't pursue it. She got back to the reason for her call.

"The news people will soon move on to another story, but it might be a good idea to get in touch with Daisy's solicitors. I imagine they won't want the cottage left empty."

"I'll do that." Fay sounded marginally brighter. "They might want me to stay on as a caretaker until probate is granted — that can take months."

"Possibly." Abby wasn't going to encourage any hopes in that direction. If Patrick Farrell inherited, it was likely that he'd want her out of both houses without delay. Or could Daisy's long-time agent and friend, Tessa Anderson, be a beneficiary? Whoever it was wouldn't want Fay getting settled.

"Did Daisy ever say how she was planning to look after you?" Abby asked.

"She said that I wasn't to worry, I'd be all right."

"Then I'm sure you will be and if you need anything in the meantime—"

"Actually, since you're going into the show and I'm stuck here, would you mind picking up Daisy's things from Beaumont Court? It's not much — a change of clothes, her handbag. Your book will be there, too. I feel so bad about that. I'll ring the show office and let them know," she added, not waiting for a reply.

"What do you want me to do with them?"

"Bring them to the cottage. I'm sure the television people will have given up by this afternoon."

Aware that she'd brought it on herself, she had little choice but to agree.

Once she'd ended the call, she switched her attention to the local television news. Unsurprisingly, Daisy's unexplained death was still headlining. There was someone reporting from outside the hospital, talking about her long-running problems with hay fever and then questioning a medical expert via a zoom link on whether it could have been a contributory factor.

While admitting that any severe allergy, including an acute attack of hay fever could, in extreme cases, cause the victim to go into shock and die, the expert thought it unlikely unless there was an undiagnosed underlying medical condition.

Questioned on the symptoms, he suggested that they would resemble flu or pneumonia.

Daisy had complained of a headache, appeared to have some trouble swallowing and a sensitivity to light along with a severe bout of sneezing. On the other hand, her chest hadn't been congested, her nose hadn't been blocked — although the spray might have dealt with that — and she hadn't appeared feverish.

But this was typical air-filling time when there was nothing new to report.

When the presenter asked the doctor if Daisy's reported problems with alcohol might have had any bearing on her death, Abby, disgusted, switched off.

CHAPTER TEN

Arriving at Beaumont Court, Abby stopped at the east wing to check in with Major Clive Elliott, the show secretary.

"Mrs Finch." He rose to his feet. "Fay Bingley called to let me know you'd be stopping by to pick up Miss Dashwood's belongings. It's been such a shock for everyone. More so for you," he added, "but the way you leapt to Miss Dashwood's aid was magnificent."

Abby did a mental eye-roll but said, "It's very sad. Daisy was no age and she's always been such a live wire on the television."

"My wife is a huge fan," he said. "I noticed that Miss Dashwood didn't look at all well when she returned from her tour of the show. I asked if there was anything she needed but her assistant said that she just needed to put her feet up for a while."

"Did she?" Abby was surprised by that. Fay had told her she'd wanted to call a doctor.

"To be honest, I was concerned that Miss Dashwood was on her own when she left here just before the television broadcast was due to start. She was very pale and didn't look quite . . ." He searched for an appropriate word. "Steady?"

Abby had seen how unsteady she was but ignored his invitation to speculate on whether Daisy had been drinking. "She was suffering very badly from hay fever when I saw her. It must have been quite a strain for her to keep going when the pollen was so bad. I believe she made a point of visiting everyone?"

He shifted awkwardly. "Yes, very dedicated . . ."

"She didn't say anything? Before she left?"

Clive Elliott shook his head. "Not to me. I did call out to her, but I don't think she heard me, and then the phone rang and I had to answer it. That woman of hers normally sticks to her like glue, but she'd gone off somewhere."

"She was in the marquee, checking that everything was as it should be. It seems that there have been a few mishaps recently. Gremlins messing with props."

"That was nothing to do with the show organisers," he said, immediately on the defensive. "Of course the insurance company requires us to have a paramedic team on standby. People fall over things, overdo it in the heat. That's why help arrived so soon."

His relief that Daisy hadn't died in the marquee was understandable. If she'd died in there, where other events were booked to take place, it would have seriously messed with the programme. As it was, once she was aboard the ambulance and on her way, things were able to go on pretty much as scheduled.

"I know how busy you are, Major. If you could show me the room Daisy was using?"

"Yes, of course. This is very good of you." He took a key from the desk of his drawer. "I locked it as soon as we knew Miss Dashwood was . . . that she wouldn't be coming back, but I do need the room for other guests. Today's celebrity, that potter fellow, will be here soon and I thought I'd have to put him in the green room, but now the cleaner will be able to get in before he arrives."

He led the way to the end of the flag-stoned corridor and unlocked the door to a small sitting room.

"It used to be the housekeeper's sitting room, but now this wing is used for events and the room has been converted for VIP guests. There's a small kitchen area for making hot drinks and a private bathroom. Can you manage? I can't leave the office unattended."

"Yes, of course."

"No need to lock up when you're done. I'll give the cleaning staff a call to let them know they can get in."

With that he hurried away and Abby took a look around.

The room was not large but there was a small area with a sink, kettle, a coffee machine in one corner and a small fridge under the work surface. It was comfortably furnished with a chintz sofa with cushions, easily large enough for Daisy to put her feet up.

Under a window looking out over the car park was a table that could be used as a desk. The chair had a cream linen jacket draped over the back. Abby's old hat was on the seat and she rolled it and tucked it into her own tote slung across her shoulder.

The dress that Daisy had been wearing was on a hanger hooked behind the door. It had stains down the front — something rust coloured, no doubt blood from her nosebleed.

She'd been wearing an identical dress when she'd staggered into the marquee so presumably she carried a spare with her in case it got marked during filming. Easily done when you were handling plants and compost.

The bathroom had a walk-in shower and toilet at one end and a large vanity unit with a mirror and basin, providing plenty of room for the expensive designer handbag lying on its side, the contents spilling onto the surface and the floor.

Her phone had fallen among a number of nasal sprays that looked as if they had been flung away with some force, as if Daisy had been trying them one after the other in a desperate attempt to get some relief.

Did the effect wear off if you'd been using it for a long time?

Or if you overused it?

Fay had warned her . . .

She bent to gather them up and returned them to the hand-bag along with a card wallet, a comb and a small make-up bag. She glanced around to make sure she hadn't missed anything.

There was a suitcase beside the table, which must have contained the spare dress.

She picked it up, put it on the sofa and opened it. There was nothing in it but a few sheets of tissue paper and an empty shoe bag.

Having checked the pockets of the jacket for anything that might cause a stain, and finding nothing but a small linen handkerchief, she folded it carefully and put it in the case. She covered it with a layer of tissue paper and then did the same with the dress.

A pair of plain, high-heeled court shoes that exactly matched the shade of her dress stood beside the door, ready to be put on as she left the room. Daisy had been wearing a pair of flat walking shoes for her tour of the gardens and presumably these shoes were for the television appearance, but she'd still been wearing the flats when she arrived at the marquee.

Because Fay wasn't there to help her, or because she didn't feel steady enough to walk in them? Or, maybe, she had just forgotten to change.

Abby tucked the shoes into the bag and added them to the case along with the handbag.

There was a fine bone china mug on the table that she recognised from the kitchen in Weir Cottage. It was empty but for the faint discoloration to show that it had been used for some kind of herbal tea.

She sniffed it, wondering what herb Daisy had used. Mint? Something else that she didn't recognise . . . She swilled it out at the sink, dried it on a paper towel and tucked it, for safety, between the dress and jacket in the suitcase.

There was only an unopened carton of milk and some unopened bottles of water in the fridge, no doubt supplied by the Beaumont Court events team.

She looked around for the book that had got her into this situation in the first place and finally found it where it had slipped between the arm of the sofa and the wall, standing upright and open.

Interested to see what Daisy had been looking at, Abby turned it over. Daisy hadn't just been looking. She'd been scribbling in the margins.

Torn between annoyance at such a cavalier attitude to someone else's property and interest in what she'd been planning, Abby snapped it shut and added it to her bag to look at later. If she'd been writing there must be a pen somewhere and, doubting that Daisy used the kind of pen you bought in a pack of ten at the supermarket, she got down on her knees to look under the sofa.

She spotted a glint of gold and her fingers touched it, but only to push it further under. After a fruitless grope, she pulled the sofa out.

The pen was a black-and-gold Montblanc rollerball. Sleek, beautiful and very expensive. She picked up yet another discarded spray that had rolled under the sofa and a lipstick.

She dropped them all in her bag, pushed the sofa back in its place and, having brushed the dust from the knees of her trousers, picked up the suitcase and returned to the office.

Clive Elliott's door was shut although the green room set aside for visitors was empty. It was still early, the gates not yet open to the public.

She reached her show garden, stowed the suitcase out of sight in her workman's hut and sat down for a moment, going through everything that had happened since yesterday morning and Daisy's arrival.

She'd started sneezing almost immediately and, ignoring Fay's warning, had used the spray but seemed to get no relief from it.

"Nothing seems to be working today . . ."

CHAPTER ELEVEN

Abby was distracted by the sight of a discarded chocolate wrapper blowing across her garden and she leapt up to retrieve it. Then, spotting a dandelion that had gone to seed overnight, she reached for the small can of hairspray she carried in her bag and carefully sprayed it, to prevent it blowing away.

She plucked out a weed that was not part of her design and was smoothing out stones disturbed where someone, taking advantage of her absence, had stepped onto the garden for a closer look, when a shadow made her look up.

It was Megan, holding a cardboard tray with two cups of coffee and a bag that promised to be something carb-heavy.

"Abby . . . How are you?" she asked, clearly concerned.

"All the better for seeing you. It seems like for ever since breakfast. Come on over to the hut."

Megan stepped over the low boundary rope. Although she'd seen the garden take shape, she hadn't been inside the hut since it was finished.

"I love the effect of a tumbledown shack outside and this comfortable reading nook inside. Where did you get these lovely old arts-and-crafts wooden armchairs?"

"I noticed them in the attic at Linton Lodge when the estate was being valued for probate. And the old cricket table was among abandoned garden furniture in one of the work-shops in the walled garden." She shifted the copy of Daisy's autobiography, a gardening book and a potted plant to the top of a low bookcase to make room for the coffee. "Cal cleaned it up and fixed one of the legs."

"What will happen to the hut after the show?" Megan asked. "I'd quite fancy this in my garden."

"Too late, I'm afraid. Someone saw the design in the newspaper and the entire garden is going to be rebuilt in his garden."

"Really? Who wants a quarry in their garden?"

"I could tell you, but then I'd have to kill you."

"Kill me?" She thought for a minute, then laughed. "Wait. I sold that vast mansion on the other side of Little Hinton to an old rocker a few months ago. It's just his style."

Abby grinned. "Got it in one."

"Well, that's good news." Megan put down the card-board tray and gave her a hug. "How are you really? A client gave me last-minute tickets for a show and Iain and I spent the night in London. I only saw the news this morning when we were on the train home."

"Oh, nice. What did you see?"

"A comedian at the O2. Iain enjoyed it . . . I'm so sorry that you were on your own."

"I wasn't. Jake demonstrated his superpowers once again by turning up exactly when he was needed."

"The man is a keeper." She removed the lid from her coffee cup then, spotting the suitcase, said, "I hope that means the two of you are taking advantage of the absence of children to have a weekend away somewhere romantic?"

"Sadly, no. I have to put in an appearance here and it's May's first birthday on Sunday. As her godmother I've had the royal summons from Katherine Hamilton."

"That'll be fun."

"It's okay. Izzy had already been in touch. She wanted the children there."

"How do they feel about that?"

"They adore May," she said. "They've made her a memory box for her birthday. Pictures of their father from a baby. Things that belonged to him. Things that they remember about him."

"That's a lovely idea. And everything considered," Megan said, "Izzy's not that bad."

"No, she's not." There was always going to be edge in their relationship, but she'd been with Izzy during May's birth and their children had the same father. There was a bond. "The suitcase belongs to Daisy Dashwood," she said, changing the subject. "It contains the stuff she left behind in Beaumont Court. Fay Bingley, her personal assistant, asked me to pick it up."

"Why?"

"She's at Daisy's cottage with a television news van parked outside. She's hoping that if she keeps her head down they'll accept that no one is there and go away."

"I don't imagine they'll hang about for long, but I meant why *you*. I know you drove the woman to the hospital but surely that was an end to it?"

"Not exactly but it's a long story. What's in the bag?"

Megan ripped it open to reveal doughnuts. "I thought you'd probably need the full works. Carbs, fat *and* sugar."

"I can feel my thighs expanding just looking at them."

"You'll soon work it off now Jake's home."

Abby rolled her eyes but said nothing more until she'd licked the sugar off her lips. "Maybe I should pick up a couple for Fay on my way home," she said. "She's in a pretty bad way."

"Isn't the Dashwood place by the weir near Longbourne Reach? That isn't on your way home."

"No, but Fay wasn't the only one hiding out from the press. I was there when Daisy collapsed so I took refuge in the houseboat."

"Good plan. They're all going to pester you to tell them what she said to you when you went rushing to her aid. She did say something, didn't she?" She didn't wait for an answer but took a cautious sip of her steaming coffee. "Give it a minute," she warned. "It's very hot." She sat back against the cushion. "So what's this long story?"

Abby shook her head. Daisy's relationship with Patrick would probably be all over the media in days, but it had been her secret and nobody's business but her own.

Megan, who until then had ignored the second doughnut, picked it up. "I wonder what's going to happen to Hartford Manor now."

Abby felt her heart pick up a beat. "Hartford Manor?"

"I discovered, quite by chance, that Daisy Dashwood had bought it."

"And you didn't tell me?" Abby asked.

"It was just a few days ago and let's face it, you've been so focused on your garden for the last few weeks that there hasn't been time for a cosy gossip."

"The only thing on my mind at the moment is this doughnut," Abby replied, "So gossip."

"We keep a close eye on planning applications in the office and there's been a lot going on since the Hartford estate was divided up and put on the market. The Dower House and the house on the home farm were put up for sale separately, along with a couple of cottages. It was the application for planning permission to build new homes on the farmland that interested us."

"Did it go through?"

"No, it's prime green belt, but there's a demand for housing in the area and it will probably go through on appeal. As for the Manor, a holding company applied for change of use to a spa hotel and restaurant. The old stable block is being extended for the spa and indoor pool area. The outdoor pool is being renewed and new bathrooms created so that each bedroom is en suite."

"But it's Grade I listed," Abby pointed out. "How could they have got all that past English Heritage so quickly?"

Megan shrugged. "Good question. The wiring is probably well past its best and a fire risk, the plumbing will be in the dark ages but turning the rooms into en suites while preserving the architectural integrity of the building isn't going to be easy. EH will be watching every detail down to the last screw. It'll take for ever and cost a fortune."

Abby frowned. That seemed to contradict what Fay had told her. "If the application for change of use was made by a holding company, how did you find out that it was Daisy Dashwood who'd bought it?"

"Pure chance. I was in Lower Haughton at the weekend valuing a cottage that backs on to the woodland on the edge of the estate. I was outside taking photographs when I heard voices, and being nosy — well, everyone has been wondering who bought the place — I took a little walk through the woods and spotted Daisy. She was talking to someone about felling some ash trees that have succumbed to dieback and didn't sound happy."

"Well, that is hot news, Meg. Have you told anyone?"

"I mentioned it to Iain. He wasn't interested until I told him who she was with. You are never going to guess," she teased.

"Could it have been Patrick Farrell?"

Megan's eyebrows shot up. "You knew?"

"He was at Daisy's cottage yesterday."

"Wait . . . You actually met him?" Megan, all ears, doughnut forgotten, fanned her face. "I only saw him at a distance. Is he as fit as his photographs in the lifestyle mags?"

"Tall, dark, with the kind of smouldering good looks that are danger to any woman within range of those blue eyes?"

"That's the one."

"He didn't smoulder at me," Abby said. "Just demanded to know who the hell I was."

"Well . . . Celebrities." Megan was clearly willing to give him the benefit of the doubt. "They guard their privacy and some stranger walking in . . ."

"He was equally rude to Fay. She'd tried calling him to tell him what had happened but he wasn't picking up.

She was desperate to get to the hospital herself but she knew Daisy would want him there."

"Perhaps he's just stressed, it can't be easy being in the spotlight all the time."

"Don't make excuses for him. Believe me, his manners don't match his looks. He ordered Fay to stay put and field any calls — something that the answering machine could have dealt with. He never even considered the fact that she was close to Daisy and would want to be there. He just drove off."

"Really?" she asked, evidently disappointed.

"The poor woman was distraught, Meg. And then, as if things weren't bad enough, there was an anonymous call asking if the old witch was really dead."

"No! Who on earth would do such a thing?"

"Who knows? Fay said she didn't recognise the voice."

"Did you believe her?"

"Why wouldn't I?"

"I don't know. You sounded a bit doubtful. Male or female?"

Abby ran the message through her head, trying to remember exactly what she'd heard, then shook her head. "Honestly, it was over so quickly and muffled. It could have been either."

"You heard it too?"

"The answering machine clicked in before Fay could get to the phone. The voice was low and, as I said, a bit muffled. She was going to delete it, but I suggested she leave it in case Patrick recognised the voice."

"Why was he there when Daisy was out? Working on the plans for the restaurant, I suppose," Megan said, answering her own question.

"Not so you'd notice. He was in the garden on a sun lounger with headphones clamped to his ears when we arrived."

Megan put her head on one side. "Am I missing something?"

"It's supposed to be a secret but once the tabloids get stuck in . . ." She drew in a breath. "According to Fay, the opening event at Hartford Manor was to have been Daisy and Patrick's wedding, and quite soon from what I gathered. They've sold the event to one of the big lifestyle magazines and they've demanded absolute secrecy. You know how zipped-up they can be when they've got a scoop. They don't want the competition sneaking in an undercover photographer."

"Wait, wait, back up — Daisy Dashwood and Patrick Farrell were getting married? To each other?"

"You're thinking about the age gap?" Abby took a swig of her coffee. "No one would lift so much as an eyebrow if it was a good-looking younger woman hooking up with a wealthy man old enough to be her father."

"What's good for the goose . . ." Megan mused. "Well, I hope she enjoyed it while it lasted, but whether it was love or money that made Farrell's heart grow fond, if his name isn't on the deeds to the Manor, his grief won't be faked."

"Tessa Anderson acted as agent to both of them and so presumably she's tied up a legal partnership agreement. Something to cover every eventuality," Abby added. "It would be crazy not to."

"Maybe." Megan finally took another bite of the dough-nut. "Although surely working for both of them is a conflict of interests? It would be interesting to know who got the best end of the deal. And who was paying for it all. Patrick Farrell was bankrupt and homeless a few months ago."

"I think that answers your question. Daisy has to be the more valuable client — television, books, appearances," Abby pointed out.

"But with a limited shelf life," Megan suggested. "The agent will already be getting fifteen per cent of everything Daisy has ever done. It's Farrell who has endless potential. Chefs are hot property these days, and with his looks he's made for television. There'll be cookery books, a ghost-written 'autobiography' involving a dreadful childhood . . ."

"We are both cynically assuming that he's only in it for the money."

"How did they meet?" Megan asked. "Did the ever-in-formative Fay tell you that?"

"Tessa introduced them." Abby, with a sinking feeling, told her exactly how.

"Single cash-rich woman whose confidence has taken a knock is introduced by a woman who has a financial stake in both their careers, to a seriously good-looking, ambitious but broke potential star in need of a cash injection to get his career back on track," Megan said, giving voice to that feeling.

"You think Tessa planned it?"

"Maybe she saw the potential benefit of getting them together to create something along the lines of the Le Manoir aux Quat'Saisons and it was Farrell who saw the possibility of taking it a step further. Did Daisy have any family?"

Abby shook her head. "Only a cousin living in Spain who died last year."

"Was she married, the cousin? Children?"

"Married but there were only stepchildren. They met when she was on holiday. He was widowed with children and Daisy was convinced he'd only married her cousin to get a housekeeper and nanny on the cheap."

"So, if we're following the money that must mean we're ruling out Patrick. Unless he's a substantial beneficiary of her will, he needed her alive."

"Megan . . . No one has suggested that there's anything suspicious about her death."

"So far." She finished the doughnut, took a pack of wipes from her handbag and handed one to Abby before cleaning her own fingers. "Something's bothering you, Abs, and you have good instincts for what doesn't feel right."

After what had happened before Christmas, the last thing Abby wanted was to be involved in another unexplained death, but the same unease that had driven her to find out the truth then was nagging at her now.

"Okay," she admitted, "I admit, I'd really like to take a look at Hartford Manor to see what's going on."

"That can be arranged. I have someone who wants to view the property at four thirty this afternoon. While I'm meeting her, you could take a walk up through the woods. I'm not sure how close you'll be able to get but I'll give you a big tape measure so that you'll look official in case anyone stops you."

Abby laughed. "You want me to say I'm from the council, checking the boundary?"

"Wear your show identity lanyard. That looks wonderfully official."

"So long as they don't look too closely." Abby sipped her coffee. "Fay told me that Poppy Jensen has been trying to push Daisy out of *The Potting Shed* and grab the show for herself. And Kevin Tarr, the show's director appears to be totally smitten."

Megan looked doubtful. "It's a big step up to murder."

Abby was aghast. "I'm not suggesting murder!"

"Then what are you suggesting? That one of them might have laced her tea with something designed to keep her off air long enough for Poppy Jensen to establish herself and overdid it?"

"I don't know, Meg. I just don't know, but apparently there have been incidents on the set. That's why Fay wasn't with her. She was checking to make sure that nothing had been tampered with," Abby explained. "And there's been some nasty stuff on social media implying that Daisy was past it and it was time for the compost heap."

"That's a classic undermining technique. Keep saying it often enough, with sufficient conviction, and it will eventually be accepted as the truth."

"It's outrageous. Even Katherine Hamilton remarked that Daisy looked a little the worse for wear, but it isn't true. She was in Switzerland having a facelift."

"Fay told you that?"

"She did, but Quentin remarked on the fact that she'd had some work done and they've known each other for years."

"Oh, right . . . Then I suppose it's possible that someone slipped her something to make her appear unsteady? Something to keep her off stage and make her look bad?" Megan sipped her coffee.

"The only person to benefit from that would be Poppy Jensen."

"So why didn't she take over when Daisy didn't turn up yesterday? Surely that was her big chance."

"She'd tripped carrying a cup of coffee and was taken to hospital." She raised her own cup. "You said yourself how hot it was."

"Tripped?" Megan repeated.

"Over a cable."

"*The Potting Shed* sounds like a dangerous show."

"Maybe, but whatever Daisy was suffering from yesterday, I'd swear that it wasn't an overindulgence in alcohol." Hearing a murmur of voices as people began to arrive, she finished her coffee and rose to her feet. "Time to face the public. What time do the Pony Club events start?"

"Ten thirty and I've got the rosettes so I'd better be off."

"Will you be around all day?"

"Just until lunchtime. The Marshall half of the partnership is on this afternoon. Steve's daughter is taking part in the pony racing. I spotted a food stall making Taiwanese bao that are calling my name if you fancy meeting up. Or are you meeting Jake for lunch?"

"No. He'll be busy catching up at the office. I'll see you over there. About one?"

"Perfect."

Megan gathered up the debris of their picnic and bore it away to the recycling station while Abby replaced the books and left the hut.

She was greeted by Quentin Latimer-Blythe standing on the path, waiting to speak to her. He raised his Panama hat. "Good morning, Abby."

"Quentin. I wondered if you'd be here today."

"Yes. I'm staying with Katherine Hamilton this weekend to talk about her new border and I couldn't let her down."

"Unlike Daisy," she replied pointedly. "Did you decide not to appear because she invited me to join her?"

"No! Not at all. I'm here to apologise for running out on you yesterday. Especially in view of what happened. But Daisy and I . . ." He gave a little sigh. "Well, you saw how she was, but I won't speak ill of the dead. I'm just sorry that my bad manners left you alone on the stage."

Abby hadn't forgotten his snide remark about her gold medal being the result of local advantage, but she was too interested in his history with Daisy to let it show.

"Fay told me that you'd known each other for a long time."

He shrugged. "We started at university the same year and were on the same course. We had a little fling that ended badly," he said. "My fault entirely, but I was young and struggling with my sexuality. I was trying to fit in, be one of the lads, but you can't fight your nature. It ended when she caught me in a compromising situation with one of our lecturers."

"That must have been a shock. Poor Daisy."

"She doesn't need your pity," he said. "She's never forgiven me. Even after all these years, she never misses a chance to put in the knife as you no doubt heard yesterday morning."

Abby, lost for a response, realised that someone was lingering by Quentin's garden, clearly anxious to talk to him. "You have a fan," she said.

He followed her gaze. "So I have. If you'll excuse me, dear lady." He raised his hat, instantly back into the role he played so beautifully.

And maybe he was not the only one.

Beneath the image of the sweet woman with the warm smile whom everyone loved there lurked a darker Daisy Dashwood. A woman who could hold on to a grudge for what must have been the best part of forty years.

CHAPTER TWELVE

The morning flew by. When Abby wasn't talking to people about her garden, chatting with friends and neighbours who stopped by for a chat, she was checking texts and voicemail messages. Most were from newspapers wanting a quote about Daisy. They were careful to sound concerned and sympathetic, but she deleted them.

There were a couple of messages from gardening magazines who said they'd loved her garden, had looked at her website, seen the photographs of the restoration of the Victorian walled garden and were interested in doing a feature. They might even have been telling the truth.

Her first brush with fame hadn't ended well but, unwilling to let Lucy down, she suggested they call her the following week when the show was over. She'd soon shut them down if their real interest was Daisy's last minutes.

Megan had managed to grab a table in the food court area and had cold drinks ready and waiting. "Sparkling apple or elderflower pressé?"

"I'll take the apple," Abby replied. "And I'll get the buns."

The queue moved quickly and it wasn't long before they were sinking their teeth into the pillowy buns and groaning with pleasure over the crispy filling of pork belly, pickled vegetables and peanuts.

"I hope that's going spare." Acting Detective Sergeant Dee Newcombe dragged a spare chair to their table and sat down.

It was Megan's second bun but she said, "I can see your need is greater." Then, as Dee devoured it as if she hadn't eaten for week, "I didn't think CID bothered themselves with events like this."

Dee finished the bun and wiped her mouth and fingers on a spare napkin. "We don't. I was looking for Abby."

Megan and Abby exchanged a look.

"Well, you've found her," Megan said. "What's up?"

Dee didn't respond.

"Okay . . . I can take a hint, and it's time I got back to the office." She stood up. "Good to see you, Dee. We should all get together one evening very soon." Backing away, Megan lifted her hand to her ear and mouthed, *Call me.*

Picking up on the silent exchange, Dee turned but Megan was already walking away. "I'm sorry if I interrupted something."

"Just lunch. She really does have to get back to her office. Is this about Daisy?" Abby asked. "Is there a question about the cause of her death?"

"Why would you think that?" she replied, all innocence, but the fact that Dee's face had the expressionless look that officers adopted when they were interviewing suspects — Abby had been on the receiving end of a few of those — was enough to heighten her interest.

"Because a CID officer is asking questions?" she suggested.

There wasn't so much as a twitch to suggest Dee was biting. "The last I heard," she replied, "was that her hay fever had triggered a severe allergic reaction."

"Death by hay fever? That sounds unlikely. There must be more to it than that," Abby pressed.

"It has raised a few eyebrows, to be honest. And Daisy Dashwood is not just a local celebrity." She shrugged. "The truth is that the Chief Constable has sent down word that he doesn't want her death to come back and bite him on the bum so I'm here to tidy up details for the coroner."

Abby raised an eyebrow. "And that takes a detective sergeant?"

Dee shook her head, but she was grinning. "There's no fooling you, is there? You're right, it would normally be the job of a PC, but a uniform turning up to ask you questions would attract attention. I imagine you have been getting some attention from the press? You were there when she collapsed, at her side until the first-aiders arrived. They'll be hoping for her last words . . . ?"

She left what was almost a question hanging.

"I've had a load of voicemails," Abby admitted. "I've ignored them all except for a couple from gardening magazines who I'd like to think are genuinely interested in my show garden. If they are only hoping for famous last words," she said, "it will be a short interview."

"Were there?" Dee finally gave up working around the question and, very casually, came out with it. "Any last words?"

Despite Dee's attempt to play it down, it was obvious that Daisy's death was giving rise to concern.

"She was trying to say something," Abby told her. "It sounded like 'Rick' which didn't mean anything at the time, but when Fay Bingley, her PA, told me that Daisy and Patrick Farrell were planning to open Hartford Manor as a hotel and restaurant I realised that she was probably trying to say 'Patrick'."

"Patrick Farrell? The bad-boy chef with the film star looks? Are you saying that he and Daisy are business partners?"

Dee was a friend, but she was also a detective sergeant, if only acting for the time being, and Abby wasn't about to be coy with her. "According to Fay they are partners in every sense of the word."

Dee sat back. "You have got to be kidding me. Wasn't he dating that model? Susie something?"

"Susie Grainger."

"Yes. And Daisy has to be old enough—"

Abby raised an eyebrow and Dee, who was almost certainly about to say "his mother", thought better of it.

"Her solicitor has been in contact with the hospital about the death certificate. No one has mentioned Farrell. Only that Daisy's next of kin, a cousin, died last year without offspring. Apart from some distant cousin there doesn't appear to be any other family," Dee informed her.

"The relationship was a closely guarded secret. Fay told me that they were planning to open the hotel with their wedding for maximum impact."

"The tabloids would have gone crazy," Dee agreed. "They'll go crazy anyway if this comes out. It's the kind of publicity that won't go down well at Headquarters."

"No. I wonder who'll inherit Hartford Manor."

"Abby . . ." Dee warned.

She raised her hands, palm out, in a defensive gesture. "Just interested. Fay mentioned that Daisy made a new will after her cousin died and I just wondered who'll get the bulk of the estate."

Dee shrugged. "I'd say it depends on how long Patrick Farrell has been part of her life. Was his arrival on the scene before or after the new will, I wonder?"

"We were under the impression that he was racing to her side yesterday," Abby said. "I'm surprised no one mentioned it."

Dee sighed. "Well, whatever's going on, you said it yourself — a fatal case of hay fever is rare. There'll be a post-mortem, but so far no one seems to be able to pinpoint the cause of death."

"Really? I thought maybe heart or stroke."

"Apparently not. There's nothing on her records other than a slightly raised blood pressure for which she was prescribed medication and the coroner isn't willing to sign the death certificate without more tests."

"Hence the gold-braided panic stations."

"No comment," Dee said, but she pulled a face, clearly of the opinion that this was a job for a PC. "You saw her yesterday, Abby. You talked to her when she visited your garden. Did you notice anything out of the ordinary?"

"There's no doubt she was suffering badly from hay fever. When she used her nasal spray Fay warned her that she was exceeding the dose, but Daisy complained that nothing was working. The local news team were filming it all."

"Good point. I'll get them to send me a download of what they shot." She hesitated. "I did a quick online search and picked up on some rumours — was there any chance she'd been drinking?"

"Fay told me the Priory story was malicious gossip, that she'd actually been having a facelift, which Quentin Latimer-Blythe certainly made a snide comment about. But the drink rumour, whoever started it, has taken hold," Abby said. "*The Potting Shed* director, Kevin Tarr, implied that the reason she didn't turn up before the show was because she was drunk."

He was a man who would be glad to see the back of Daisy, so that scenario would have suited him very well, Abby thought. She would have liked to talk to him, but he wouldn't have hung around.

Maybe she could use the excuse of calling the production office to ask him for a copy of *The Potting Shed* tape for Lucy. He'd probably think she was angling for more airtime but since she'd held the fort for them, taking a moment to say thank you was the very least he should do.

"You were there," Dee said. "Do you think she was drunk?"

"Honestly? I suspect people have been pushing the story for their own reasons. Someone has been spinning that line on social media and I saw this morning that it had gone viral."

"Oh, that's sad. As you know, I live in a flat, so I don't do any gardening, but my father is a huge fan."

"It's not sad, it's nasty," Abby said. "Daisy wasn't well but I doubt if strong drink was involved. She was struggling with her eyes and she *was* a little unsteady. Blinking a lot. It reminded me of something but I can't think what."

"Keep thinking."

"I will. But I can confirm that she wasn't slurring her words and she carried on like a trooper, determined not to disappoint anyone." She finished her second bun then looked at Dee. "Won't a post-mortem show up alcohol in her blood?"

Dee nodded. "Everything's backed up and Forensics are centralised these days, but we're pushing for the lab results."

"Fay did mention that she'd had a nosebleed after they returned to Beaumont Court, but she refused to see a doctor saying that she just needed a lie down."

"Was Fay with her all yesterday morning?"

"You'll have to ask her. I know she left to check the set before the show started."

"Surely that's the job of the production people. The director?"

"According to Fay, there have been a few incidents where props have been tampered with. She distrusts Kevin Tarr, who to her mind was very keen to get Daisy off the show and put Poppy Jensen, her assistant, in her place."

Dee's eyebrows rose. "You're suggesting he had a motive?"

"I'm suggesting nothing. Just passing on what Fay told me."

"Is she reliable?"

"She's been with Daisy a long time," Abby said. "She may be prejudiced but I heard Tarr tell Fay that if Daisy wasn't on set when the titles rolled she was finished." Before he'd rushed off to be with Poppy. "When Daisy didn't turn up, Fay tried raising her on the phone, but then went to look for her. She arrived back at the marquee just after Daisy collapsed."

"I'd better have a word with her," Dee said, "get a statement of exactly what happened yesterday. Do you know where she's staying?"

"She's at Daisy's cottage. She asked me to pick up Daisy's things from Beaumont Court. If you're going there maybe you could take them with you?"

"Yes, of course. It was a bit of a cheek her asking you to do that, though."

"It was, but she's in a shocking state and was obviously very attached to Daisy."

"I don't suppose you could spare half an hour?" Dee asked. "I don't have the address and since she evidently trusts you, it might make it easier for her as well as for me if you were there."

"That cheek thing," Abby said, not wanting to be appear too eager, "there's a lot of it about."

But while Dee talked to Fay, she was going to take a look at Daisy's herb garden and try and pin down what was in the tea she'd been drinking.

Purely out of professional interest.

CHAPTER THIRTEEN

Abby loaded Daisy's things into Dee's car.

"Why on earth did Daisy Dashwood need a suitcase full of stuff?" Dee asked.

"It's a change of clothes, a jacket and her handbag. She has two identical dresses, presumably in case one gets marked during filming. It's a sensible precaution. Poppy Jensen spilled coffee down herself yesterday morning."

"Is that why she didn't run the show?"

"No. The coffee was very hot and she needed a trip to A&E."

"It was a bad day all round at *The Potting Shed*," Dee said, then frowned. "Is that her real name?"

"Daisy?"

"Daisy, Poppy . . . All these gardeners with flower names. It seems a bit coincidental."

"Daisy might have been a Margaret or Marguerite — that's French for 'daisy'. I imagine it was quite popular back in the day because of the Queen's sister. I've no idea about Poppy. Take a left here." Once the turning was safely navigated Abby said, "What about you?"

"What about me?"

"Dee isn't a name," she pointed out. She and Megan had long speculated on what it was short for. "It's an initial."

"It serves."

"Is your actual name something cute that wouldn't suit the job?" Abby teased. "Something like Debbie? Or something hippyish like Daydream?"

Dee's lips tightened ominously.

"No? No, I've got it. You're a flower too. Dahlia? Daphne? Delphinium? Or was your mother a fan of *Cold Comfort Farm* and decided to call you Delphine?"

"Highly amusing."

Or not. Dee wasn't smiling and, whatever her name, Abby realised that she wasn't going to tease it out of her. Fortunately, they had arrived at their destination.

"Nice spot," Dee said. "Television gardeners do a lot better than coppers. The location alone must be worth seven figures."

"Daisy was born in Maybridge. This was her parents' home," Abby said. "Maybe even her grandparents'. It's been extended more than once."

"It will, as you suggested, be interesting to find out who's going to get lucky."

Dee had checked her for wondering just that, but it wasn't just Weir Cottage. There was the house in London and Hartford Manor, and the first rule when investigating a suspicious death was to follow the money — if it was suspicious — and whatever she said, Dee's presence suggested that it might be.

Daisy could easily have lived for another twenty or thirty years. That was a long time to wait for an inheritance, and Patrick Farrell's arrival on the scene had thrown everything up in the air because, whatever was in the present one, there would have to be a new will once they were married or he'd get it all by default.

Could the prospect of losing it all to the new man in her life have prompted someone to hurry nature along?

Abby knocked on the door. "It's me, Fay. The news people have gone. I've got Daisy's things and DS Newcombe is with me. She'd like a few words."

The door opened a few centimetres and, with the security chain in place, Fay peered cautiously through the gap. "Oh, it is you . . . I'm sorry, but I've had no peace. The phone hasn't stopped ringing and there have been all sorts of people knocking and creeping around."

"Have there been any more unpleasant calls?"

She shook her head.

"There's no one about at the moment," Abby said. "Can we come in?"

"Sorry." She slipped the chain and stood back. "Oh, you've brought Daisy's things. That's so kind." She took the suitcase and stood it in the hall. "Come on through and sit down. I'll make some tea."

They followed her through to the sitting room where, despite the warm, sunny day, the French windows were closed and the curtains drawn.

Fay saw them looking. "I locked the side gate but someone must have climbed over. He came to the French windows with a camera and started taking pictures. I saw him from the hall and kept very still, but my heart was thumping. He even tried the door but I'd checked that everywhere was locked. When I was sure he'd gone, I closed all the curtains."

"Is there nowhere else you could go?" Dee asked. "The cottage is quite isolated."

"I have a flat in the basement of Daisy's townhouse but it won't be any better there."

"Family? Friends?" Dee asked.

"No . . . Did Abby say you were from the police?"

"Acting Detective Sergeant Dee Newcombe," she confirmed. "Abby told me that you were with Daisy during the morning before she died."

Fay took out a tissue, blew her nose and sank into an armchair. "Yes . . . No. Not all morning."

"Why don't you run me through what happened that day?" Dee sat on the armchair opposite.

"I'll go and make the tea, shall I?" Abby suggested.

"Oh, yes. You'll find teabags in the cupboard over the kettle," Fay said. "Daisy only ever drinks . . . drank her own herbal tea, but she bought English Breakfast for me. Patrick just has coffee," she added as an afterthought.

"That would be Patrick Farrell," Dee suggested.

Fay glared at Abby. "You told her?"

"Where is Patrick Farrell now?" Dee cut in.

"I've no idea," Fay said sulkily. "He wasn't at the hospital when I arrived. I haven't heard from him and unless he wants something, I don't expect to."

"But he stays here?" Dee persisted. "Has he left any of his belongings here?"

"He stays most weekends," Fay said. "There's some of his stuff in the guest suite."

"They didn't sleep together?" Dee asked. "I understood they were about to be married."

Oh for the authority to ask such questions and not have to be tactful, Abby thought, enviously.

"When they . . . um . . ." Fay struggled to answer but finally managed, "They shared the bed in the guest room. Daisy's bedroom and bathroom were her special place."

Abby left them to it, crossing the hall to the kitchen, where she filled the kettle and set out three of the pretty mugs that were hanging from hooks on the dresser on a tray. She found the teabags in the cupboard and a packet of shortbread biscuits. Concerned that Fay might not be eating, she put some on a plate and added them to the tray.

She went into the larder for milk, and as she shut the fridge door and turned around, Abby found herself facing the array of herbal teas.

If Daisy only drank herbal tea, it stood to reason that she would have taken some with her to Beaumont Court. And she would have needed something to make it in — either a small teapot with an infuser to contain the leaves, or maybe just an infuser . . .

The mug had definitely been used and her mind was racing as she made the tea, disposed of the teabags and carried the tray into the sitting room, where Fay was telling Dee about the social media campaign. They paused while she put the tray down.

"Fay, did Daisy take one of her herbal teas with her yesterday?" Abby asked.

"Yes, of course. She has a little silver tea caddy and infuser which she takes everywhere."

Abby felt a little jolt of concern. "She had it with her yesterday?" she pressed.

"Yes. Daisy asked me to make her tea after we'd visited the showground."

"What blend was it?" she asked, certain that it was important.

Fay shook her head. "I don't know, I wasn't here to pack it up for her. Is it important? If I check the tea caddy I could probably tell you what it is."

"I'm sorry, Fay." Abby glanced at Dee. "When I cleared the sitting room at Beaumont Court, I didn't find either the caddy or the infuser."

CHAPTER FOURTEEN

"Someone stole them?" Fay was on her feet. "That's outrageous! They were very precious to Daisy. She bought them on the day she signed the contract for *The Potting Shed*. How could someone just walk into her room and take them?"

"Fay, I know it's distressing," Dee said quickly, "but it's possible that a cleaner washed them and, aware that no one would be coming back that afternoon, put them both in a cupboard for safety."

"More likely someone took them for a souvenir," Fay replied, sinking back into her chair. "Probably that creepy man in the office. 'Can I help you, Miss Dashwood, just ask, Miss Dashwood, anything at all, Miss Dashwood . . .'"

Dee glanced at Abby, who was doing her best not to smile at Fay's surprisingly accurate mimicry of Major Elliott. "Do you have a photograph? In case they have gone missing?"

"There's a video on YouTube of Daisy making her tea when she was doing a book signing. It shows the caddy and the infuser."

"That's useful." Dee produced her card. "Will you send me the link?"

Fay's hand was shaking as she took the card.

"Maybe we could take a break," Abby suggested. "Have some tea and a biscuit." She picked up the plate and offered it to Fay, who shook her head. "I really think you need to eat something," she urged.

"Everything chokes me." she said, gingerly taking a piece of shortbread and holding it between her fingers, making no attempt to eat it.

"How did you come to work for Daisy?" Abby asked, hoping that conversation rather than Dee's questioning would get a better response.

"Oh, that was so strange," Fay said, finally smiling. "I saw her struggling with a bag as she was getting on a train and I stopped to help her. I put it up on the overhead rack for her and then, since I had a standard class ticket, I wished her a good journey and started to walk to my part of the train. She called me back and asked how she was going to get the bag down when the train reached London."

"Anyone would have got it down for her," Dee said.

"I knew that, but she looked as if she wanted company and she said she'd pay the difference when the guard came through. It was a bit odd but who would pass up the chance to travel first class?"

Dee smiled. "No one."

"When the guard reached our carriage it was obvious that he recognised her and greeted her by name — 'Good afternoon, Miss Dashwood' — She smiled, then told him that I was her assistant and had bought myself a standard class ticket as I thought I'd be travelling separately and offered to pay the difference. I was so shocked at the way she could just smile at him and lie like that without blushing, but he was a big fan and said taking the fare was more trouble than it was worth. She had one of her books in her bag and she signed it and gave it to him. That's when I realised who she was."

"You hadn't recognised her?" Dee asked.

"She'd just said to call her Daisy," Fay said, instantly on the defensive. "When she produced the book I recognised the name and I knew she was on television, but I was living in a bedsit. I didn't watch gardening programmes."

"You were going to London," Abby said. "Where did you get on the train?"

"Manchester. Daisy had been there for an event. I'd been to the wedding of a girl I knew who did the same business course as me at sixth form college. It was a very small wedding. Her parents didn't approve," Fay gave a little sigh. "We weren't close friends. I think she must have gone through her address book to find people to bulk up the numbers on her side of the register office."

"When was this?"

Fay gave her the exact date and the time of the train.

"So you travelled all the way back to London with Daisy?"

"It was lovely." Fay smiled at the memory. "A steward brought a menu. You didn't have to pay. Daisy had scrambled eggs and smoked salmon and I had a cheese toastie. Daisy asked me about the wedding and where I worked and what I did and where I came from, even my star sign. She always read her horoscope. I told her things I'd never told anyone. And then, when we reached London, before we got off the train, she told me that I should come and have tea with her."

"Oh?" Dee sounded doubtful.

"She really meant it," Fay insisted. "It wasn't one of those throwaway 'come and see me sometime' invitations, the kind that doesn't mean anything. She checked her diary on her phone, set a date with me to have tea with her the following week and gave me her card with her address."

"Heavens," Abby said. "How exciting!"

"Then what happened?" Dee asked, not excited at all.

"She took me for a walk around her garden. I knew nothing about plants, but she showed me her favourite flowers . . . We had tea under the rose-covered pergola in her garden. I said how lovely the scent was and she told me the rose was called Zéphirine Drouhin, and told me that it been first grown more than a century ago. Then, when her housekeeper had cleared away the tea things, she asked me if I would like to work for her."

"Just like that?" Dee raised her eyebrows. "She was taking a risk on a stranger."

"I'd told her that I was a shorthand typist and about the office where I worked, and she was frank about having had someone check me out. When I asked her why she'd bothered — she could have got someone with a degree from one of the top agencies — she said . . ." Fay stopped, momentarily overcome. "She said that she valued kindness above everything."

"That's an extraordinary story," Abby said. "How long have you been with her?"

"Eleven years next month. I've never let her down. Until yesterday." She was still clutching the biscuit and it disintegrated in a shower of crumbs. "I should have been with her."

"You were doing your job, Fay."

Dee gave Abby a 'leave this to me' look. "Fay, can you tell me about Daisy's relationship with Mr Farrell?"

Abby, who'd heard this before, said, "Is it okay if I take a look around Daisy's vegetable garden while you're talking, Fay?"

She sensed rather than saw the almost imperceptible protective gesture. Fay wanted to guard Daisy from the world, but she wouldn't be able to do that. "I won't touch anything. No cuttings — gardener's honour," she said and, as she'd hoped, Fay laughed.

"There isn't a gardener alive who doesn't have a pair of sharp scissors or a small pair of secateurs in her bag," she said.

"Guilty as charged!" She had a small pair of secateurs in her bag for keeping her show garden in pitch-perfect condition. "I'll leave my bag here," she said, "as a guarantee of my good behaviour." In any case, her phone was in her pocket and it was photographs she wanted.

"No," Fay said. "Daisy admired your garden. She'd show you around herself if she were here and she was always generous with cuttings. Help yourself. I know you'll be respectful."

"Thank you. It would be an honour to have something of Daisy's growing in my own garden." She picked up her bag, glanced at the closed curtains and said, "I'll go out through the back door."

She went through the kitchen cupboards looking for a plastic bag, into which she splashed a little water for the cuttings, and then let herself out into the garden. The main garden was just lawn with large weeping willows at the water's edge, nothing to distinguish it from its neighbours or attract special attention. She stood for a moment listening in case there was anyone creeping around hoping to snatch some photographs, but the only sounds were the chug of engines and laughter from boats passing by on the river below.

She opened the gate to the hedged-off vegetable garden. There was a large greenhouse filled with a variety of heritage tomatoes and Mediterranean vegetables that needed the extra heat to ripen in an English summer. Impressive, but they weren't what interested her.

Outside, raised beds contained the more common vegetables all in bright growth and a long cane wigwam row of sweet peas for cutting. Again, they were lovely, but she was looking for the herbs.

Among the commonly used culinary herbs there was a wonderful selection of sages, thymes and varieties of mints. She brushed her hand over the feathery fennel to release the scent into warm air alive with the noisy buzzing of the bees on the French lavender and marjoram but once she snipped cuttings, she didn't linger.

Phone in hand, she quickly set about taking photographs of everything so that she would remember exactly what was there, sniffing as she went, searching for the elusive scent, before moving on to a second bed containing medicinal herbs.

There were all the more common herbs she expected to find: chamomile, feverfew, evening primrose and valerian, but also gingko and turmeric, which Lucy had been urging her to grow. Was Daisy using the root to make tea for arthritis in her hips or knees?

The glossy green foliage of the less common Vinca rosea was an unexpected addition but it was the Conium maculatum growing in a damp corner that was holding her attention when Dee came to find her.

"I'm ready to go. Have you seen enough?" she said, clearly anxious to be off.

"Nearly. I need a photograph of this." She took a picture of the plant in place and then knelt down to get a close up.

"What is that?" Dee asked.

"It's sometimes mistaken for chervil," Abby said, getting to her feet, "but its common name is hemlock."

"Hemlock?" Dee repeated. "Even I know that's poisonous."

"Deadly," Abby confirmed.

"So why would anyone grow something like that in their garden?"

"Fay mentioned that Daisy was in the process of writing a book on herbs. She may have grown it to take photographs."

"Maybe so, but hemlock isn't the sort of thing you'd add to a stew. At least not one you were going to eat yourself," Dee added.

"She was probably going to use it as a warning comparison. Daisy does — did — use a lot of herbs, but I imagine her book was more about the history of their use. A lot of these plants were once used in folk medicine, including hemlock."

"Kill or cure?" Dee said, thoughtfully. "What are the symptoms of hemlock poisoning?"

"I'd have to look it up, but pretty nasty from memory. Should Daisy have taken some by accident I think it would have been obvious."

But something toxic could have found its way into Daisy's tea, either by accident or design. Farrell had access here, but then so did anyone who was in the east wing of Beaumont Court yesterday morning, which would presumably include all of *The Potting Shed* production crew and probably Quentin Latimer-Blythe, as a celebrity, had been given access.

It might not have been meant to kill but to incapacitate her so that she couldn't take part in the show and top of that list had to be both Kevin Tarr and Poppy Jensen.

It was just Poppy's bad luck that she'd been unable to take advantage of Daisy's absence.

Abby looked across to a large shed tucked away in a corner. "Can you hang on for a couple of minutes while I take a look at where Daisy dries her herbs?"

"Go ahead but should you discover that Daisy Dashwood has been secretly growing cannabis — just for the book, you understand," Dee added, straight-faced, "I'd rather not know."

CHAPTER FIFTEEN

Having discovered that the shed was locked, Abby found Dee at the bottom of the garden standing on a small landing stage, looking out over the river. It was screened from the garden by one of two magnificent weeping willows, underneath which the lounger that Farrell had been using and the abandoned headphones were still in evidence.

There was a gap to take advantage of the view across the river to the hills, but the trees successfully blocked out most of the house and garden from anyone passing on the water.

"I was just wondering if the nosy photographer might have come this way," Dee said.

"If you knew which was Daisy's cottage, it would be a very simple way in. Perfect for anyone wanting to snoop."

She hoped it wasn't Gary Jackson or someone from the *Observer*, but the local newspaper would certainly know the location of the homes of local celebrities. And they must surely have been sniffing around Hartford Manor hoping to catch sight of the new owners.

Farrell must have been keeping a very low profile indeed, although with builders and decorators in and out she was surprised that the news hadn't leaked — maybe not about his relationship with Daisy, but about his presence.

Dee broke into her thoughts. "There's not much we can do. A police tape would only attract attention, but I'd have thought that Daisy would have some security systems in place."

Back in the house, they found Fay, still surrounded by crumbs, nose red, tissue crumpled in her hand, just as Dee had left her. When asked about security she shook her head. "There's a burglar alarm, and we installed lights that come on when they sense movement." She pulled a face. "The problem was that they came on if anything bigger than a mouse ran across the garden, so they're only switched on when the cottage is empty."

"Daisy didn't live here full time?"

"No. Daisy spends — spent — most of her time in London, although she was here more often since she bought the Manor. And despite insisting the Manor was taking all his time, I'm sure Patrick Farrell spent time here when she was away."

"That's not unexpected," Abby pointed out.

"No, but . . ."

"But?" Dee pressed.

"I'm sure he used to go through the desk in the study. Papers weren't always where I left them."

Abby glanced at Dee but she moved on without comment.

"There's no CCTV? Not even covering the river?"

"There's never been a problem so Daisy never saw the point although Patrick insisted that something be installed. He said that once their relationship was public knowledge there were bound to be paparazzi trying to get pictures of them together." She sniffed. "He was going to talk to someone about it. I don't know if he ever got around to it."

"Will you be staying on here?" Abby asked. "I don't like to think of you here on your own if there are people snooping around."

Fay momentarily brightened. "Daisy's solicitor didn't think it wise to leave the house unoccupied at the moment and they've asked me to stay on."

"Maybe you should ask them about getting some cameras installed," Dee advised. "Or I could give them a call if you'd prefer?"

"Would you? They'd take more notice of you." Fay drew a shuddering breath. "I don't suppose it will be long before ghouls find out where Daisy lived, where she was born, coming to look at the house, probably trying to get into the garden to take cuttings or even dig up plants."

"I'll speak to her solicitors about security and you have the card I gave you," Dee reminded her, quite firmly. "If you're bothered by anyone poking around, give that number a ring and someone will come out. And turn the security lights on."

"Yes, I will. Thank you." She looked up. "And if Patrick Farrell comes for his things, can I give them to him?"

"Why wouldn't you?" Dee asked.

She shrugged. "I thought maybe . . ." She stopped. "I don't suppose he will. I imagine he's hoping to move in soon."

"Daisy has left the cottage to Patrick Farrell?" Dee asked.

"I don't know," she said. "I don't know anything."

"But she said she'd take care of you?"

"She set up a pension plan, but that won't be any use right now, will it?"

"How will you manage for essentials, Fay?" Abby asked before the threatening tears overwhelmed the woman. "You don't have much milk."

"There'll be some in the freezer. And bread. There's plenty of food."

"Make sure you eat," Abby advised, "and you have my number if you need anything."

Fay swallowed and managed a smile. "Thank you, Abby. You've been so kind. And you will try and find Daisy's missing things?" she urged.

"They may have been put away somewhere. I'll go and ask," Abby assured her.

They let themselves out, neither of them speaking until they were in Dee's car.

Abby spoke first. "I really don't like leaving her like that."

109

"She's a grown woman, Abby. And if you pressed me, I'd say she's putting it on a bit."

"Really?"

"That 'I don't know anything' seemed a bit overdone. She's been living rent-free in Daisy's house so unless she's got a shopping habit, she should have saved something. And with her employment history she should get a job easily enough. But meanwhile she's got you running around after her."

"You weren't concerned about Patrick Farrell snooping around her desk?"

"He was probably looking for an envelope or some stamps." She snapped in her seat belt. "Did you find anything incriminating in the shed?"

Abby gave her a side-eye. "I thought you didn't want to know."

"Not officially."

"I didn't find anything. It was locked."

"What were you hoping for?"

"Nothing," Abby said. "I was just being nosy. Can you take a detour past Earthly Designs? I need to get these cuttings potted up."

"As you said, there is a lot of cheek about this morning," Dee replied, but she was grinning and took the detour.

Abby called ahead and the gate was open. She handed Kate the cuttings. "Any problems?"

"No, but I was in the office just before you arrived when a message came through on the answering machine. Someone called Kevin Tarr. He said he's the director of *The Potting Shed*?"

"Yes, he is. What did he want?"

"He's staying at the Queen's Head over the weekend and asked if you'd get in touch. He said it's quite urgent. I was just about to text you when I got your call." She gave Abby his number. "Maybe he wants to apologise for abandoning you at the recording."

"It's more likely that he wants to make sure I don't run to the press with the story," she replied.

"That's a touch cynical, Abby, but if that's the case, twist his arm for another spot on the show. They'll be looking for another presenter."

"He's already got Poppy Jensen lined up for that. I imagine a long weekend in the luxury of the Queen's Head is a celebration with benefits."

Kate's eyebrows shot up. "But she's—"

"Young enough to be his daughter? There's a lot of it about."

Dee gave a toot on her horn. "Abby, I'm wanted at Headquarters," she called. "Can you make your own way back?"

"I'll give her a lift," Kate called.

Dee raised her hand and was gone in a scatter of gravel. "She's in a hurry."

"So am I." Abby checked her watch. It was two thirty. "I just need some stuff from the office. Stick the cuttings in water for me, they'll keep until tomorrow, and then you can drop me off at the Queen's Head on your way home."

The opportunity to talk to Kevin Tarr or Poppy Jensen was too good a chance to miss.

She picked up a couple of plant books and fifteen minutes later Kate dropped her off in front of the Queen's Head, an old coaching inn near the river that was now a very expensive hotel and restaurant. The receptionist recognised her from an earlier occasion. "Good afternoon, Mrs Finch. How can I help you?"

"Hello, Cindy. I'm here to see Kevin Tarr. Is he in?"

"I think you'll find him in the bar with Miss Jensen."

"Thanks." She walked through to the bar, all oak beams and intimate little corners. There were very few people about at this time in the afternoon, but Kevin was leaning forward in an armchair beside the vast inglenook fireplace attempting to placate a furious Poppy.

"I'm really sorry, Poppy," he was saying, his eyes darting to the other people in the bar, "I tried—"

"You promised me!"

"And I meant it." His voice was low and urgent. "Every word. The production team love your input, but they're adamant that you're too young to present to the show's demograph—"

"It isn't only the middle-aged who garden," she replied, cutting off his attempt to calm her and seemingly not caring who heard. "I wasn't too young when you were talking me into bed with your promises." She picked up her bag and stood. "You're pathetic and I'm a fool to have listened to you!"

He was rising to his feet, but she turned, glared at Abby and stormed past her.

"Poppy!"

Tarr, looking shaken, made to follow her but, seeing Abby, who made no pretence that she hadn't witnessed the scene, gave an embarrassed shrug. "I'm sorry about that. She's had a career disappointment."

"She's not going to be replacing Daisy Dashwood on *The Potting Shed*?"

That got his attention. "Who are you?" he demanded, Poppy momentarily forgotten. "If you're the press—"

"Abby Finch, Mr Tarr. You left a message saying that you wanted to talk to me? I was in town so I thought I'd take a chance on finding you here."

"Oh, yes, I'm sorry, but you can imagine . . ." He glanced towards the door, clearly desperate to follow Poppy.

"I'd give her a minute or two to calm down," Abby advised. "She's young. She'll get over it." Although it looked as if it was the end of his directorial benefits. She would have liked to follow Poppy's example and leave rather than sit down with Tarr, but her sleuthing instincts were on high alert.

If Daisy had been somehow poisoned — and the books in her bag might give her an idea of what with — he had motive. And, in and out of Beaumont Court on the morning she died, the opportunity.

Means? Well, he directed a gardening show. He must have learned something over the years, although the internet was a mine of information.

The same applied to Poppy. A fellow gardener, she would certainly know what to put in her tea to make Daisy too ill to appear. There were plenty of options — the difficulty would have been finding something to use that she wouldn't notice.

Tarr made an effort to smile. "Poppy is right, of course. Young people have taken up gardening in a big way since the pandemic. Perhaps they need a show that speaks to them." He looked thoughtful.

"Young people with their first gardens?" Abby suggested. "Window boxes, indoor plants, maybe dial down a bit on the glamour? It's likely to antagonise the women watching."

That provoked a sigh. "She'd look glamorous in a black bin bag, but it's an idea worth thinking about. Please, sit down, Mrs Finch. Can I get you something? Tea, coffee?"

"No, thank you. I have to get back to the flower show."

"Of course. You're a busy woman. Congratulations on your medal, by the way. I'm so sorry I wasn't there." He cleared his throat. "Poppy . . ."

"Scalded herself," Abby said when he hesitated. "I was there when Fay told you what had happened. I could see how upset you were."

"It was a nasty scald, a real shock," he assured her. "She was lucky that Ross was there and acted so quickly or it could have been much more serious. But I couldn't leave her at the hospital on her own."

Abby made no comment.

"Anyway, I wanted to thank you in person for stepping in the way you did. I've seen the recording and you totally saved the day until . . . well . . . And even then, you were the one who took action."

"Actually, Mr Tarr—"

"Kevin, please."

"Kevin, I was going to ask if there's any chance of a copy of the recording? My daughter is hoping to get an internship with a PR company and she worked very hard to engage Daisy. You have her to thank for getting me on the show."

"With pleasure. Give me your details and I'll get it to you."

Abby reached into her tote for her business cards and her fingers touched a sleek pen. Daisy's pen. And she had her lipstick . . . Could that have been doctored in some way?

"I imagine, with Poppy out of the running, it's too soon for a decision about who will replace Daisy on *The Potting Shed*," Abby suggested as she handed over her card. "Or will you cancel the rest of the season?"

"We can't do that. The sponsors . . ." He pulled a face. "The production company have already been in touch with Quentin Latimer-Blythe and he's agreed to step in, at least until the end of this season. After that, well, who knows."

"Quentin?" How he must be relishing that.

Kevin caught her surprise. "He was the obvious choice."

"Yes, I can see that he would be," Abby said. And so, no doubt, could Quentin. "He and Daisy were the same age. He told me that he knew her when they were students together."

"Were they?" He shrugged. "It appears that the suits had already been talking about asking him to take over should Daisy decide that she didn't want to continue. In view of her problems."

That was interesting. He was someone else with motive to help her on her way.

"I imagine you're referring to the social media rumours about her drinking?" Abby said. "Had she been struggling on set before this week?"

He shrugged. "She's been . . ." He sought for a word. "Let's be kind and say she's been distracted. Turning up late, not on top of that week's topic. Anyway, the reason I wanted to talk to you, Mrs Finch . . ."

He paused, presumably waiting for her to invite him to call her Abby. She did not oblige.

"Well, the company that produce *The Potting Shed* would like to offer you a guest spot on the show."

Taken aback, Abby was still absorbing this information when he said, "I've looked at your website and understand you've renovated a Victorian walled garden where you have your own design studio. This is an absolutely shameless request but we were wondering if there's any chance we could film the next show there?"

Abby's head was yelling "No, no, no" while her heart was hearing Lucy shouting "Yes, yes, yes", and for a moment she was at a loss. "I don't know what to say," she finally managed. Which was nothing but the truth. "When were you thinking?"

"I realise that this is very short notice but we were hoping we could film it next week, since we're all here, and Quentin is staying with friends in the area."

"Next week!"

"It will be very relaxed," he assured her. "Just a chat as you show Quentin and the viewers around. It's felt that it would be a very touching segue from what happened this week. A chance to offer a tribute to Daisy. Your inspiration?" he pressed. "I saw the run-through of the last show and the lovely story about the book token. You were so natural."

"It didn't feel as if I was on television," Abby said. "There were people in the audience that I knew and it felt as if I was talking to friends."

"And that's the way it will be in your garden. The viewers are your friends and you'll be giving them a tour of something special you've created."

When she didn't immediately answer he said, "I can see you want to think about it but for obvious reasons I do need a quick answer. Unless it will be too painful?"

"No," she said, quickly. Not only would Lucy be over the moon, but it would mean she could spend some time with everyone who had worked with Daisy. It would give her a chance to talk to them. "No, you're right. I was hoping to invite Daisy to come and meet my team and see how we've utilised all the latest energy-saving technology."

"That would be perfect. I've checked the forecast for the coming week and the weather is holding until Thursday. Monday or Tuesday would be most favourable."

"Monday," she said. The high school had an inset day so Lucy could be there. And Tom if he was interested.

"Excellent." He smiled, rose to his feet and offered her his hand. "I'll be in touch."

CHAPTER SIXTEEN

Abby, with her phone out to summon a taxi to take her to Beaumont Court, spotted Poppy Jensen trailing a suitcase as she headed for reception.

Cindy smiled. "Are you checking out, Miss Jensen?"

"I'm leaving. You'll have to ask Mr Tarr what his plans are. He'll be the one paying the bill. What I need is a taxi."

"Of course. Where are you going?"

"Oh . . ." In full flight mode it was obvious that she hadn't thought beyond getting out of the hotel.

"If you're returning to London," Cindy offered helpfully, "you'll probably want to take the train. The nearest stations are Bath or Chippenham."

"The train?"

"They are both direct lines to Paddington," Cindy said. "It's nine miles to Bath, eleven to Chippenham," she added to give an indication of the likely fare. "Or there is a regular bus service to Bath that stops right next to the railway station."

Poppy hovered indecisively, belatedly considering the cost of her decision to walk out of her job, looking around as if desperate for someone to help.

Abby caught the receptionist's eye. "Will you organise a pot of tea, please, Cindy?" she asked. "I think Miss Jensen could do with a minute to decide on the best option."

Poppy turned to look at her. Despite attempts to disguise the fact with make-up, it was clear that she had been weeping, no doubt more in anger than sorrow, as she'd packed. It was also obvious that she wasn't quite the ingenue she appeared on-screen. Nearer thirty than twenty.

"Who are you?" she asked. "You were in the bar. Were you snooping? Are you a reporter?"

"No," she said, "I'm Abby Finch. Cindy knows me."

"Mrs Finch is a garden designer," Cindy confirmed. "She won a gold medal for her show garden at the Maybridge Show."

Poppy frowned, uncertain.

"I was left holding the fort on *The Potting Shed* when Daisy didn't appear and you had to go to the hospital," Abby prompted.

"That was you?"

"Yes. I called in here today because Kevin wanted a word. Why don't you sit down and catch your breath?" She indicated a table tucked into a corner by a window overlooking the garden. "Give yourself a moment to think."

Poppy sank into one of the comfortable armchairs. "You're the woman Kevin wanted to speak to," she repeated. "He wanted to thank you."

"Yes, I got his message and here I am. Not great timing on my part." She took the other chair.

Poppy shrugged. "I imagine half the hotel heard me. I was just so angry!"

"Understandably," Abby replied. "How are you, Miss Jensen? I heard that you had a nasty scald."

"It was agony," she said, "and Fay Bingley will be hearing from my solicitor."

"Fay?"

"Daisy's little poodle. Have you met her? Ghastly woman. She looks as if butter wouldn't melt in her mouth, but it's all an act. She hooked up that cable with her foot to trip me."

"Are you suggesting that she did it deliberately?"

"I'm not suggesting anything. It's a fact," she declared. "I was too busy trying to save myself to realise what she'd done, but Ross saw everything. He couldn't get hold of Kevin so he called a taxi and poured cold water over me until it arrived to take me to A&E."

"That was quick thinking." Abby discovered that she was nowhere near as shocked to discover that Fay had been involved as she should have been.

"I'm going to put in a complaint to the production company," Poppy said. "Not that they'll give a damn now I've quit."

"No." And Abby doubted that the production company would want to be involved in something that nasty now that Daisy was out of the picture and Fay history. "Where was Kevin when this was happening?"

"He said he was in the green room at Beaumont Court working but Ross got no response to his call. Kevin insisted that he hadn't missed a call. Maybe there was a problem getting a signal in the house. All those thick walls."

"I saw how shocked he was when Ross told him what had happened," Abby said. "He left him in charge so that he could come to you."

"Ross is very experienced. Too experienced to be an assistant at his age but jobs are tight and he was keen to work on the show." She shrugged. "And Kevin was very upset," she admitted. "He took care of me afterwards, which is why he didn't find out about what happened to Daisy until we heard it on the car radio on our way back to the hotel."

"Quite some time later then."

"I had to wait to see a doctor," she said, "but Fay must have known that Daisy was in a bad way and was unlikely to appear so she made sure I was out of it," she said bitterly.

Was that true? Had Fay realised that Daisy wasn't fit to appear some time earlier and made sure that Poppy couldn't take her place? She'd said that Daisy had just wanted a lie down . . .

"And now they've given *The Potting Shed* to that old queen Quentin Latimer-Blythe." And with that a large, fat tear spilled over and ran down her cheek. "All that planning."

"Planning?"

"From the minute Daisy went into the Priory her cards were marked. I wasn't sleeping with Kevin for fun," she said.

Whoa . . . That was frank.

"But she wasn't in the Priory," Abby said.

Poppy frowned. "Wasn't she? Well, something was up with her, and I saw the way that Kevin was looking at me so I played up to him. I know how that must sound, but this a tough business."

"I'm sure it is."

"He promised I would get *The Potting Shed* if Daisy got dropped — and I thought he could do it or I'd never have—" She caught herself, dashed away the tear then sighed. "I've been such an idiot!"

Fortunately, a tray of tea arrived, saving Abby from the need to respond.

She set out the teacups and gave the pot a stir. "What are you going to do now?"

"I don't know." Poppy waved a vague hand, taking in the lobby with its comfortable armchairs and the well-heeled women who'd called in for afternoon tea. "I can't stay here with him."

"Awkward," Abby agreed.

Poppy's jaw tightened. "If I walk out in the middle of the season my television career will be in the bin."

"And if you make a complaint against Kevin?"

"A complaint?" She pulled a face. "I can hardly do that and Ross is going to be . . ."

She looked as if she had been about to say more.

"Ross?" Abby prompted.

"He warned me." She shook her head. "Television has been my dream for as long as I can remember."

"Really?" Horticulture might be big on television these days but it seemed an odd choice if a media career was your goal. "Mine was a gold at Chelsea," Abby said, pouring the tea.

"And you're on your way," Poppy replied, "while I'm finished."

It was clear that she was bitterly regretting her rush for the exit and looking for a way back and Abby, who thought that she probably knew a lot about what went on behind the scenes on *The Potting Shed*, decided to help.

"Kevin wants to film me in my walled garden on Monday with Quentin. A follow-up to my appearance on the show," she explained when Poppy looked doubtful. "There'll be a tribute to Daisy, how she inspired me, a chance to tell the viewers that she and Quentin have been friends for forty years and she'd want him to step into her shoes . . ."

Poppy nodded. "A soft introduction," she said. "It makes sense although he and Daisy loathed each other."

"So I gathered. I did wonder if he was behind the online trolling."

"At his age? Would he know how?"

Somewhat ageist, but Abby shrugged. "Maybe he knows a person who does," she said. "Somebody was going out of their way to give Daisy's reputation a bashing."

She looked up, wondering if she'd catch Poppy in a blush. On the contrary, she'd taken a compact out of her bag and was busily repairing the damage to her face.

"Forget about Quentin for a moment," Abby said. "You were part of Daisy's show. You worked with her. It would seem odd if you weren't there on Monday."

"I suppose."

"As for Kevin, I understand why you wouldn't want to make a complaint, but his disappearing act when the programme was about to start means he's already got some explaining to do. And how will it look for him if you walk out on the show?"

Abby had no doubt that he would come up with some believable excuse, but Poppy nodded. "He should have sent Ross. I wish he had."

"Oh?"

"Kevin made such a fuss when he arrived, even though it was obvious that there were people who needed to be seen before me. Ross wouldn't have done that. He would have just sat and held my hand. He was always so nice whenever Daisy was mean to me." She looked up, a tear hovering on her lower lid. "She could be mean, you know."

Who wouldn't be if they saw themselves being pushed out by someone younger, more glamorous?

"I was robbed of my big chance by Fay Bingley," Poppy continued, blinking back the tear. "And Kevin owes me." She sipped her tea. "I can't stay here with him, though."

By 'with him', she obviously meant in the same room.

"He won't expect you to." She looked up. "Cindy, do you have a room available for Miss Jensen through until Monday?"

Cindy checked. "I have one overlooking the garden?"

Abby raised a questioning eyebrow at Poppy.

She shook her head. "No. I won't need that." She took out her phone. "Ross, sweetie, please don't say 'I told you so', but that spare bunk . . ."

CHAPTER SEVENTEEN

Abby texted Megan to tell her where she was, slipped on her dark glasses and waited outside the Queen's Head to be picked up.

"You're having a busy day. What were you doing in the Queen's Head?" Megan asked as they drove towards Lower Haughton.

"I went to Weir Cottage with Dee first," she said and told her about that, then about the phone call from Kevin Tarr and the tea and sympathy with Poppy.

"So Fay Bingley isn't Daisy's poodle after all. She's her rottweiler," Megan said.

"Maybe she has good reason. She's convinced that Poppy and Kevin are behind the social media campaign to discredit Daisy. Maybe Poppy is right. Having realised that Daisy was in trouble, Fay decided to take direct action to prevent her from taking over. It's possible that the hot coffee spillage was an unexpected bonus."

"It would have taken some nerve," Megan said, "but maybe she saw her chance and went for—" She braked hard as someone pulled out across the road in front of her.

Banging furiously on her horn although they were already long gone, she restarted the car and raised a hand to thank the driver behind, who'd managed to pull up before running into her rear. She drove on, expressing herself forcibly on the subject of people who were so desperate to get to their destination that they risked getting a pair of wings. For a little while neither of them spoke while they recovered from the near miss.

At last Megan picked up the thread again. "Is it possible that Poppy orchestrated the campaign herself? Even if, as Fay suggested, Tarr had his tongue hanging out and she led him on to get the big job, I doubt he'd risk his career when an investigation would quickly expose him. Was he even in a position to give her the job?"

"He told me that he tried and I believed him." Abby's heart was still beating a little faster than was comfortable. "Apparently the production company had already been talking about offering Quentin the job in the event of Daisy dropping out — a conversation that he hadn't been part of."

"So, basically, no."

Abby nodded. "It's pretty obvious that he wasn't thinking with his brain. Poppy is too young for the show's demographic and the powers that be have already confirmed that Quentin is taking over until the end of the season. They're going to play on the fact that he and Daisy were old friends and it's what she would have wanted."

"Friends!"

"People close to them might know the truth, but when they met in front of the cameras at Chelsea or elsewhere, they played the game and it was all smiles." Until yesterday.

"So—" Megan was slowed to a crawl by a tractor — "if Poppy was spreading the rumours she must have been acting on her own."

"It's a risk," Abby said.

"Not much of one. I had a look at the posts and you have to be a lot nastier than that — make real threats — to disturb any of the tech giants." Megan thought for a minute. "What about Tarr? I wonder if he has history with young vulnerable women."

"Poppy is a lot younger than him," Abby agreed, "although, close up she's older than she looks. And she was frank about her motives. I wouldn't describe her as vulnerable."

Megan finally managed to pass the tractor. "Women are always vulnerable," she said, with feeling, "and he was in a position of power. He could have been doing this for years, with colleagues turning a blind eye and women too worried about their careers to make a complaint?"

"It's possible, although he seemed genuinely distressed. I think he is totally smitten."

"And she's staying put. Was the walkout just for the drama, do you think? Was he supposed to chase after her and beg her to stay?"

"He was going to, but I was standing in his way. He was torn," Abby told her, "but I suggested he take a few minutes to calm down, introduced myself, and he had no choice but to talk to me."

"It was fortunate you were there to stop her flight, then."

"There's no doubt she was angry. She must have thought *The Potting Shed* was hers for the taking. But the moment Cindy started offering train options she seemed to panic so I waylaid her with tea and sympathy, which she didn't resist. Once she was sitting down it took her about ten minutes to work out where her best interests lay, career-wise."

"While you, Mrs, despite your horror of publicity, are doing your career no harm at all by making another appearance on *The Potting Shed*."

"It's for Lucy," Abby said. "She's got an inset day so she can be there, which will be good experience for her. And it will give me a chance to talk to everyone. According to Poppy, Ross saw Fay trip her." Which went a long way to explain the look he'd given Fay when she rushed off to find Daisy.

"Assuming he wasn't lying," Megan said, "it does seem an incredibly risky thing to do, and what difference would it make? Daisy would still be in trouble."

"She saw an opportunity and acted on the spur of the moment?" Abby suggested. "And why would Ross lie?"

"I don't know, but he was the person who told Poppy that he couldn't get hold of Kevin and meanwhile he was the hero of the hour, dousing her in water and getting her off to hospital."

"Maybe he wanted some attention from her. Men are hard to age but he's got to be in his late thirties at least. Even Poppy remarked that he's old for an assistant director on a show like *The Potting Shed*."

"It's still a bit of a stretch."

"Hmm," Abby said. "The friend Poppy was calling as she left the hotel was 'Ross, darling' . . ."

"You think he might have a tendresse for Poppy?"

"What a sweet way of putting it. It would give him a strong motive for getting Daisy out of the way," Abby said, her mind spinning with the possibilities, "but it's a big step up to murder. He's more likely to be the online troll."

"But again, if the campaign had worked, it would be Tarr handing her the job. Tarr who'd get the reward."

"Stop picking holes in my perfect motive," Abby grumbled, knowing that she was right.

"Isn't that my job? Do you really think there's something suspicious about Daisy's death?" Megan asked. "What did Dee say?"

"She said the cause of death was unclear and the coroner wouldn't sign the death certificate until they'd carried out more tests. She implied her inquiries were all about the gold-braid mob covering their backsides."

"Really?" Megan sounded doubtful. "Surely checking what happened and when is a task for someone way below her pay grade. Someone in uniform."

"Pretty much my response, but she said they're keeping a low profile. Uniforms would excite press attention."

Even as she said it, she didn't need to turn and look at Megan to know that she'd just raised her eyebrows in disbelief.

"Just be careful, Abs," she warned. "Think about what happened last Christmas before you go poking a stick into a hornet's nest."

Despite the heat, Abby shivered. As if she'd ever forget how close she'd come . . .

"Lesson learned," she promised.

"Are you still staying at the boathouse?"

"Just for tonight. It's rare for us to be there on our own and it feels a bit special. We're having a champagne and fish and chip supper on the deck."

"You're a cheap date, Abby Finch."

"It's very good champagne," she replied, "and we can't all go swanning off to London to take in a show at the drop of a hat."

"I'd stay over and keep the offspring from burning the house down in your absence whenever Jake feels like treating you," she offered. "Tell me what you'd like to see and I'll drop a hint."

Abby laughed. "It wouldn't need a hint but I may take you up on staying over one night. Meanwhile it's not all gold medals and television appearances. Sophie and Tom will be home tomorrow. I need to stock up the fridge first thing, and there'll be enough dirty clothes to keep the washing machine in business for a week."

"All that and an unexplained death to investigate. It's just as well I bought you a summer sleuthing hat."

"It's just a Panama, Meg," she said, straightening it. "An exceptionally nice one, which I love," she added, "but it's to keep the sun off my head and out of my eyes. Nothing more."

Megan just laughed. Five minutes later she pulled into the driveway of a pretty house set well back from the road, with woodland at its rear. "Great, I'm here first so I can flick a duster round while you go off a-sleuthing."

"Will I have to climb over the fence?"

"No. Someone, sometime must have been a fisherman and put in a gate so that they could take advantage of the footpath down to the Hart. With or without His Lordship's permission."

"Whichever, I'm grateful."

"Be careful, Abby." Megan suddenly looked anxious. "Jake will never forgive me if you get into trouble."

"If I get into trouble," she said, "he'll ground me until I draw my pension."

"Wait!" Megan said as Abby headed towards the rear of the house.

She stopped, looked back.

"You're wearing an Earthly Designs T-shirt. If anyone sees you . . ."

"Oh, Horlicks!"

"Not to worry. Like Daisy Dashwood I carry spares — I have been known to get through three shirts in one day when I've been climbing through loft hatches." She opened the rear door of her 4x4 and handed her a white shirt still in its bag from the laundry. "Try not to get it covered in green stuff. Where's your lanyard?"

"I'm not going to risk saying I'm a council official." She peeled off the polo shirt and buttoned herself into the crisp white cotton just as a car drew in alongside the 4x4, giving Megan no time to quiz her on her story. The trick was to keep it simple . . .

The gate squeaked. There was a squawk and a beating of wings as a startled pheasant flew up, then silence as she stepped onto a well-worn path. Since she couldn't see the manor and wasn't sure exactly where it lay, she walked quietly along it, tucking the shirt into her waistband. The soundtrack of the woods gradually restarted: wood pigeons, squirrels scampering along the branches, the rat-a-tat-tat of woodpecker, a blackbird proclaiming his territory.

She walked on, automatically noting the plants in the undergrowth. Holly, brambles, wild clematis. Rhododendron was spreading and could become a nuisance if not checked. There was a white spread of wild garlic scenting the air, dog roses and honeysuckle winding around the trunk of an old oak. It was unbelievably peaceful.

She caught a glimpse of tall chimneys through a gap in the trees and left the path to push her way through, doing her best to avoid the brambles, which were throwing out vigorous new shoots to catch the unwary.

She wasn't entirely successful. Having carefully unhooked her jeans, she looked up. In front of her stood a grand Jacobean manor built from the local buff stone. It was not open to the public, but she had once visited the place with her primary school, the same one that Sophie now attended, while doing a local history project.

There was a large ornamental pool in front of wide stone steps leading up to a terrace the length of the magnificent frontage, which was now partly obscured by scaffolding and tarpaulin. A large sign declared *DANGER FALLING MASONRY*.

There was no one about so she crossed the lawn to take a closer look. She was staring up at the roofline, which looked solid enough, when she heard a voice behind her.

"Can I help you?"

CHAPTER EIGHTEEN

Abby jumped. Anyone would jump, she told herself. It was a natural reaction to being caught where you shouldn't be and she wasn't about to deny that. And the voice, while cool, was polite. Not the least bit threatening, unlike the last time she'd heard it when its owner had been asking her who the hell she was.

She took a breath and turned, hoping that Patrick Farrell wouldn't remember her without her Earthly Designs T-shirt. "I'm so sorry. I realise I'm trespassing but my dog saw something — a squirrel or a rabbit — I only caught the movement out of the corner of my eye. The stupid thing just took off through the trees."

"Your dog?"

She wasn't the only one wearing dark glasses and a hat, although Farrell had gone for a baseball cap with a good-sized peak that shaded his face.

"She's a spaniel," she said, sticking to a dog she knew, "and terminally stupid, I'm afraid. I was with a friend who's looking at a house that's for sale." She waved vaguely in the direction from which she'd come.

"You didn't have her on a lead?"

A lead . . . She wasn't carrying a lead.

"No. We were in the garden chatting and she was happy just snuffling around. My friend has gone looking in the direction of the stream." She didn't want him to think she was totally on her own. "She'll probably come back covered in mud."

"Dogs will do that."

"This is a wonderful house." She turned back to face it rather than him. "I came here once, years ago, on a school trip. We were doing a project on local history," she rattled on, nerves making her talk too much. "Not nearly as interesting as the more recent past. Did you know that Edward VIII and Mrs Simpson cavorted naked in the Hart?"

"That piece of gossip had somehow passed me by," he said, "but it will be an interesting note to add to the website when we open."

"Open?"

"The Manor is going to be a hotel and spa."

"You're converting your home? Is that what all the scaffolding's about?

"As you can see, it needs a lot of work."

Except there was no sign of builders. There were no vans in sight. There was no sound of machinery, no sign of the essential skip, no sound of men working. No noise other than the birds.

"It's being surveyed before we begin," he said. "Dry rot, wet rot, you name it. But this is a private garden and while I hope you find your dog, as you can see, it's not safe to wander around."

"No — yes, I mean. Of course. The stupid animal will have probably found her way back to the car by now."

"Covered in mud."

"And panting for a drink."

"I'll give you a call if I find her. What's her name?"

"Maisie." The name slipped out and her mouth dried. The man's sheer physical presence was threatening. She wished she could see his eyes, see what he was thinking.

"Maisie?" he repeated. One sound away from Daisy. "And I imagine all the contact details are on her collar?"

"Yes, but I'm sure one of us will find her. Good luck with the survey. I hope you don't find any rot. Dry or otherwise," she added before she walked briskly back the way she'd come, calling out "Maisie, Maisie . . ."

She had to force herself not to look over her shoulder to see if he was following, told herself not to break into a run but walk calmly away as if she really was a woman looking for her lost dog.

"Maisie!" Just a few more steps.

She reached the trees and pushed through the brambles, not caring as they caught her clothes and skin, until she was back on the path, where she hung onto her hat and ran.

She was gasping when she closed the gate behind her and stood in the safety of the cottage garden.

Megan was still inside the house with the woman whose car was parked alongside hers and Abby climbed in, grabbed a bottle of water from her bag, took a long drink and then found some antiseptic wipes to clean up the scratches.

Ten minutes later Megan waved off the house viewer and climbed into the driving seat of her 4x4.

"How did it go? The viewing?" Abby asked.

"She wants to bring her partner back for a second look." Then, with a sigh, "What did I say about the shirt?"

There were smears of blood and snags where the brambles had caught. "I'm sorry. I just wanted to get away. I'll buy you a new one."

"It's okay. I've got a dozen."

"Really?"

"Office uniform. So, what happened to have you running scared?"

"There's scaffolding and tarpaulin covering large parts on the frontage and a big 'danger' sign, but there are no trucks, no skips and no workmen. However—" she dabbed at a tear on the back of her hand that was still oozing blood — "I did run into Patrick Farrell, hiding behind dark glasses and baseball cap."

Megan groaned. "Jake is going to kill me. What did you say?"

"That I was looking for my dog. It was the first thing that came into my head. Of course he immediately spotted that I wasn't carrying a lead but I said I was chatting with my friend — I wanted him to know that I wasn't alone — and she'd taken me by surprise chasing after a squirrel. I'm not sure he believed me."

"Do you think he recognised you?" Megan asked.

"There was a moment . . . I was thinking of Emma's dog and said she was called Maisie."

"Oh." The sound escaped Megan in a little huff of breath.

"He said he'd call me if he found her, and I couldn't think of a thing to say, and then the way he'd asked if all the contact details would be on her collar . . ."

"Abby?"

"There was something in his voice. As if he knew I was lying."

"What kind of something?"

Abby shrugged. "Something that made me want to get out of there."

"You were wearing a hat and sunglasses. He couldn't possibly have recognised you."

"I was wearing the hat and the sunglasses when I took Fay to the cottage and he was there."

"Damn it." She took a deep breath. "Okay. Suppose he did remember you? What's he going to do? If there's no sign of workmen just weeks before the place is supposed to open, he's obviously up to some funny business. If he thinks he's been rumbled, he's not going to waste time hunting you down to stop you talking, he'll be too busy putting some distance between himself and Maybridge. With luck, it will be somewhere without an extradition treaty."

"Let's hope you're right," Abby said.

"Trust me, I'm an estate agent."

That got the intended laugh. "Can you drop me back at the show?" she asked. "I need to pick up my van."

And go home. She needed a hug.

* * *

Fay had sent her the link to the YouTube video showing Daisy using the tea caddy and infuser, with a text urging her to check at the Beaumont Court events office.

Definitely not a poodle, Abby thought. More a rottweiler with terrier tendencies. Time was getting on but another ten minutes wasn't going to make much difference one way or the other and she wanted a word with Major Elliott.

His door was shut. She tapped before opening it and then began to back out when she saw he was on the phone, but he said, "Hold on," to his caller and waved her in.

"Mrs Finch." The 'again' remained unspoken but it was there in the tone. "How can I help you?"

"I'm sorry to be a nuisance, Major Elliott, but Fay Bingley is insisting that some of Miss Dashwood's belongings are missing. An antique silver tea caddy and infuser," she added. "They are not only valuable but they are strongly associated with her brand."

"Brand?" he repeated.

"She always had them with her at events," she explained, "but they weren't among the things I collected from the sitting room and returned to her home."

Flushed with indignation, the major drew himself up to his full height. "Is that woman suggesting that I've taken them?"

A voice from the phone demanded to know what was happening, and he raised it to his ear. "It's nothing, dear. I'll let you know." He cut the connection. "My wife," he explained, "wanting to know when I'll be home this evening."

Abby sympathised. "An event like this must mean long days for you."

"It goes with the job."

"I think you said your wife was a big fan of Daisy Dashwood? Did she get a chance to meet her?"

"I was able to take her to the breakfast reception and Theresa met her then," he said, a little less stiffly, "and of course she had a ticket to the recording of *The Potting Shed*. She was in the front row and saw everything."

"I'm so sorry."

"She was absolutely distraught and I was going to call someone to take her home, but fortunately a guest arrived by private taxi just then and the driver agreed to take her home."

"That was fortunate."

"I imagine it was off the clock . . . But what's this nonsense about a tea caddy?" he asked, impatiently.

"Oh, yes, sorry. Acting Detective Sergeant Newcombe is going to follow it up, but she's been called away and since I'm here now I thought it was worth checking in case it's been tucked away somewhere?"

Clive Elliott became alarmed. "That woman has involved the police?"

"No, not at all. DS Newcombe just happened to be there when I told Fay that I hadn't found it. She was very upset."

A lift of his eyebrows indicated what he thought of Fay Bingley. "Are you certain that Miss Dashwood would have brought something so valuable with her?"

"It seems that she takes it everywhere. It's with her on the photograph on her website. She has it at book signings and when she's running workshops. As I said, it's part of her brand image." Abby called up the YouTube video on her phone of Daisy making tea at a book signing and showed it to him.

"I see. Yes. But no one would have seen it here," he pointed out.

Someone had, Abby thought. "Daisy blended her own herbal tea and she certainly made some here. I washed out the mug she had also brought with her and I could smell it. But the caddy containing the herbs and the infuser she used were not there."

"No one could have taken it from here. As soon as I heard that Daisy had been taken ill I locked the door." He seemed affronted at any suggestion of carelessness on his part. "And I haven't found her pen either."

"Pen?" Abby's hand went to her own tote bag.

"Fay Bingley rang and asked if I'd found Daisy's pen," the major said.

"Don't worry about that. I have it safe," she assured him. "It's just the silver tea caddy and infuser. It's possible that Daisy put them out of sight in a cupboard for safety before she left for the show. I don't imagine the room is in use at the moment." She was well aware that the events were over for the day. "Can we check it now?"

"If you insist," Major Elliott said, grudgingly. He took a key from his desk and led the way to the sitting room, standing back while Abby checked the cupboards under the kitchen work surface and the refrigerator. There was no sign of the caddy or the infuser.

"I should think there were people coming in and out all morning?" Abby said. "Only I've noticed that you shut your door when you're taking a telephone call."

"Not always, but there was a lot of noise from the green room that day. Television people," he said, as if that explained everything.

"And, of course, if it was a personal call . . ."

"Well, yes." The muscles worked in his jaw.

"So," Abby said, ignoring his growing irritation as she recapped, "someone could have slipped in, seen the silver and taken it while you were on the phone."

"That would take some nerve."

"Would it? They are small pieces and there are strangers in and out all day during an event like this." She turned to the door as a couple walked down the corridor. "How many people are permitted to use the facilities?"

"A few," he admitted. "All absolutely trustworthy. That was Mrs Forsyte, a judge at the dog show, with her husband."

"Quentin?"

"Well, yes . . ."

And with the door shut he wouldn't know if someone not on his approved list had walked in, and his expression suggested that he knew it.

"I'm sorry to have taken up so much of your time, Major. The police will circulate photographs to antique shops in a wide area. An opportunist thief will want to move them on so we may get lucky."

"I sincerely hope so. It would reflect very badly on the show, and on me personally, if they are not recovered."

"Unfortunately, if it was a fan — someone hoping for a moment with Daisy but seeing something so iconic just sitting there —" Abby shrugged. "If that happened then they'll never see the light of day again."

Major Elliott shifted uncomfortably. "We do get fans hanging around. I hope it was insured, although of course, nothing could ever replace them."

"No. I'll let DS Newcombe know that I've checked with you."

They walked back to the events office.

Abby adopted a casual tone. "I noticed you were using your mobile phone, rather than the landline, when I arrived. Do you get a good signal in the house?"

"It's very good here," he said, happy to be on safer ground. "In the house and even at the furthest reaches of the showground." He glanced at her. "You haven't had any problems?"

"No. It's just that someone mentioned a poor signal in the green room."

"Try it for yourself and you'll see." He returned to his office and closed the door.

Abby tried and Major Elliott was right. There was nothing wrong with the signal.

There could be two reasons for Kevin Tarr's unanswered call. Either he didn't answer it in the green room because he didn't want to, or he didn't answer it there because he wasn't in the green room but down the corridor removing evidence.

Alternatively, the person who said there was no answer might have been only pretending to make the call to prevent Kevin from coming back to take care of the lovely Poppy.

CHAPTER NINETEEN

The sun had slipped beyond the distant hills leaving the sky golden and Abby was lying back in a deckchair replete with a perfectly battered fish and rather too many chips.

"This is perfect," she said.

"It has been special staying here on our own for a couple of nights."

Since Jake had been invited by the children to come to stay at Christmas and somehow never left, the houseboat had become a family weekend retreat and they rarely had it to themselves.

He lifted the champagne bottle from a bucket filled with ice and shared the last between their glasses. When he put the bottle down he picked up her hand and ran his thumb over the long scratch. "How did you get this?"

"I had an argument with a bramble and lost."

"Brambles always win," he said, keeping hold of her hand. "Where exactly was this bramble?"

"There are some on my show garden," she said, "but it's been a bit of a crazy day. Dee asked me to go with her to talk to Fay. I met with Kevin Tarr at the Queen's Head and then I went to Lower Haughton with Megan. She's got a house on the market there. It backs on to Hartford Manor so I thought I'd take look."

His hand tightened around hers. "Abby . . ."

"Patrick Farrell caught me in the garden," she admitted. "I said I was looking for my dog. A spaniel." She ignored his exasperated huff. "Daisy might have thought she was having a wedding reception in a beautifully converted Jacobean manor in a few weeks, but although the place is draped in scaffolding and tarpaulins there's absolutely no sign of building work."

"But Daisy must have been there?"

"Megan saw her there with Patrick Farrell and she wasn't happy. You'd think she'd be all over it but she has been very busy. It wasn't just *The Potting Shed* and appearances, the book she was working on was scheduled to go out in the autumn to coincide with harvests, and she was negotiating with the company who were to produce her teas and cordials for sale in the spa."

"So she was leaving the hotel side of things to Farrell?"

"Presumably. I imagine she saw the designs and signed off on them, but didn't want to be involved in managing the work — not when she had Farrell to do it for her. And there was a big-money deal with a lifestyle magazine to cover the wedding. They were concerned that rival magazines would have time to get people in undercover to take photographs and rush out copies if the news leaked so they were paranoid about secrecy."

"But there isn't going to be a wedding," Jake said. "And from what you saw today, there isn't going to be a hotel either."

"No."

"You think it was all a lie, don't you? Right from the start."

"If it looks like a duck, walks like a duck . . ."

"I hope you didn't quack at Patrick Farrell."

"No, I acted as if I thought it was his home. I told him I'd been there on a school visit as a kid, which is true, by the way."

"I don't remember that."

"It was primary school, before you came to live in Maybridge."

His jaw tightened. Jake had shared the bare bones of how his mother had taken him into a Bristol shopping centre and, while he was looking at a toy, had walked away and left him. Abby had to swallow down a lump in her throat.

"Pushing your luck, Abby," he said, not bothering to hide his exasperation. "One of these days . . ."

"He told me that the house was being surveyed before work started. Dry rot was mentioned. I suppose it's just possible that the scaffolding is set dressing and the survey a ploy to put off anyone getting too nosy, but there was something a little too smooth about him. I was glad to get out of there."

"Without the dog?"

"I'm afraid so. The stupid animal didn't come when I called."

"Oh, what was his name?"

"Hers," Abby said. "Maisie."

"You have got be joking."

"I had to come up with something on the spur of the moment," she said, "and when I said it was a spaniel I was thinking of Maisie, Emma's dog. It just came out."

"Damn it, Abby, I'm tempted to get Sophie the puppy she's been begging for just to teach you a lesson."

"Only if you're prepared to take it for walks for the next ten-plus years."

"Don't tempt me," he said. "I always wanted a dog when I was a kid."

"Did you? What kind?"

"Any kind," he said. "A scruffy mongrel."

Something to love that would love him back unconditionally, she thought as he held her gaze before abruptly changing the subject. "Would it help if I picked up Tom from the station tomorrow?"

"It would," she said, "and he'll enjoy talking to you about what he's been doing because, obviously, being a woman — no, make that being a *mother*, which is even worse — I couldn't possibly understand the difference between a googly and a doosra."

He gave her an old-fashioned look but then, as she'd hoped, he laughed. "I'll text him in the morning and check what train he's on."

"And then it's back to normal."

"Normal does it for me," he said, with feeling.

Abby smiled, sipped her champagne then sighed. "I'm afraid I've let things slip over the last couple of weeks. The fridge is Mother Hubbard, and I need to check the laundry and make sure everyone has a clean school uniform for next week. Thank heavens for Pam or there'd be cobwebs hanging from the ceiling."

"I'd offer to cook, but I'm giving a talk at the Bath Rotary Club tomorrow evening."

Abby looked across at him. "How come? According to the calendar you should still be in Ireland."

"I added the extra days so that I could surprise you. Epic fail."

"No, perfect timing," she assured him, and, loving him for being so thoughtful, she leaned across to kiss him. His response led to a spillage of champagne and a retreat below deck.

* * *

They were up early the following morning but Dee had already texted to tell Abby that Patrick Farrell was no longer at Hartford Manor.

"He must have recognised me," Abby said.

Jake looked up from reading the paper on his tablet.

"Patrick Farrell. When Dee followed up my message, he'd flown the nest."

"Definitely dodgy business, then. I wonder where he's taken cover."

"I suspect it will be France," Abby replied.

Dee probably knew that but she'd sent her a quick text just in case and one to Megan to update her before realising that Jake was watching her.

"His agent has a house there," she explained. "It's where he met Daisy. Any requests for dinner this evening?"

His brow flicked up at the abrupt change of subject. "If you'd been paying attention you'd remember that I'm speaking at the Bath Rotary Club."

"Yes, sorry, I've a lot on my mind."

He looked away.

"It's short notice, isn't it?"

"The speaker they booked has gone down with covid. Zaida asked if I'd step in at the last minute."

"Zaida is a member of Bath Rotary?" Jake's office manager, who had done so much to help relocate his business to Maybridge, had recently been made a director.

"She is and she's doing her best to recruit me. You're welcome to come?"

"If you're going to scare the pants off them with dire warnings about the danger to their business posed by a cyber-attack, I'll pass, but give my best to Zaida. We should have them all over for lunch soon, fix a date. Or are you going away again?"

"I'll be spending a day in Scotland next week and Paulo has set up some meetings in Rome. I'll check the calendar and let you know." He glanced at her. "Why don't you come with me?"

"To Scotland?"

"If you want to look around Glasgow, but I was thinking of Rome. Penny will be back from her cruise in a few days and she'll stay at the cottage while we're away."

"Let's see how it fits in. I've the rebuild of the show garden . . ."

Jake shrugged and returned to his newspaper, cutting off Abby mid-excuse. Without stopping to think how she would manage it, she said, "I am busy, Jake, but I will always find time for a couple of nights in Rome with you."

His smile was enough to make however many extra hours she had to put in worth the effort.

"When he was here at Easter Paolo offered the loan of his villa during the summer holidays," she said. "If I take him up on it will you be able to get away for a couple of weeks?"

"Family holidays, preferably without an internet connection, are mandatory for my employees and now I have a family, if only at second hand, I plan to lead by example."

That 'second hand' clutched at her heart a little. "I'm glad to hear it. This year will be the last with Lucy, assuming she hasn't already made other plans with Cal or her friends."

"She may not be able to get away at all if she lands the internship," Jake said.

"I suppose not. Fingers crossed the filming on Monday will help."

"That's why you're doing it?"

The question was casual enough, but Abby wasn't fooled for a minute. "What other reason could there be?" she asked, waiting for the other shoe to drop.

"Most garden designers would give their eye teeth for the opportunity," he said, "but you're not most garden designers and you have a strong aversion to publicity of any kind."

Abby waited.

"And there's the fact that you've become rather heavily involved in this business with Daisy Dashwood. I'm surprised Dee took you with her to interview Fay Bingley."

"I was going anyway, to deliver Daisy's belongings," she said, "and the police wanted a timeline of what happened that morning. An idea of where everyone was when she collapsed. Fay has been knocked sideways and Dee thought it would help if there was someone with her that she knew. And, if I'm honest, I was keen to get a look at Daisy's garden."

"Why?"

"Well, as I said, she's in a bit of a state—"

"Why do the police want a timeline?" he asked, antennae twitching. "And what were you looking for in her garden?"

There it was. A great big size-eleven shoe hitting the deck.

"She's a gardening legend. I took photographs. I'll show you." She picked up her phone.

"Nice try, but you can't distract me with pretty pictures."

Ignoring his dismissal, she flipped through the photographs and held the phone above his tablet so that he couldn't avoid looking. "That's hemlock."

"Hemlock?" He frowned, then looked up at her. "Isn't that what Socrates took when he was condemned to banishment or death?"

She was grinning as she put down her phone. "Distracted in one."

"Abby." Jake looked so concerned that she relented, reaching out for his hand.

"I'm sorry. The truth is that Dee told me the coroner is unwilling to issue anything but a temporary death certificate as the cause of death is unclear. And Daisy's a celebrity. The top brass are keen to ensure that every 't' is crossed and 'i' dotted."

Jake frowned. "They still don't know why she died?"

"The post-mortem hasn't come back yet. Besides that, there's been social media nastiness suggesting a drink problem, her assistant who desperately wanted *The Potting Shed* has walked out, and I found out Daisy apparently had a student fling with Quentin that ended very badly. They've been at daggers drawn ever since."

"Over a fling that happened nearly forty years ago? What the hell happened?"

About to say that enquiring minds would like to know, she thought better of it. "I have no idea, but guess what? He's got *The Potting Shed* gig. It seems that the production company had already decided to put out feelers to see if he would be interested should Daisy be unable to continue."

"Because of this alleged drink problem? Have they looked at her liver?"

"Don't be unkind. The rumours are unfounded."

"How do you know that?" He shook his head. "Stupid question. And now you'll be filming with him on Monday."

"I'll be seeing him sooner than that, and so will you. He's staying with Sir Mark and Lady Hamilton. It seems he's an old friend of Katherine's and about to design a new border for her, so he'll be at May's birthday party on Sunday. You hadn't forgotten about that?"

"It's imprinted on my memory," he said, without enthusiasm. "I'm going to have Sir Mark trying to get me to donate to his damn party, or, worse still, join it, and Her Ladyship patronising the kid from care made good."

"Don't take it personally, she patronises everyone." Abby grinned. "But bear up, Izzy will be there and she won't be able to resist flirting with you, if only to annoy me."

"You two have a very weird relationship," he said.

"We do," she agreed, "but it works."

"You won't be popular with Her Ladyship if you grill Quentin about Daisy at the party," Jake warned.

"I wouldn't dream of it."

He gave her a side-eye.

"No, honestly." She put on a fair imitation of Her Ladyship's cut glass accent. "Absolutely infra dig, darling." Jake laughed.

Abby was keen to learn more about what had happened between Quentin and Daisy at college, or, more to the point, what Daisy did after she'd found Quentin with his trousers down. But a children's birthday party was not the place for that kind of conversation.

Although it would be interesting to observe him. Beneath that avuncular exterior would Quentin be triumphant? Or on edge?

And what the heck was going on at Hartford Manor? There was no sign of a hotel ready to be open in a few weeks. Maybe it was going to be a staged opening. Restaurant first, then the spa, then the rooms.

"The big question is who, apart from Quentin, actually benefits from Daisy's death? Or, like Poppy, believed they would," Abby said without thinking.

"You think she was murdered and on Monday you're going to be seeing everyone who was there that day."

"Not everyone," she said pointedly. Not Daisy. And not Patrick Farrell.

"Nearly everyone. And you'll be asking the kind of questions that we both know can get you into all kinds of trouble." He held her gaze, his face serious. "I worry about you, Abby Finch."

"We're just filming the garden for *The Potting Shed*," she said, with what she hoped was a reassuring smile. "What could possibly happen?"

"Do you want me to remind you?"

"No." There was no need. There were still occasions when she woke sweating from a nightmare and grasping at the invisible hands around her neck.

CHAPTER TWENTY

Jake had just left when Abby received a call from DI Iain Glover.

"Abby, are you busy?"

"You could say that, but fire away."

"Could you call in at the station sometime this morning? I need a favour."

"I can squeeze you in before I hit the supermarket. In half an hour?"

This arranged, she gathered up her things and set off, wondering what the DI had in store for her.

She arrived and was shown to Iain's office. Iain rose to greet her. "Thanks for dropping in, Abby. I know how busy you must be with the show. Congratulations on your medal, by the way."

"Thanks." It was just two days ago but it seemed a lifetime. "Is this about Daisy? Has the pathologist come to any conclusion about what might have caused her death?"

"You know I can't discuss that."

"But you're not ruling out a poison of some kind," she pointed out, "or you wouldn't have asked to see me."

"Dee mentioned that you were interested in Miss Dashwood's herb garden."

"It was a professional interest, but you might want to have someone check what she puts in her herbal teas."

"Oh?"

"Daisy dries — dried — her own herbs. There are a number of caddies in her pantry containing not just single-herb teas such as mint, chamomile, lemon balm, but she created blends to aid sleep, focus, that sort of thing."

"Oh, right." He nodded. "Megan's been trying to get me to cut my coffee habit and use them, too. Chamomile?" He pulled a face and Abby hid a smile.

"Very calming," she said, "but Meg buys commercial blends from the supermarket. Daisy creates her own.""

"I see. Is it possible that something could toxic have got into one or more of them by accident? Dee mentioned hemlock?"

"Daisy wouldn't make that kind of mistake," Abby assured him. "She was writing a book on the subject. According to Fay Bingley, her assistant, she had a keen interest in the historical use of herbs in folk medicine."

"It would help if we knew what she used. I'm sure the lab could sort it out, but they're under pressure and it will take time."

"She must have kept notes," Abby said.

"Notes?"

"She'll have conducted trials to see what was the most effective combination of herbs. Not just what she was using, but the quantity and combination. They'll be among her records, but you'll need an expert to look at them."

"I'm looking at an expert. If I get you her paperwork can you look through it?"

About to protest that she wasn't qualified, she hesitated. A chance to look through Daisy's papers was not to be missed.

"I have to put in at least a token appearance at the show, Iain, and I've got the children coming home . . ."

She trailed off, realising she hadn't really talked herself out of it.

"I'll get the papers sent to you," Iain said, the decision apparently made. "They're being logged at present but once that's done they're all yours." He got to his feet. "What do you make of Fay Bingley?" he asked as he walked with her to the door. "Dee said that she seemed grief-stricken."

"I get the feeling that her whole life revolved around Daisy," Abby said. "And there's the likelihood that having lost her job, she will also lose her home."

"So she would have no reason to cause Miss Dashwood harm?"

"No, on the contrary."

Of course, you couldn't discount jealousy, anger, thwarted love, Abby thought as she climbed into her van.

Before driving off, she took a moment to check her phone. Lucy had sent a clip of Cal and his band performing and she sat for a moment watching it before sending back a row of clapping emojis.

She'd be interested to look at Daisy's papers, diaries, whatever, but Sophie and Tom would be home today and Lucy and Cal on Sunday. This was what was mattered. Her family. Jake.

She put the car into gear and drove to the showground, where she found someone waiting at her garden.

"Mrs Finch? Martin Green from *Gardening for the Future* magazine. I left a message but I imagine you've been busy."

"I have, Mr Green. What can I do for you?"

"Maybe talk about how you think we should all be gardening for the future?"

About to tell him that she was too busy, she changed her mind and indicated a stone slab, where they sat and talked for half an hour, during which Daisy Dashwood's name was never mentioned once.

When he'd gone, Quentin came over. "Telling the tale about Daisy?" he asked. "How much are they paying you?"

He sounded bitter and Abby, beyond annoyed, said, "If you hadn't slunk off in a sulk ignoring your commitment to *The Potting Shed*, Quentin, you'd have been there when Daisy collapsed. And, assuming you could have brought yourself to go to her aid, it would be you everyone wanted to speak to."

His shoulders slumped and shockingly, his eyes filled with tears.

"If only you knew . . ."

* * *

Abby finally found a moment to call Fay to let her know that she'd drawn a blank on Daisy's silverware. "I'm really sorry, but it looks as if someone walked off with it."

"I knew it, but thanks for checking. It just makes me so angry that anyone would do that." She sighed. "If I'd been there—"

"Don't do that to yourself, Fay. You were doing what was best for Daisy." Or what she thought was best. "And before I forget, I've just realised that the last things I picked up, after I'd closed the suitcase, were Daisy's pen and lipstick. I put them in my bag and forgot about them."

"That's a relief. I phoned Major Elliott about them but he clearly thought I was making a fuss over nothing and was rather sharp with me. But the pen was expensive. A Mont Blanc. I was going to ask if I could keep it. It was something that Daisy used every day."

"Have you seen or heard anything of Patrick Farrell?" Abby asked, in an attempt to divert her from dwelling on Daisy.

"Nothing, but Tessa Anderson phoned me yesterday morning to let me know that she'd be coming down today to pick up his belongings."

So, his agent *was* in touch with him.

"Has he left Hartford Manor?" Abby continued her digging mission. "It can't be more than fifteen miles from the cottage. Obviously he will be avoiding the press but it seems crazy for Miss Anderson to drive all this way just to pick up a few things."

"I don't think he ever went to the hospital," Fay said. "I think he wanted to put as much distance between himself and Daisy as possible."

"Why would he do that? I realise that things have changed but the Manor has to go ahead, surely?"

"Maybe. Daisy arranged to meet a tree surgeon there about ten days ago. Patrick was furious with her. He said that anyone could have been there, seen them."

He was right, Abby thought. They had been seen. By Megan.

"The way he spoke to her—" Fay was undeniably angry — "The way she apologised. He was all over her, then, saying he understood her impatience, that he couldn't wait until they could share their love with the world, promising to cook her favourite dish. I don't know which was more sickening, her cringing apology or his fawning over her."

"But they were all right after that?"

"He was in control and Daisy would have done anything to keep him, Abby. If he'd told her the sky was pink she'd have agreed with him. Is that all right?" She didn't wait for an answer. "I should have done something, told someone."

"Did you handle the payments for the work?" Abby asked.

"No. I kept the books for her day-to-day expenses, but Daisy set up a separate business account for the Manor. Patrick drew down from that to pay the contractors."

The non-existent contractors.

"Daisy's solicitors want to talk to me," Fay went on. "I'll mention it to them."

"That's a good idea."

"I offered to deliver Patrick's things to Tessa then, but she wanted to pick up Daisy's papers, diaries, laptop and everything that Daisy had written for the new book and her notes. She was hoping there'd still be enough to pull it together for publication."

"That makes sense." Abby thought that she would need to let Iain know.

"She asked me to get everything together for her and I did," Fay said. "I had it all in Daisy's laptop bag, but then I had an email from the solicitor's office to tell me that the police would be picking it up. That woman who came here with you turned up an hour later and had a good look around the cottage to make sure I hadn't overlooked anything before she left." Fay sniffed. "She even asked for the key to the drying shed. I don't know what she thought she'd find in there."

Unwilling to speculate, Abby asked Fay if she'd told Tessa that the police had taken away the paperwork.

"I sent her a text and she wanted to know if they'd taken everything."

And had they? Dee had looked around, but there would have been plenty of time since Daisy's death for Fay to have gone through all her papers and hide anything she might think useful. Or could sell.

Daisy was big news at the moment and any uncomplimentary diary entries about television personalities she'd met, any letters, emails or texts between her and Patrick Farrell or photographs of them together would be worth a lot of money.

"I told her they had but she's coming anyway to check for herself. I don't suppose you could . . . ?" The plea trailed off.

There was nothing more than Abby would have liked to do than meet Tessa Anderson but her day was already fully booked.

"I really wish I could, Fay, but my children are coming home from their half-term camps this morning and I have to be there. I'm really sorry. And I'm afraid this won't be easy to hear but I think you ought to know that Quentin Latimer-Blythe has been asked to take over *The Potting Shed*."

"What!"

"They're filming in my walled garden on Monday. There's going to be some sort of tribute to Daisy."

Fay groaned. "If Daisy were in her grave, she'd be turning in it. Thank goodness that you'll be there. At least one of you will be sincere."

"I'll do my best," Abby assured her.

"You do realise that someone killed Daisy?" Fay insisted. "Why else would the police have taken her papers? It could even have been him!"

Abby frowned. "Quentin?"

"Yes. I've listened again and I'm sure he made that phone call."

"I'll listen again when I drop off the pen, but it's much more likely that Daisy's death was at worst an unfortunate accident," Abby said. "The concern surrounds the possibility that something toxic found its way into her tea."

"Only if someone put it there." Fay was emphatic. "They should be looking for the tea caddy."

"I'm sure they're doing everything possible," she said. "You didn't see anyone near Daisy's room that day? Anyone who shouldn't have been there?"

She didn't immediately answer.

"Fay?"

"Sorry," she said. "I was trying to think. *The Potting Shed* people were there and that woman doing a baking workshop — but honestly, I wasn't paying that much attention."

"Why would you?"

Besides, it didn't have to have happened at the show. The tea could have been tampered with any time before that. If it was the tea.

"Have a think about it," Abby said, "and I'll drop the pen off as soon as I have a moment. Is there anything you need?"

"No. You have your family to take care of," Fay said. "Don't worry about me. I'll be fine."

CHAPTER TWENTY-ONE

Having filled her boot with food, Abby pulled onto her driveway and began to unload. June, pottering about in her front garden opposite, gave her a wave.

"We saw Jake arrive home in a taxi and called out to tell him where you were."

"Thanks," Abby called back. "He said."

June crossed the lane to talk to her. "There have been a few people nosing around while you were away," she said, "but when one of them started looking into your front window Beattie went out and saw them off."

Beattie, June's partner, who'd kept order in the local library until she retired, famously had a voice that carried to the back stacks if she thought teenagers were fooling around. She could still use it when roused and, now she had a new hip and was back to full mobility, took no nonsense from anyone making a nuisance of themselves in the lane. But she was in her late sixties and shouldn't be taking that kind of risk.

"I thought you were going to call Harry if there was any trouble," Abby scolded. Bona fide newsmen wouldn't do anything stupid, but hot news attracted all kinds. "You never know how people will react."

"There wasn't any trouble. She waved her hoe at them and one of them laughed and waved back, which made her even madder. But they did leave."

"Well, please be careful. I'd hate it if anything were to happen to either of you." Especially if it was because of some drama she had attracted to their usually quiet street.

She carried her shopping through the gate to the back of the house. The grass had grown while Tom had been away and flowers had been fading in the heat and needed dead-heading. It wasn't just the inside of her house that had been neglected for the last couple of weeks.

Patch rubbed against her legs, happy to see her. Princess, very much the diva of the two cats, turned her back.

Inside, the cottage was hot and airless from being shut up and once she'd put everything away she went through the cottage opening windows and the folding doors to let the light breeze carry in the scent of the roses.

Then, having prepared a pasta bake that she could slide into the oven when needed, she went through to her study. Kate was covering the show garden and Pam Lewis was now cleaning for her on a regular basis, so she had a couple of hours to hunt down the answers to some questions that were burning a hole in her brain.

The first thing she did was put Daisy's name into the search engine and click on her Wikipedia biography to find out where she'd done her horticultural degree. There was a photograph taken about five years ago with the Chancellor, when they'd awarded her an honorary doctorate.

Quentin Latimer-Blythe had his own Wikipedia page where she discovered that they'd been born in the same year, within weeks of each other. There was a photograph of him as a very young man and he was stunningly handsome. It was hardly any wonder that Daisy had fallen for him. He could have had his pick, but maybe Daisy had been less predatory, less sexually demanding, safer . . .

More surprisingly, she discovered that he'd graduated two years earlier than Daisy.

There could be a perfectly straightforward reason for that if it hadn't been for the fact that she had been awarded her degree in horticulture, landscape and design by a different university from Quentin.

He'd said they'd started university together, but from the dates, it was clear that Daisy had started her degree in the autumn two years after Quentin had started his. There was no mention of a false start, a delay because of illness, and clearly she hadn't asked for a mid-year transfer, which was easy enough if you were staying on the same course. So why had she walked away and started again from scratch, two years behind?

Had the humiliation and anger from her relationship with Quentin brought on depression, possibly even a breakdown, while Quentin had carried on as if nothing had happened? It would explain the resentment and why Daisy had still harboured a grudge after all these years.

She was wondering how to find out what had happened after Daisy left when she saw the Guides minibus pull up in front of the house. Pushing all thoughts of suspicious deaths to the back of her mind, she went out to gather up her youngest, who emerged, hauling a rucksack almost as big as her. She looked happy but grubby.

"Thanks so much, Emmy," Abby said to the Guider who'd climbed out of the passenger seat to see her charge safely home. "I hope they were all well behaved."

"They were a nightmare. Vaping, drinking, hanging out in the woods with the Scouts the minute my back was turned."

"Emmy!" Sophie protested, grinning. "That is such a big fat fib!"

"Just kidding," Emmy conceded. "Did you have a good time?"

"Brilliant. Thank you. And thank you, Mrs Grey," she called to the Guider who was driving. "Especially for the abseiling. When can we go to the climbing centre?"

"I'll see what I can fix up."

Abby leaned in to offer Mrs Grey her own thanks, thanked Emmy, asked the girls still in the van if they'd had a good time, then watched as Mrs Grey backed into her drive, gave a toot on the horn and drove away.

"You stink of woodsmoke," Abby said, smiling, as she ushered Sophie inside. "Come and sort out your rucksack, then into the shower with you. Are you hungry?"

"Starving." Sophie had tipped the contents of the rucksack onto the utility room floor and was quickly sorting her dirty clothes into piles — something that would normally require nagging — while Abby put aside the sleeping bag and ground mat and added the camping utensils to the dishwasher. They looked clean but she was taking no chances.

"You've going to have to wait until Tom gets home for the pasta. Will a sandwich hold you?"

"A Dagwood?"

Thankfully this was not the original, from the comic strip, but their own version consisting of piled-up ham, cheese, tomato, onion, lettuce and mayonnaise. It had been a favourite of Sophie's dad and she always asked for it.

"It'll be waiting for you."

It was close to lunchtime so she decided to have one herself and had cut them in two and piled them onto plates by the time Sophie came downstairs, wet hair hanging down her back, wearing clean shorts and a T-shirt. She added the clothes she'd been wearing to the washing piles.

A week of Guide camp discipline had clearly worked magic. How long it would last was another matter.

While they were eating Sophie told her all the exciting things she'd done while she was away but as soon as she'd finished her sandwich she grabbed her phone to check in with all the friends she hadn't seen for an hour.

Not yet a teenager but already behaving like one.

It did mean that when a young constable arrived with a package, she was tucked up in the den and didn't see him, for which Abby was grateful.

* * *

156

A note from Iain explained that the package contained copies of everything handwritten, including Daisy's diaries. They had kept Daisy's computer but had downloaded the folder with her book file onto a USB stick that was also enclosed.

She had a couple of hours before Tom arrived home, so she put the USB stick into its port and settled down to examine its contents.

There was a file labelled *A History of Herbs Through the Ages* which proved to be working documents for Daisy's new book. It was nowhere near complete but Abby skim-read, hoping that something would leap out at her, and quickly realised it wasn't just herbs.

There were all the plants that had been used medicinally from ancient times. Abby knew a lot of them, although some made her wince.

There were all the usual suspects that could be used to good or ill. Foxgloves, poisonous but valuable for the treatment of heart problems. Henbane and hemlock were there, both poisonous but once used for all manner of things. Hemlock, the witch's brew with its psychotropic effects gave the user the sense of flying, while henbane, mixed with honey, was prescribed in Roman times for parents who had lingered too long.

That one had a jokey red tag in capital letters that read: *DO NOT TRY THIS AT HOME.* But that was the big question.

What exactly had Daisy been trying at home?

CHAPTER TWENTY-TWO

Abby's brain was too fired up to sleep. Jake was late home from Bath and, not wanting to disturb him, she was up when the sky was still pre-dawn pale.

She made a mug of tea and took it with her laptop to the table under the roses in the pergola.

She'd hoped the manuscript of Daisy's book would give her some ideas about the teas blended from the herbs she grew, but so far nothing, and there was a lot still in note form.

Vinca rosea, once classed in the family Apocynaceae, or periwinkle, was one that caught her eye. The entire family was toxic to some degree but had powerful medicinal properties too. Vinca rosea, the Madagascar periwinkle, produced a valuable compound that was used to treat cancer, while back in the seventeenth century Sir Francis Bacon had recommended wrapping the leaves of the green periwinkle around the leg as a cure for cramp.

Abby already knew that one of Vinca rosea's folk names was the 'flower of remorse', as it had once been used to garner confessions from suspected criminals.

Daisy had noted down that it was 'the plant that kept on giving' and a final note mentioned that in some societies the leaves were used to make a tea to keep the brain alert and ward off dementia.

That made Abby sit up. Afraid of dementia, would Daisy have added that to one of her teas? She tried to remember the names on the little caddies on the larder shelf. It wouldn't be in her 'sleep' blend. That would be chamomile, lavender, maybe valerian . . .

There had been one for 'vitality', she remembered, which she'd quite fancied trying herself. What would Daisy have put in that?

Abby sifted through the stack of paper copies hoping to find Daisy's tea recipes. There were none, but she must have done some research, tried various mixtures, and would have kept detailed notes about flavour and results.

She'd had a desk in her workroom. And a MacBook. Neither Iain nor Dee had mentioned it. Nor, for that matter, had Fay.

Abby picked up the phone and sent a text.

Dee, I don't think all Daisy's papers are here. There was a MacBook on her desk in the larder/workroom off the kitchen. It will contain notes of her experiments with herbs and her recipes. A x

It was early — Dee wouldn't be at Headquarters yet — and she sat back, trying to picture the row of herbs in her mind's eye. Single herbs: lavender, chamomile, the mints, sages, lemon balm. Then there were the mixes. Sleep, vitality . . . and memory!

That was it. Memory.

Daisy would have done background research for her book, and she was about to do the same, when her phone rang.

It was Dee.

"Good grief," Abby said. "You're up early."

"I could say the same about you," Dee replied, sounding weary. "I'm sorry, Abby, I have some very bad news. Fay

Bingley's body was pulled out of the river a couple of hours ago."

"Fay?" The news hit her like a shockwave. "No . . . I knew how upset she was, Dee, but I had no idea."

"Upset? More than when we saw her?"

"Maybe, I don't know. It was just a phone call but Tessa Anderson was going to the cottage yesterday to gather up Daisy's papers, that is, before they were taken away by you. Fay seemed anxious and I wondered if she'd hidden stuff."

"What kind of stuff?"

"Photographs, letters — the kind of things that she could sell to the tabloids. That MacBook with her recipes."

"It's possible," Dee admitted. "I had a good look, but there must have been a dozen places where Fay could have hidden stuff."

"She asked me if I could be there when Tessa arrived but I said I was too busy. I should have realised—"

"Don't," Dee cut in.

Easy to say. "The last thing she said to me was *'Don't worry about me. I'll be fine'* — but she wasn't . . ."

"You think it was suicide?"

"Well, yes." Why wouldn't she think that? "Patrick's arrival on the scene broke up the close relationship she and Daisy had. She blamed herself for not being there when Daisy needed her. And Fay hadn't just lost Daisy, she'd lost her job and almost certainly her home."

Abby felt sick as she remembered saying that she was too busy to be with her yesterday morning. While she'd been browsing the supermarket shelves, Fay had been in despair and thrown herself from Daisy's dock, maybe, in her distress, wanting to be with her.

"You did more for her than anyone else, Abby," Dee assured her. "You would have nothing to reproach yourself for even if she had taken her own life."

If?

Abby's guilt-ridden thoughts slammed to a halt. "Are you saying that she didn't?"

"We're waiting for the pathologist, but she received a blow to the head and was almost certainly dead before she went into the water."

Bile burned in her throat.

She swallowed it down. "You're saying that someone killed her?"

Was that better or worse?

Stupid question.

It was worse. Much worse.

"I imagine the killer hoped that if her body was found it would be taken for suicide," Dee said. "She could have got the head injury as she was swept downriver."

"But she didn't."

"She didn't drown and the lack of rain we've had lately means that the river is low. She was caught in some reeds a mile or so downstream from the cottage."

Abby stirred herself. "When did it happen? Do you know?"

"Sometime yesterday afternoon or early evening. We'll have a better idea after the PM. What time did you speak to her?"

Abby thought for a moment. "I was at Beaumont Court, so late morning?"

"Unfortunately, there's no CCTV close to the cottage. She didn't even have a doorbell camera. When was she expecting Tessa Anderson?"

"Just at some point during the day," Abby said. "She was coming for whatever Patrick Farrell had left there and she'd asked Fay to put together all Daisy's papers. She'd said she needed them to see if there was enough of the new book to rescue it."

"She asked for all her papers? The book I can understand," Dee said, "but why would she want the rest? That would be accounts, financial stuff, her will."

"Have you got those?"

"No. There's some stuff on her laptop but now we've opened a formal inquiry into her death we'll be asking her solicitor and accountant for everything when their offices open tomorrow."

"I wonder . . ." Abby was thinking out loud. "Is it possible that when Fay was going through Daisy's papers she found something that got her killed? She'd told Tessa Anderson that the police had taken them all, but she still planned to go and pick up Patrick's things."

"It's a long drive from London for a few of Farrell's belongings," Dee agreed. "Unless there was something among them that he didn't want the police to find."

"I imagine Fay had been through them," Abby said. "Were they gone when you searched the cottage?"

"Yep. There was nothing in the guest suite. Even the bed had been stripped."

"And there's the missing MacBook Air. Did the cottage look disturbed? I wonder if Tessa had keys to the cottage. Did she actually see Fay?""

"The French windows were open but there was no sign of any disturbance. Scenes-of-crime officers are going through the place now and we'll be talking to Tessa Anderson." Dee paused. "I need hardly add that this is all highly confidential information. I'm only telling you because you're involved."

"Yes, thank you." She and Dee had become friends, but she appreciated the trust built through their dealings together. "One of the last things Fay said to me was that you needed to find the tea caddy."

"It's a priority. Iain is concerned that rather than our first thought that it was removed by an opportunistic thief, it might have been taken to cover up the fact that something toxic had been added."

"Surely the pathologist would find anything harmful enough to kill?"

"We're trying to speed things up, but when I spoke to Iain earlier he asked me to stress the urgency of looking at the papers he sent you."

"In other words you are now treating Daisy's death as suspicious?"

"That, too, is confidential, but under the circumstances we have to, which is why it's important that we find out what herbs she was using. And whether there's anything in her diary that might offer some explanation."

"The diaries might be useful, but the MacBook would give me more information. It was where Daisy worked on recipes for her teas, syrups, preserves. She would have experimented, made notes about what she used and in what quantity."

"Maybe that's what Anderson was after."

"Daisy will have had them backed up somewhere. Maybe on a stick drive? I imagine Patrick Farrell has keys to the cottage," Abby said. "Have you located him yet?"

"Not yet. He must have been staying at Hartford Manor when he wasn't with Daisy, because he'd been forced to sell his London flat to cover his debts. But when I went to interview him the place was deserted and none of Daisy's keys fit the locks."

"Apparently, he was angry when she turned up unexpectedly with a tree surgeon," Abby told her. "Megan saw them. She'll be able to tell you exactly when that was."

Dee sighed. "We've been slow off the mark on this one, Abby. We should have listened to you. And Fay. She was convinced Daisy had been murdered and now we've let Farrell slip through our fingers."

"He may have gone to Tessa Anderson's house in France. She's his agent, too, and he'll be her number-one priority now. Fay will have the address," she said, without thinking, and then, hand to her mouth, gave a little groan.

"Let us worry about Farrell," Dee said, gently. "Just concentrate on the paperwork."

"Yes . . . I'll do that."

But she didn't return to the laptop when Dee ended the call.

Instead, she took her secateurs for a walk around the garden, snipping away at faded blooms, leaving her subconscious to poke around in her memory, looking for something she might have missed.

163

CHAPTER TWENTY-THREE

Jake found her there a little while later.

"I'm sorry," she said. "I didn't mean to disturb you."

He grinned as he placed two steaming mugs of coffee on the bench. "That ship sailed twenty years ago."

She made an effort at a smile and sat down. "How was your evening?"

"Well, they were expecting someone who's on the television and famous for scandalous anecdotes, so I came as something of a disappointment."

"Zaida hadn't warned you?"

"She's too smart for that," he said. "But they were polite and several people wanted to talk to me afterwards. Not a bad evening, considering. She suggested getting together for Sunday lunch at the Italian on the Quays very soon. It's child-friendly and she'd rather talk to you than have you slaving away in the kitchen."

"I'll give her a call," Abby said and then, unable to help herself, shivered.

"Hey, sweetheart . . ." He put his hand to her cheek so that she had to look at him. "What's up?"

"Fay's dead," she said. "Someone killed her yesterday and threw her in the river hoping it would look like suicide."

He didn't answer. He just put his mug down and his arms around her, holding her, until finally, a little comforted, she pulled back.

"She wanted me to go there yesterday, be with her when Daisy's agent arrived to collect some things."

"What things?" he asked.

"Daisy's papers, the book she was working on. Iain sent copies for me to look over and see if I can spot anything — any plant that might have caused her death."

"Iain has employed you as a consultant?" Jake asked.

"Employed might be overstating it. He asked as a friend, since getting an expert on board would take time."

"And money."

"And money," she agreed. "But it gives me a chance to look at her book, her diaries."

"That's no small task," he said, sympathetically.

"No, it's a privilege," she said, grateful for his understanding. "I just feel so bad. I told Fay that she could call me anytime and she seemed nervous about Tessa Anderson's arrival but when she asked me if I could be there I told her that the children were coming home and I was busy. She said not to worry. That she'd be fine." She looked at him. "That was the last thing she said me. 'I'll be fine' . . ."

"You think this woman Tessa might have killed her?" he asked. "Seriously? What motive would she have had?"

Abby shook her head. "I don't know. This whole business is a mess. There are any number of people who appear to have had a motive to kill Daisy but who on earth would want to kill Fay?"

Poppy might want to sue her, but murder . . . No one deserved to die like that.

She was palming away a tear that she couldn't stop from falling when Tom wandered out of the kitchen, swigging orange juice from the carton.

"Who is this?" Jake checked the time in mock astonishment, shielding Abby while she recovered. "And what have you done with Tom Finch?"

He pulled a face. "They got us up at sparrow's fart at cricket camp."

"Tom!" Abby warned, doing her best to ignore Jake's desperate attempt not to laugh.

"What?" He rolled his eyes. "Anyway, the body clock has been brainwashed and here I am, wide awake at some ridiculous hour on a Sunday."

It was like Guide camp discipline, Abby thought. She'd give it until Tuesday when everyone was back at school for things to return to normal. In the meantime . . .

"Breakfast will be a while so why not use the time productively and wash the van for me?" she suggested.

"Will I get paid?"

"You'll get breakfast."

* * *

The rest of Sunday flashed by with breakfast, the arrival home of Lucy and Cal, lunch, and then it was time to leave for May's birthday party.

Abby, Jake and the family were met at the door of the Hamiltons' ancient manor house by the housekeeper who directed them to the garden, where everyone had gathered on the lawn.

May, one year old and now walking, saw them and tottered towards Abby, arms outstretched.

"Happy birthday, sweetheart." Abby stooped to gather her up and give her a hug. "And happy giving-birth day to you, Izzy," she said, taking Izzy's hand and leaning forward to kiss her cheek.

"Luceeee!" May squealed and leaned towards her.

Lucy, delighted, took her. "Happy birthday, little sister."

"It's lovely to see you all." Izzy's smile lingered just a little longer on Jake.

"Izzy." He kissed her cheek.

"Come and join us. Mummy has laid on a champagne tea and I think Lucy is now old enough to have a sip."

"Lucy is just back from a music festival where I'm sure she'll have had something rather stronger than a sip of champagne," Abby said.

"Who knows if the water was safe to drink?" Lucy grinned and Izzy laughed, delighted.

"Come with me, Lucy, and let me lead you astray."

"Can I come, too?" Sophie asked.

Izzy caught Abby's eye. "I have some delicious elderflower fizz, which I think you'll like a lot more."

Tom self-consciously offered her the bag of gifts he was carrying, and Izzy was for a moment lost for words. He was now as tall as his father and every day looked more like him. The silence lasted only a moment before she managed a laugh.

"Good heavens, Tom, are you ever going to stop growing?" She turned to her mother. "Do you think we've got enough food?"

"The caterers can always put out an emergency call for cow pie," Lady Hamilton replied, demonstrating an unexpected familiarity with Desperate Dan. "Abby. I think you know everyone?"

She and Jake had met the grandparents and other godparents at May's christening. There were also local political figures and their partners present, whom Abby knew through her late husband. Unusual at an infant's birthday celebration, but then Sir Mark Hamilton was the local chair of the party and every social event was an opportunity to network. Jake knew some of them through business and joined them.

And then there was Quentin.

"Abby, how unexpected. I didn't realise you were a personal friend of Katherine's," he said.

"More Izzy's. I know Katherine in my capacity as May's godmother," she explained. "Why don't you show me where you're going to put the new white border she's so excited about?"

"It's going to be over here." He led the way to a long-established and colourful herbaceous border that was backed by an old wall built from the same buff-coloured local limestone as the house.

"There are a lot of valuable plants in this border," Abby said. "And white isn't going to show up well against that wall."

He shrugged. "It's her decision." Then, apparently eager to change the subject, "You seem an unlikely friend for Izzy Hamilton."

"We have a lot in common. We shared a husband — mine — and our children have the same father."

"Oh . . ." he said, evidently at a loss.

"He died before he could marry her and Izzy's waters broke while we were discussing arrangements for his funeral so I was the one holding her hand while she gave birth to May. On a hormonal high she asked me to be her godmother. Katherine has just about got over it," she said with a wry smile before changing the subject. "Many congratulations on getting *The Potting Shed* gig."

He was clearly relieved at the change of subject. "You've heard about that?"

"Kevin Tarr mentioned it when I saw him yesterday."

He shrugged. "The production company contacted me back when the rumours started about Daisy's drinking to see if I'd be interested in stepping in if needed."

"Who wouldn't be?" Abby said. "Although, in light of the latest tragedy, I imagine the police will be interested in who started them. Since they were rumours without any basis in fact. And the unpleasant phone calls. She wasn't cold when someone called and asked Fay if the old witch was dead."

"Really?" He sounded sceptical.

"Really. I was there. I heard him."

He took off his hat and fanned his face. "They're the kind of thing you have to expect when you're in the public eye. I'm sure if you looked at your social media you'd find a few unpleasant comments. People do seem to resent success."

"That's my daughter's province. I stay well away," she said. Although she'd better check. If there was anything nasty she didn't want Lucy involved.

"Of course, poor Daisy was so vain that she'd rather have people think that she was in the Priory drying out than admit that she'd been in a Swiss clinic having her face lifted back into place."

For someone who disliked Daisy so much, Abby thought, he seemed to have taken a great deal of interest in what she was doing.

"A lose–lose situation for her either way." With her best attempt at a nonchalant shrug she added, "Although it did look as if someone was trying to get her out."

"Kevin Tarr was hoping to shoehorn the delectable Poppy into Daisy's size fives," he agreed, "but then you've done very well out of her death, Abby. Do you have ambitions in that direction? You certainly took to fronting *The Potting Shed* like a duck to water and I had a note this morning informing me that we'll be filming in your walled garden tomorrow."

Insinuation fielded and effortlessly returned.

Before she could think of a suitable response Sophie rushed up and grabbed her hand. "Come on, Mum, May is going to open her presents."

"Good luck with the border, Quentin." She allowed Sophie to lead her back up the lawn, conscious every step of the way of the man's eyes boring into her back.

"Garden conference?" Katherine asked.

"Yes," Abby said. "Quentin is too afraid to tell you, but we both think that's the wrong place for a white border. It really needs a darker backdrop to show it to its best advantage."

There was a dangerous moment before Her Ladyship unexpectedly nodded. "You're not afraid of anything, are you, Abby?"

CHAPTER TWENTY-FOUR

Abby, not sure which way this was going to go, said, "I'm scared of any number of things, Katherine, but if I was afraid to tell someone they're making a mistake in their garden I wouldn't be worth the money my clients pay me. However if you do go ahead, I'd like first refusal on the flag irises. You have some rare specimens and I'd give you a good price."

"You'd buy them?" she asked, astonished.

"Gladly. There are a lot of valuable plants in that bed. It's worth a lot of money."

Katherine Hamilton gave her a thoughtful look. "Is it true that you've sold your show garden to some rock star who's bought the Armstrongs' old place?"

"Where did you hear that?" Abby asked.

"Izzy went to school with his latest wife."

"I haven't met her yet, but I heard that she's a lot younger." There was, it seemed, a lot of it about. "I haven't mentioned it to Quentin."

"No? Probably wise." She smiled. "Come and sit with me while May opens her gifts."

Jake had bought her the complete works of Beatrix Potter in a slip case, which delighted her grandmother. "I used to read these to Izzy."

Abby's gift was a little silver bracelet with a mayflower charm that had been made by a bespoke jeweller in the craft centre. It was infant-sized but there were extra links to increase its diameter as needed.

The children had bought a wooden box with a hinged lid from the craft shop in Silver Street and Lucy, the artist in the family, had stencilled *Memories for May* on the lid and decorated it with images of May blossom. Then she, Tom and Sophie had filled it with photographs and personal things that had belonged to their father. A watch he'd worn before he could afford his precious Rolex, which had now been set aside for Tom. His school tie. A well-thumbed copy of *The Lost World* they'd found in his childhood bedroom in Linton Lodge, along with some sea glass and shells from a Cornish holiday, his first swimming certificate when he was five years old and other small but prized possessions.

"Charming. A kind and lovely thought," Katherine said while Izzy was struggling to hold back tears. "Izzy, darling, do you want to go and let the caterers know that we're ready for tea? Why don't you take Abby with you and tell her your news."

"I'm sorry if that upset you, Izzy," Abby said as they walked towards the house.

"No . . ." She blinked hard. "Your three must have given up some of their own precious memories of their father."

"They have years of memories, Izzy. When May asks them about the things in the box, they'll talk to her about him." Then, because it looked as if more tears were imminent, "What's your news?"

Normally the most confident of women, Izzy was hesitant. "It's taken them a while to persuade me, but I wanted you to know before it's officially announced next week. I've been adopted as the party candidate to stand in Howard's place at the next election."

Abby had always thought a woman with Izzy's education and steely determination would have been wasted as a political wife. "That's absolutely brilliant," she said. "Katherine and Mark must be so proud of you and Howard would be delighted to have you stepping into his shoes."

"Do you really think so?"

"Without a doubt." Abby had no idea how Howard would have felt about it, but it was what Izzy needed to hear and she gave her a hug.

* * *

"So," Megan said, when Abby zoom-called her later that evening to bring her up to date, "Izzy's standing for parliament? That explains the long delay in announcing a candidate. I imagine there were a lot of old buffers who had to have their arm twisted by Sir Mark, or, more scarily, Her Ladyship."

"And a few who thought it should be them," Abby said. "But there's plenty of precedent for a constituency being taken over by the partner of the deceased incumbent. Nancy Astor led the way when she stepped into her husband's shoes after he'd succeeded to a peerage and did a brilliant job."

"Will you vote for her?"

"She doesn't need my vote — this is one of the safest seats in the country. But she's bright, intelligent and decorative, not some tired old has-been being handed a safe ticket because it's his turn."

"Young and photogenic with a family history in politics, she'll soon be on the front bench whichever side of the house her party finds itself on after the next election. So how was it apart from that?"

"A champagne tea on the lawn," Abby replied, "and Katherine was unusually mellow. It would have been perfect if I hadn't brought up the social media campaign against Daisy when I was talking to Quentin."

"He thought you were accusing him?"

Abby didn't answer.

"*Were* you accusing him?"

"Not exactly, but I did bring it up just after I'd congratulated him on taking over *The Potting Shed*."

"Not exactly subtle," Megan suggested. "How did he react?"

"No visible reaction, but he retaliated by saying that I'd done very well out of Daisy's death, implying that I had ambitions in that direction. Since he has no idea just how reluctant I've been to get involved throughout, I suppose, from his point of view, it must look that way. Lucy had better get this internship."

"You've gone above and beyond," Megan replied. "Whether she gets it or not, you couldn't have done more."

"No, but now I have to work with him tomorrow and it'll serve me right if he trips me up the same way Fay tripped Poppy."

"Stay away from hot coffee," Megan advised. "It's shocking news about Fay. The internet is buzzing with the suggestion that she killed herself out of grief or — if you read the more scurrilous rags who'd never spoil a good story by telling the truth — guilt about Daisy's death."

"Dee told me that she was dead before she went into the water.

"You're saying it wasn't suicide?"

"Surely Iain mentioned it?"

"Work stops at the door, although he did seem more than usually distracted when he came over last night," Megan admitted. "One unexplained death might be down to natural causes, but a second one, clearly linked to the first . . . How likely is that?"

"Not likely at all," Abby said, grimly. "If it had been suicide Fay would certainly have a left a note. A very long note. She'd want the world to know her story."

The unlikely meeting on a train. How kind Daisy had been to her. How aggrieved she had been at being pushed aside by Patrick. How people had been trying to dislodge Daisy from *The Potting Shed*. How guilty she was for not being there when Daisy needed her.

And she'd have named names . . .

"But why would anyone want to kill her?" Megan asked. "Could she have seen something?"

"Or someone," Abby said. "Someone going in or out of the room Daisy was using. They were away socialising with the show committee first thing and then they were out for quite a while touring the gardens."

"The room wasn't locked?"

"The public didn't have access. Only guests like Daisy, who were major attractions to the show. The stallholders were booked in somewhere else. And Major Elliott, the show secretary, was there all the time."

"All the time? Unless he had iron control of his bladder he'd have taken the occasional comfort break. And I'm sure he'd have made himself a cup of tea during the morning. Could Fay have run back to get something for Daisy and seen someone then?"

"It's possible, although she seemed to have everything but the kitchen sink in the bag she was carrying." Including her book. She needed to check it and see what Daisy had written. "She certainly didn't mention going back and Major Elliott said he hadn't seen her. On the other hand, he did shut his office door to cut out the noise when he was on the phone."

"Not an entirely reliable witness then."

"No."

"You talked to Fay," Megan persisted. "If she had seen someone, do you think she might have been tempted to go in for a little blackmail?"

"That's a horrible thought."

"And yet, with her life apparently about to go down the pan . . . ?"

Abby hated the idea and yet the Fay Bingley who'd seized the opportunity to trip up Poppy Jensen might well have decided to take the risk.

"The missing tea caddy has to be important," Megan said. "We need to find out who took it and you're going to be with most of the people involved tomorrow. It will be the perfect opportunity to see how everyone is reacting to the news."

"I'll keep my eyes and ears open," Abby assured her, "but what I'd really like to know is what happened after Daisy discovered Quentin *in flagrante* with his tutor."

"Really? After all these years?"

"He said they started their course at the same time, but her wiki profile has her graduating at a different university two years behind Quentin."

"You're saying that she was so upset that she left her course?" Megan huffed with disbelief. "I know it must have been a shock, but that seems an excessive reaction. Unless she made such a scene that it was impossible for her to stay."

"She was very young and Maybridge was much quieter then, a bit slow," Abby said. "It was a different world. This happened nearly forty years ago, remember, and although the law had changed by then, the legal age of consent was twenty-one. Quentin would have been eighteen — nineteen at the most."

Megan gave a little nod. "And did you say that the man involved was one of their lecturers?"

"That's what Quentin told me. The question is, what did Daisy do next?"

Megan thought for moment. "I imagine the university authorities would have wanted to hush the whole thing up and let the man resign, if only to protect Quentin from the scandal, but if she wouldn't play ball it would explain his animosity."

"If there had been a prosecution it might have been reported in the local press," Abby said. "Would it be online?"

"That long ago? Unlikely unless the local newspaper is big enough to have digitised its archives. Where was Quentin at uni?"

Abby told her.

"Okay. I know someone who lives in that area so leave it with me, but I wonder what Daisy was doing during the gap. Is there anything in her autobiography to cover that period?"

"It starts with a quote from Tolstoy — *'Happy families are all alike . . .'* — Then *'Chapter One: The day I graduated'.*"

"That's it? Nothing happened in the first twenty-odd years of her life that was worth writing about? No childhood angst or teenage rebellion to boost sales?" Megan asked. "Her publishers can't have been happy. That story about Quentin would have done wonders for publicity and, bearing in mind her hatred of him, I'm surprised she didn't use it."

"Maybe she wanted to, but the lawyers wouldn't wear it."

"Or maybe she did something she wasn't proud of," Megan suggested. "Ruining a man's career over something like that wouldn't go down that well these days. Assuming it was a one-off and he wasn't a serial seducer of undergraduates."

"Quentin did give me a rather soft-focus *mea culpa* description of what happened but I doubt it was that simple. Why, for instance, if she wanted to leave, didn't she just transfer to another university?"

"You don't suppose . . ." Megan hesitated. "Might she have been pregnant? From what you've told me Quentin didn't sound as if he was that clued up."

"Confused, fumbling, a couple of innocents—" Abby's heart broke for the two of them — "Quentin trying to be something he was not. Daisy falling for a very beautiful young man."

"Quentin was beautiful?"

"Hold on, I'll show you." Abby found a photograph and did a screen share.

"Tall, slender, fair curls and a smile to die for. A golden lad." Megan sighed. "I imagine he was the target of every girl and quite a few of the boys on campus. I wonder what Daisy was like. A girl from a small rural area."

"Both out of their depth? You're thinking they may have latched on to each other for safety?"

Megan shrugged. "It's possible, but surely, under the circumstances, she'd have had a termination."

"Maybe not. She might have had strong feelings on the subject, although I do wonder what sort of state she'd have been in," Abby added. "She'd obviously fled the campus but where did she go? It's possible that she refused to admit what was happening to her until it was too late. It would be an added reason to hate Quentin."

"It's all supposition, but if she was pregnant do you think she would have told him?" Megan asked. "Since there is no sign of any family, the baby — assuming there was a baby — must have been given up for adoption."

"Adoption papers are sealed. Adoptees can apply to the court to see them but no one else. Unless there's evidence of the birth in her papers there's no getting around that."

A thought struck her. "I wonder if she confided in Tessa Anderson. Any offspring would have a claim on the estate."

"You think that's what she might have been looking for? It would be really interesting to know what's in her will," Megan said. "Someone might have a very big motive for losing that information."

"They would," Abby said. "It's certainly something to think about."

"And maybe talk to Beattie and June. They've lived in Maybridge all their lives. It was much smaller forty years ago, a place where everyone knew everyone. And their business."

"That's an excellent idea, but right now I need to go and sort out what I'm going to wear for the filming tomorrow."

"Gardener casual," Megan advised. "Good jeans, shirt and a gilet so that you have pockets for your secateurs and plant ties — they'll give you something to do with your hands if you get nervous. And remember that someone there might be a murderer, so be careful what you say."

CHAPTER TWENTY-FIVE

Monday morning wasn't quite the usual scramble. Sophie was disgruntled that the high school had an inset day so her siblings not only had an extra day's holiday but were going to be able to watch the filming of *The Potting Shed*. But then the excitement of telling everyone at school took over.

By the time Abby arrived at her design studio in the walled garden, Lucy, Tom and Cal were already there, hard at work watering and helping Kate to remove any weed that had dared poke its head above ground and any faded flower or leaf that didn't look perfect.

They'd just tidied away the last of the tools and fastened the hoses into reels when *The Potting Shed* team arrived. Kevin Tarr seemed subdued, but he looked around and said, "This is perfect, Abby. We'll just wait for Quentin and then run through what we're going to do."

Lucy stepped forward. "Can I offer anyone coffee? Tea? A cold drink?"

"My daughter, Lucy," Abby said.

"Your PR guru." Kevin found a smile as he took something from his pocket. "I have something for you, Lucy." He handed her a USB stick. "Your mother thought you could use a recording of *The Potting Shed*. Good luck with the internship."

Lucy blushed. "Thank you, Mr Tarr. I was planning to watch it on catch-up, but it's not there."

"It's Kevin, and no, the network didn't think it was appropriate given what happened." He allowed Abby to introduce the rest of the team — Poppy, Ross, and a new cameraman called Mo.

Poppy looked around. "I'm having walled garden envy, Abby," she said. "Is it okay if I take some photographs for my social media?"

"Be my guest."

"Would you link them to our pages, Miss Jensen?" Lucy produced an Earthly Designs card from her pocket.

"Oh, call me Poppy, and it will be my pleasure to share them." She tucked the card into a pocket then touched Abby's arm. "I owe your mother."

Lucy looked interested, but Abby reminded her that she was taking orders for drinks. Once she had gone to fetch Poppy some water, Abby said, "You decided to stay after all."

"Yes, and I've you to thank for that. If you hadn't been there . . ." She drew a slightly shaky breath. "It could have been a bit sticky with Kevin, but it's all sorted now."

"You're not going to make a complaint?"

"And get a reputation as a troublemaker? Besides, he's right. *The Potting Shed* is for the over-forties. The only reason I'm there is to keep the men watching but Kevin is going to pitch an idea for a programme for a younger audience so fingers crossed."

"You have talked to him, then?"

"He called me. He feels so bad about letting me down. He didn't know the suits were already talking to Quentin. Obviously we're not . . . I'm not . . . But we have to work together."

"Well, good luck with the younger generation," Abby said. "While you're here, can I ask you something?"

Poppy opened the bottle of water Lucy had brought her and took a swig. "Go ahead."

"Fay told me that there were things going amiss, stuff out of place, on the show — incidents designed to make Daisy look foolish. Was that anything to do with you?"

Poppy, far from taking affront, pulled a face. "I know what you're getting at, but that would have backfired on me. I know you shouldn't speak ill of the dead but I'm pretty sure it was Fay trying make *me* look bad. As if I hadn't done my job properly."

"Oh?"

"Kevin had asked Daisy to keep her off the set, but she was always oiling her way in with some excuse or other."

"Well, as her assistant, Daisy would have wanted her close by," Abby pointed out. "And there was some unpleasantness online?"

"Oh, that . . . Some fan who didn't get the full Daisy Dashwood treatment when he accosted her in the street, no doubt. I stick to posting pretty pictures of me holding flowers or large vegetables, with the cleavage front and centre," she said. "I've become a bit of an influencer, too. Hand creams, hats, sunscreen. That's too valuable to risk. Let's face it, we've all seen people's careers crash and burn for hitting 'send' before their brain is engaged."

Poppy Jensen wasn't just a pretty face, Abby decided. She was ambitious, which is why she'd decided to fall into Kevin's arms, and, if it suited her, she'd no doubt fall into them again."

"How did you manage yesterday?" Abby asked. "Was your friend able to put you up?"

"Friend? Oh, Ross. Yes, he's staying on a boat moored just along the river and when I explained what had happened he invited me to stay with him."

"Ross has a boat?"

"It's not his," Poppy said. "It belongs to a friend who lets him use it whenever he fancies a weekend on the river."

"It's a houseboat?" Abby asked hopefully.

Poppy shook her head and laughed, a world away from the tearful young woman in the Queen's Head.

"Living on a houseboat would be so cool, but it's just a cabin cruiser for pootling about on the water." She took out her phone and showed Abby the photographs she'd taken. "It's called the *Lucky Duck*. Isn't that fun? We've had a couple of trips down the river and stopped for a drink in the garden of a pub Ross knows called the Pike and Heron." She flipped the screen to a photograph of the old inn sign that would probably find its way onto Poppy's Instagram page. "Do you know it?"

"I was there a couple of days ago," Abby said. "The food's very good." Then, her heart thumping, "It's quite near Daisy's cottage."

"Is it?" Poppy shook her head, her blonde curls gleaming as they bounced in the sunlight. She and Ross must have made quite an eye-catching pair sitting in the pub garden. "I knew she lived on the river but I didn't know where."

Abby frowned. "But surely you've been there? Daisy sometimes broadcast her shows from her vegetable and herb garden."

"Oh, yes, but I wasn't ever needed for those." She looked thoughtful. "I'll put that another way. She didn't want me there. She threw a party there once when the show won an award, but I was booked to film a garden in the north of Scotland that weekend."

"You believe it was deliberate?"

"Wouldn't you? I did ask Ross to point out her cottage, but he said everything looked different from the water."

It did, but there weren't many properties in that part of the Reach and those huge weeping willows would be hard to miss.

"Did the two of you have a good day?"

"We did. It was so relaxing after everything that's happened."

Abby assumed she was talking about Daisy. "Yes, it's been a tough few days."

"Awful. What with the scald and Kevin . . . I told Ross how kind you'd been, stopping my mad dash out of the hotel. He was quite cross with me for throwing away my big chance."

"It's an easy thing to do in the heat of the moment." Abby turned to where Ross was standing with Kevin. He was looking at them — or rather at Poppy, who was snapping away on her phone, unaware of his intense scrutiny.

"You've obviously heard what happened to Fay?" Abby said.

"I saw on social media that she'd topped herself." Poppy said, not even looking away from her phone screen. "I'm not going to pretend I liked her just because she's dead. She could have scarred me for life." She took more photographs. "You've got to feel sorry for her though. It was obvious to everyone that she had a pash for Daisy, trailing after her, desperate for a kind word. So pathetic."

"I thought they were close?"

"Not as close as Fay would have liked them to be, if you get my meaning." Her raised eyebrow emphasised the point. Abby was not alone in having come to that conclusion . . . "And Daisy had her living in her basement. My grandmother said it sounded like something from *Upstairs, Downstairs*, whatever that is. Oh, here's Quentin!" She waved as he walked in and, all smiles, greeted him with a kiss.

The queen was dead, long live the king . . . ?

She watched her for a moment. There were some very attractive women on other gardening shows, but they were older and had solid experience. Real knowledge. She wasn't getting that from Poppy.

She'd looked around the garden but despite her protestations about being a real gardener, her only interest in the plants was their photogenic quality.

She wasn't asking questions, had shown no interest in the beds of last year's cuttings, hadn't mentioned varieties. It made Abby wonder whether her degree was actually in horticulture. If television had been her aim, surely drama or media studies would have been the way to go. She had cheerfully admitted that she'd been brought on to *The Potting Shed* to add glamour. It certainly hadn't been for her gardening skill.

Abby had written her off as a possible suspect but she had already proved herself capable of seizing an opportunity to scramble up the ladder. Maybe her agent had suggested she practise using a trowel and go for it.

She tucked a wandering tendril behind a support. "Where did you take your degree?"

Poppy raised her phone to take a photograph of the copper weathervane fixed to the roof above the studio. "Bath Spa. I'm a local girl. Warminster. Dad's an army man."

"Great university," Abby said. "Lucy is going there next year."

"Oh? Is she following in your footsteps?"

"No. Marketing, PR."

She'd checked out Bath Spa University when she was looking at day release courses for Cal. It didn't offer degrees in horticulture or anything even remotely related.

Quentin joined them. "Good morning, Abby. This is delightful."

Smooth and charming as ever, he had apparently forgotten her hint, however veiled, that he might have been behind the social media campaign against Daisy. Possibly that phone call.

Putting on a face . . . She hadn't forgotten how it had slipped after she'd won a gold medal.

"Thank you, Quentin, but it's not all on the surface," she said. "Let me show you the energy and water-collecting systems that were installed during the restoration. Poppy?" she invited.

"Actually I think Kevin wants me."

At that moment Kevin looked up and beckoned them all over and Abby and Quentin spent the next half an hour walking through the garden with him, deciding what they'd talk about and where.

A chat between two passionate gardeners — because whatever else, he was passionate about plants — reminiscing about a gardener they both admired.

When, at a prompt, Quentin turned to Poppy to include her in a memory of Daisy, she slotted in seamlessly with memories of her kindness to the newbie.

It would be easy to be fooled by Poppy. But she was shrewd, and could certainly take a cue and turn on the charm like a tap.

"Great run-through, everyone. Let's go for it," Kevin said.

Quentin smiled as they took their places.

Meanwhile, Abby reminded herself that everyone in this business was putting on a face and Quentin Latimer-Blythe was a man who, like Daisy, had borne a grudge for almost forty years.

CHAPTER TWENTY-SIX

Kevin had emailed her in advance to ask if she had any photographs of the garden before the restoration work, and Abby had sent the best before, during and after pictures to be shown as they moved around the garden.

The programme would start with the first picture, he'd explained, and Quentin would add a voiceover later in the studio.

A year ago this was sad, neglected . . . Now, after extensive restoration . . .

The picture of the neglected garden would fade and the camera would pan around the restored garden and come to rest on Quentin.

I'm here today in this magnificent walled garden with gold-medal-winning garden designer, Abby Finch, who just a few days ago told our beloved Daisy that she had been her inspiration . . .

The camera would pull back to include Abby as he asked her about the book token, giving her a chance to talk about Daisy.

"All set?" Kevin asked and, getting nods, he did a countdown.

When the camera started rolling, Quentin began as they agreed and everything went well until they came to the restoration of the walled garden.

Instead of asking Abby about the planning that had gone into restoring it, he said, "How did you come to own it?"

Out of the corner of her eye she saw Kevin jerk in reaction, but already on her guard for the unexpected, she smiled, suppressing a flicker of rage — with herself for stupidly making an enemy of him, and with him for using her husband's death to throw her off balance, maybe even to reduce her to tears.

"You don't know?" she asked. "I'm astonished that your dear friend Katherine Hamilton hasn't shared her irritation that I inherited the bulk of the family estate rather than her daughter. Not that Izzy cared about the money. Like my children, she only cared about losing the man she loved."

"Cut!" Kevin glared at Quentin. "What the hell was that?"

There was a deathly silence.

While it was possible that Quentin's flush was down to the heat, Abby didn't think so.

"I'm so sorry, the question just popped into my head . . . Most unprofessional. My apologies, everyone."

He wasn't looking at her when he said that.

That was deliberate, petty payback — not for her suggestion he might have been behind the online trolling, but for scuppering his plans to sell off Katherine's border while charging her a fortune for replanting it.

What would he do if he was seriously aggrieved? she wondered. Despite the heat she felt a cold spot in the pit of her stomach.

"Abby, are you okay to go on?" Kevin asked.

They weren't the only ones who could put on a face. She nodded, smiling until her cheeks hurt. "Whenever you are."

After that the filming proceeded with the only interruption caused by a bee that had taken a fancy to the cameraman's cologne.

As soon as Kevin called it a wrap, Quentin, having confirmed that he wouldn't be needed for two weeks and offering no more than a curt goodbye, got into his car and drove away.

"What the hell has got into him?" Kevin said. "I hope he's not going to be difficult to work with."

"I shouldn't worry," Abby said. "I'm the fly in his ointment. He didn't think my nettles deserved a gold medal."

"Put his nose out of joint, did it?" Kevin asked, with a grin.

"He's got *The Potting Shed* to console him." Then, because she was interested in where everyone would be for the next few days, "You're not filming next week?"

"No, there's a test match so something in the schedule has to give and on this occasion it's *The Potting Shed*. Today's film will go out in the regular slot and the following week we'll run a mash-up of Daisy's best bits, which gives us all an unexpected but much appreciated break."

He eased his back as if he was ready for one.

"Will you go away?"

He glanced at Poppy. "That was the plan." He shook his head. "I know how it must look but it wasn't just . . ."

Abby waited.

"I know she was only with me because she thought I could help her career and, despite everything Daisy did to thwart me, I did get her more time on the show. Those out-of-the-studio visits to gardens where Daisy couldn't interfere — she's really good at those."

"The ones where the guests are free with their technical knowledge and she just has to drop in the occasional prompt and look interested?" Abby suggested.

He gave a wry smile. "Not much gets past you, does it?"

"She's no gardener," Abby agreed, "but it does rather give you a motive for wanting Daisy out of the way."

"Motive?" He looked genuinely startled. "They don't think—"

"Fay was murdered, Kevin. It puts a whole new spotlight on Daisy's death."

"*You* don't think . . . ?"

Did she? If she did, Abby realised, she'd just said something rather stupid. Not for the first time. She managed what she hoped was a sincere smile — she'd seen enough of the fakes during her contact with television professionals to have a good go at it.

"If I thought you'd killed either of them, Kevin, I wouldn't have said anything."

"No." The tension went out of his shoulders and with an uncertain little laugh, he repeated the word. "No. Of course not."

"We're all done here," Ross called out. "Poppy is coming with me."

Kevin nodded, resigned, and Abby went across to say goodbye.

"Good luck, Poppy. I look forward to seeing more of you on the show."

"Oh, you'll see me before then. We've got some time off so we're staying on the boat and I owe you lunch." She turned to Ross. "Could we all go up to that pub again?"

"The Pike and Heron?" Ross smiled at her. "I'm sure you know it, Abby?"

Had she misread the look she'd seen earlier? He seemed perfectly genuine and, aware that she wouldn't get a better chance to talk to them both, she nodded. "Yes, my partner and I eat there quite often."

"Great," Poppy said, genuinely delighted. "Tomorrow?"

Tomorrow was going to busy. She still had a lot of work to do on Daisy's papers and Lucy had her interview. "Wednesday would be better. If you'll still be here?"

"Until the end of the week," Ross said. "Twelve o'clock at the quays? You can't miss the *Lucky Duck*, she's bright yellow."

"I can meet you there."

"Oh, no," Poppy said. "It'll be much more fun if we all go on the boat and you can point out Daisy's cottage on the way."

"I'd better take my seasickness pills, then," she joked and waved them off.

Kevin joined her. "You did well today, Abby," he said. "Maybe we could use you again in the future? Perhaps we'll even see you at Chelsea in a year or two?"

"That's very kind, Kevin, but I think I'm done with show gardens." And television, she thought, deciding not to mention the invitation to Lucy.

* * *

Lucy was sitting at the kitchen island with her laptop open, sorting out the photographs she'd taken during filming to add to the Earthly Designs media pages. More ammunition for her coming interview.

"Can you make yourself lunch?" Abby asked.

"No problem." Then she looked up. "Where are you going?"

"To Beaumont Court. Eric is more than capable of taking down the show garden, but I need to show my face. If I'm not back by the time Sophie gets home, will you sort out a snack for her?"

"Sure."

She'd left the plant Kate had wrapped in hessian outside in the shade of the pergola. She put it in the van and was about to reverse out of her drive when Jake rang.

"How did it go?" he asked, then, hearing the engine, "Oh, you're driving. I'll call later."

"No, it's okay. I'm parked." She turned off the engine. "It's safe to talk."

"The question is, am I talking to the new star of daytime gardening?"

She laughed. "You've got to be kidding."

"Was it difficult?"

"There is an art to walking and talking at the same time," she said, "but mostly it's boring with a lot of starting and stopping. If I tell you that once Lucy had some photographs she went home, Tom went to join his mates at the cricket club, and Kate shut herself in the office to update the wall schedule . . ."

"That bad? What did Cal do?"

"He took the edging shears into the Linton Lodge garden to sharpen up the lawn for a second viewing tomorrow."

"Fingers crossed on that."

"Very firmly."

The location of Linton Lodge couldn't be bettered, but the house was too big for any but the largest, cash-rich family and unsuitable for a company headquarters.

The rock star had looked at it, but with a footpath through the woods and the river frontage it was too accessible.

It had been empty for over a year and the upkeep laid a heavy cost on the estate, which was not only coming out of her inheritance but the fifty per cent that was to be divided between Howard's four children.

Then, because she didn't want to think about that, or the unpleasantness with Quentin, or any of them, she said, "Kevin was happy enough with the result of the filming to suggest that I might do more guest spots."

A sweetener? Just in case she thought about mentioning that he had a motive for Daisy's death? After all, everyone wanted to be on television.

Jake cut into that uncomfortable thought. "I'm not surprised," he said. "I saw you and you are clearly a natural."

"That's very kind of you," she replied, "and never say never. I smiled politely and said thank you."

"But you don't see yourself as the next television gardener?"

"Honestly, Jake, nothing about my close encounter with television and the people involved has warmed me to the experience. I only did it in the first place for Lucy."

In the second place . . .

"Is she all prepped for her interview?" Jake asked.

"She contacted her head of year and has permission to leave school early tomorrow. I offered to drive her into Bath but she pointed out that she'll be taking the bus if she gets the internship and that's what she's going to do."

"In other words she doesn't want her mother, a bag of nerves on her behalf, tangling with the Bath traffic."

"There is that," Abby admitted, not wildly keen on driving into the city. "But she's worked so hard and the competition

190

for these places is so fierce . . . I would have liked to be there when she came out. If only to give her a hug."

"Isn't it Cal's college day?"

"Yes." Abby didn't want to surrender her right to offer comfort but she had been no older than Lucy when Jake had been there for her. "That's the other reason for the bus. I suspect he's going to meet her and take her out to either celebrate or commiserate." She took in a long, slightly shaky breath, wishing that Jake was there to give her a hug. "It's such a long shot."

"She knows that."

"And I'll have to be here for Sophie when she gets home from school."

"You could have asked me."

"I don't expect—" she began, then stopped. "You're busy . . ."

There was an infinitesimal pause.

"You're right. I should be in a meeting."

And that was the end of the conversation.

Abby sat for a moment, wishing she'd handled that better. Then she started up and set off, but not for Beaumont Court. She had another call to make first.

Her phone rang. She ignored it until she pulled up outside her destination and called back.

"Sorry, Meg, I was driving."

"I just wondered how it went today."

"Quentin tried to trip me up, metaphorically rather than physically," she said hurriedly. "I was expecting something of the sort so I was on my guard. I didn't mention that to Jake, by the way."

"Apart from that did you manage to find out anything useful?"

"Well, underneath the impressive cleavage and the husky voice," Abby said, "Poppy is sharp as a tack and has too much to lose to risk trolling someone on social media."

"She told you that?"

"Yes, but it seems that she's doing very nicely as an online influencer. She wouldn't risk that."

"No. So if not her, who do you think might have been behind the nasty posts?"

Abby shrugged. "It could just have been a coincidence. A disgruntled fan who'd caught her at a bad moment."

"It doesn't take much to set some people off," Megan agreed.

"And then there's Ross Mason, the assistant director."

"Why would he kill Daisy?"

"Kill? No, I was still thinking about the trolling." Abby batted away a fly that buzzed in through the open window. "Daisy might have been the gardener's darling, but she wasn't popular with the crew, and I heard Kevin Tarr telling Fay that if she didn't turn up she'd be off the show."

"Oh? Is that his decision?"

"Probably not, but he as good as admitted that although Poppy is good on the outside interviews — which he did get for her — she's too young to present the show for *The Potting Shed* demographic."

"He just got her into bed by promising to make it happen? What a sleazebag."

"I thought that, but she admitted that she was the one who leapt into bed with him in the hopes that he'd get her the top spot. What man is going to tell her to hop out again because it was beyond his powers?"

"It doesn't make it right."

"No, it doesn't, but I get the impression that he really does have feelings for her."

"Be careful what you wish for . . . ?" Megan suggested.

"On that subject, while Poppy insists that she's a gardener, she told me that her life's ambition was to be on television and she took her degree at Bath Spa."

"So?"

"They don't have courses in horticulture or anything related," she said.

"So she's not a trained gardener. Would it matter? With a good script?"

"Maybe not. A lot of television is smoke and mirrors, but that was the thing about Daisy and what made *The Potting Shed* such a success. She might have had her nails gelled to a high gloss but she never hesitated to stick them into the soil. And she knew her plants."

"Poppy must have a bio on the show's website. I wonder how much of it is true."

"I'm having lunch with her and Ross on Wednesday. I'll see what I can find out about her then."

"Really? Lunch with two possible suspects? Where are you going?"

"The Pike and Heron," Abby said. "Practically home territory. And I'm not even sure Daisy and Fay's deaths have anything to do with the television programme. Most murders are about money and the money is at Hartford Manor."

"Farrell . . ."

"And there's something a bit off about Tessa Anderson. She was the one who put them together."

"And in the meantime we need to find out more about Fay. Where does she come from? Has she any family? And could she have removed the silver belonging to Daisy?"

"If she had she wouldn't have drawn attention to the fact that it was missing."

"Maybe if someone had seen it, commented on it," Megan said thoughtfully, "Clive Elliott, maybe — or anyone who'd been in and out of the east wing that morning — it would have been dangerous not to mention that it was missing. Is it possible that she killed Daisy?"

"It did cross my mind," Abby admitted. "Fay certainly wasn't the meek, biddable woman she appeared to be. She had access to Daisy's cottage and, having worked with her, typing up her notes, she must have known which plants would do the job."

"Accepting all that, why would she kill her? She'd lose her job, her home."

"Maybe just plain old anger. She'd worked for Daisy for years and then Farrell turns up and within weeks gets a fifty-grand sports car for his birthday. She really didn't like that."

"Understandable, but then you're faced with the fact that Fay herself has been killed," Megan pointed out. "If she was Daisy's murderer she might have been a danger to anyone who'd seen her, but she wouldn't be the victim."

"Maybe she saw something? Or let slip something she'd seen without realising its significance," Abby suggested. "I could see Patrick Farrell lashing out at her. He had keys to the cottage and he's disappeared."

Megan cleared her throat. "I imagine the police are on to that."

"Imagine or know?" Abby asked.

"As you know, Iain and I don't discuss work so if you happened to discover that he flew to France this morning, you didn't hear it from me."

"Oh, right. Farrell must have recognised me and, deciding Hartford Manor was no longer a safe hideout, took to his heels. Or, rather, his expensive birthday present."

"You're lucky that's all he did."

"For once I'm happy to let you say, 'I told you so.'"

Megan manfully resisted the temptation. "So what's next?" she asked.

"Well, I still have to finish reading Daisy's notes," Abby said, "check to see what she wrote in my book and find the missing tea caddy."

"Any ideas?"

"I'm working on it."

CHAPTER TWENTY-SEVEN

Parson's Row was an elegant terrace of townhouses on the outskirts of Maybridge. Four storeys high, built of local stone, with long rear gardens that ran down to the river, they were highly desirable and very rarely came on the market.

Abby had done some work in a couple of the gardens, but not for the Elliotts. She remembered the monkey puzzle tree being the focus of a neat but conventional front garden with lawns and flowerbeds bisected by a straight path from the gate to the front door.

Now the path wove between the dramatic planting of yucca, canna lilies, tall Firebird foxgloves and Melianthus major, with the stark drama of the monkey puzzle tree, an increasingly rare sight, at its heart.

Mrs Elliott was not just a fan of Daisy Dashwood, she was a skilled gardener in her own right.

Abby took a deep breath, stepped out of her van and, after pausing to admire a particularly fine Agapanthus 'Black Jack', she rang the doorbell.

It was opened almost immediately by Major Elliott.

"Mrs Finch . . ." He sounded surprised, as if he'd been expecting someone else. And looked as if he'd aged ten years overnight. "You'd better come in."

He stepped back, inviting her into an elegant hallway, and there, on a serpentine table and reflected in the deep polish and the gilt-framed mirror above it, was a small silver tea caddy and a silver infuser.

"You guessed my wife had taken them," he said.

"Let's just say that I hoped she had."

That got a reaction — a tightening of his jaw, his hands . . .

"She's a fan," Abby said. "She would have kept them safe, unlike a sneak thief who would have sold them on the same day. Once Daisy's death became a police matter they would have been melted down for scrap silver. This really is the best outcome because it's vital that the tea is tested."

"The tea?" What little colour he had drained from his face. "You think there was something in the tea that killed her?"

"Probably not," Abby said, "but the fact that it was missing raised questions. Your wife hasn't used it?"

"No." His relief was palpable. "Theresa greatly admired Miss Dashwood. As soon as I told her that the police had been asking about her silverware, she broke down and admitted that she'd gone to the room Miss Dashwood was using, hoping to find some little keepsake. A pen Daisy had used, perhaps. Nothing big. It's so out of character. I don't know what came over her."

"She'd just witnessed something dreadful, Major Elliott. You said yourself how upset she was."

He shook his head. "I hope the police are as generous. I called them twenty minutes ago. When the doorbell rang I thought . . ." His voice trailed away.

"Then I'll leave you to explain what happened. There's no need to mention that I was here." She looked at the plant she was holding. "Is your wife about? I brought her this."

"An excuse to talk to her?" He managed a smile. "She'd have liked that. After our son moved to New Zealand with his family the garden became her passion."

"Your front garden is stunning."

"Yes . . . It's greatly admired." He cleared his throat. "Theresa phoned Father O'Neill after we talked and asked him to hear her confession. She is overcome with guilt, not just for taking Miss Dashwood's things, but because I've resigned as show secretary."

He paused for a moment, and she saw his Adam's apple bob as he swallowed down what must have been a very bitter pill.

"I'm so sorry."

He acknowledged her sympathy with a nod. "She's composing herself for what will undoubtedly be an ordeal."

So much misery and shame for what must have been a moment of impulse.

"I grew this salvia from a cutting," she said, putting it down. "I hope Theresa can find a use for it, but what I do have, are some cuttings from Daisy's own garden. I can see a place where the French lavender would fit perfectly beside the Agapanthus. When they're rooted I'll bring them over." And then Abby, having her own moment of impulse said, "Or maybe she would like to come up to my studio one afternoon? She knows Kate, who works with me. I'll show her my walled garden and we can sit and talk plants over a cup of tea."

"Mrs Finch . . . Abby . . ."

She put a hand on his arm. "Tell her that I'll give her a call."

* * *

Beaumont Court was a hive of activity in the show garden area. Eric and the team had already removed the furniture from the hut and taken it down ready to reconstruct in its final location and the plants were being returned to their pots.

"Any problems?" she asked.

Eric grinned. "No. Kate had all the pots ready for us this morning. We should have all the trees and shrubs out by lunchtime tomorrow and then I'll bring in the crane to start taking down the rock."

"Good work." She looked across at Quentin's garden, which hadn't yet been touched. "If you happen to see Mr Latimer-Blythe . . ."

"Don't mention that your garden has been sold?"

"Best not."

By the time she got home, Sophie was back from school, making toast, and Tom was cutting the grass when he should have been revising. He was doing it with the kind of fierce intensity that suggested he was working off something that was bothering him and that interrupting him to suggest he'd be better occupied revising for his Maths exam would be unwise.

Then, having called the personal assistant of the rock star who wanted the quarry in his garden — who would have guessed— to discuss when Eric and his team could start work, she looked with despair at Daisy's notes and decided that supper was going to have to be a takeaway.

She had two hours, tops, before Jake got home and since Forensics would now have the tea to analyse, she decided to concentrate on Daisy's diaries. But first she checked her copy of *First Steps in Gardening*.

Daisy had made several notes with suggestions for revisions in the margins, her handwriting becoming increasing illegible. But then she found the last one. It wasn't about plants or gardening; it was about Poppy.

Patience Jensen, Drama, Bath.

She'd underlined the words so heavily that the paper was torn, which answered Dee's question about their flower names.

Daisy must have decided to investigate her and maybe someone had called with the information while she'd been lying on the sofa. There was triumph in that fierce underlining. Had she thought it would be enough to get Poppy off her show?

Abby thought it unlikely. Her main role was to interview gardeners on site and she was good at that, but she sent Dee a text to let her know that Poppy was in fact Patience, although she'd probably discovered that when everyone was interviewed.

She put the book to one side and ignored those she'd brought from her office library on poisonous plants. Whoever had done this hadn't gone for the obvious.

She turned to Daisy's diaries. There were only three of them. The rest were presumably in her London house.

They were standard page-a-day office diaries with dates and times for bookings to give talks or workshops, meetings with her agent and *The Potting Shed* production company, and filming dates. And the dates when both Daisy and Fay would be on holiday.

Two years earlier, ten days had been blocked out for a visit to the Caribbean and Abby vaguely remembered seeing a couple of *Potting Shed* programmes that had been filmed in that region. Had the entire team flown out, or did they use local talent?

Later trips to Italy and Germany had been at the same time as Fay was on holiday in Spain and on those occasions there were reminders for Fay to deliver gifts to Daisy's cousin.

A month after Fay's last visit, meetings had been cancelled for five days while they both flew out for her cousin's funeral. There was a note tucked into the page for that date. It was on headed notepaper with a Spanish name and address. It was stapled to an invoice stamped *PAGADA*. Paid.

The note, written in English, was brief. There was no salutation, just the words, *You wanted this for your accounts.* The signature was indecipherable, but the name at the top of the page was Spanish and presumably that of her cousin's husband.

With the aid of the internet she deciphered the account, which was long and basically covered the services of an undertaker, the burial, food and wine for the mourners, the cost of a memorial headstone and a donation to the church where the burial service had been held.

She knew that funerals were expensive but the final sum made Abby blink.

Daisy, who had obviously paid for it all, wasn't impressed either.

Not fooled, she had written across the bottom. *I'm not going to argue. Mateo Molina can whine poverty all he likes, he'll get no more out of me.*

It wasn't chargeable to her business, but it was odd that it had been left in the diary.

Mostly the entries were made in a neat, round, almost schoolgirl handwriting. That had to be Fay. Other more personal entries, such as the dates Daisy flew to Switzerland for consultations about her plastic surgery had been written in the same free-flowing style with which she'd made notes for her latest book.

She had also added, after meetings, notes about the people she'd met. Generally unflattering. Her public-facing persona might have been all sweetness and light, but it was clear that Daisy had a sharp head for business and didn't suffer fools gladly.

She did seem to have a very close relationship with her agent. The regular, fortnightly dates in her diary when they had dinner together were followed by descriptions of food, wine, summer evenings in the garden or sitting beside an open fire, always with a final nightcap. Tia Maria drunk through a topping of cream. The smoky taste of Laphroaig in the firelight. Amaretto warm and delicious on the tongue . . .

Abby found herself getting slightly hot under the collar as she read them and was fanning herself when the doorbell rang.

"Oh, Dee, come on in." She'd anticipated a call. The visit was unexpected. "And before you ask, I am working through Daisy's diaries."

"I'm glad to hear it but that's not why I called. I thought you'd want to know that we've recovered Daisy's missing tea caddy and infuser."

"Really?" Her voice squeaked a bit in her effort to sound surprised. She cleared her throat. "Where did you find it?"

"It was taken by a fan who was in *The Potting Shed* when Daisy collapsed. Distraught, convinced she was dead, she got into the room Daisy had been using looking for some small keepsake. When she saw the silver she couldn't stop herself from touching it. And once she'd touched it . . ."

"So not spirited away by a killer hiding their tracks," Abby said, not asking how the woman had got into Daisy's room.

"No. She finally broke down and confessed to her husband."

"Thank goodness he didn't decide to cover it up."

"No. He's a very upright gentleman. Old school."

"And his wife?"

"She was in a state of shock when I went to pick it up. It's been sent off to Forensics but I thought I'd drop in on my way home to give you the good news."

"Thanks. I'm in my office. Come on through."

"I can't stop for long," Dee said. "I've got to pick up something for supper, but I've been in the office most of the day and I'll be going home to a hot flat. Could we sit in your garden for a few minutes?"

"Of course. We can grab a drink on the way through."

Tom had finished cutting the lawn. He'd even trimmed the edges, a job he hated — she'd better check what was worrying him — but from the sound of music coming from above, he was now in his room.

"I've been so busy that my lot are getting a takeaway this evening," Abby said. She offered Dee a choice between water or a soft drink.

Dee took a can of cola.

"I'll be glad to get back to some kind of normality," she went on, automatically unhooking her secateurs from their hook by the back door as they headed out into the garden.

Dee stopped and took a deep breath of the freshly cut grass and an early flowering pink rose. "This is heaven."

"Buy a house and I'll plant you a rose just like that," Abby offered.

Dee sighed. "I have no time for gardening."

"You should make time. It's life-enhancing." She snipped off a couple of faded blooms. "What will happen to the woman who took the silver?"

"As I said, she's in a state of shock." Dee sank onto a seat at the dining bench in the pergola and ripped open the can. "She said she saw it and felt she had to take care of it."

"She had just witnessed Daisy collapse practically at her feet," Abby said, without thinking, and then, holding, her breath, snipped off the head of a newly opened flower. Damn it.

"It's a first offence so I imagine the DI will give her a caution and leave it at that." Dee took a sip of the cola. "I thought the idea was to cut off the dead flowers."

"It is. I stayed up late with the draft of Daisy's book on Saturday and then got up early because I knew I wouldn't have much time during the day." She sat down beside Dee before she did any more damage.

"How are you getting on with the paperwork? Have you found anything useful?"

"Not yet. The last two days have been non-stop. It was May's birthday yesterday, this morning I was filming with *The Potting Shed* crew and this afternoon I've been back at the Beaumont Court. Thankfully removing the garden won't take as long as building it."

"You're becoming a media star," Dee teased. "Did I see your van leaving Parson's Row earlier this afternoon? That was a bit out of your way."

They exchanged a glance and Abby decided that she really needed to drive something less noticeable than her flower-bedecked van.

"I was dropping off a plant that's been sitting in my garden for days," she said. The truth, if not quite the whole truth.

"Really?" It was obvious that Dee hadn't missed the slip and knew that she had been somehow involved in the retrieval of the silverware. "You suspected Theresa Elliott that long ago?"

CHAPTER TWENTY-EIGHT

Abby, caught with her metaphorical pants down, had no choice but to admit it. "I was talking to Major Elliott," she said. "He'd already mentioned that his wife had gone there after she'd seen Daisy collapse. When, later, I asked him if he'd seen anyone who shouldn't have been in the east wing—" She shrugged — "There was just something in his expression. A memory . . ."

"So you thought, rather than telling me, that you'd take it upon yourself—"

"I thought that if she had taken it she'd be terrified. I was just going to talk to her, but her husband had called you before I arrived."

Dee just shook her head. "No harm done, but promise me you won't go off on one of your wild goose chases?"

"I've already promised Jake."

She nodded. "What was the plant?"

"A salvia. Very pretty but too tall for a window box."

"What window box?"

"You need some plants in your life. I have some Nicotiana, which would be perfect. You've got sash cords so when you lift the window the scent will waft in."

"A lovely thought but where I live window boxes are like cats and dogs," Dee said. "Forbidden. They're a health and safety hazard."

"You're on the ground floor!"

"Same rule for everyone. And much as I'd love to sit here all evening, if I don't move you won't be the only one having a takeaway."

"Give yourself a night off."

"You are a bad influence."

"It's what good friends are for," Abby said. "Are you any further forward with Daisy's death?"

"The gold-braid lot are still hoping that Daisy's death was just one of those things that will never be explained."

"Unlike Fay's," Abby said. "What was she struck with? Do you know?"

"A fist-sized lump of stone. There's one missing from the edge of the rose hedge. We've recovered it from the river."

"It suggests a spur-of-the-moment act."

Dee nodded. "Whoever did it must have thrown her in the river hoping it would be taken for grief or guilt-ridden suicide. They must have hoped that by the time she was found the head wound would have been put down to damage from being swept down the river."

"But that would be exposed the moment it was discovered there was no water in her lungs," Abby said.

"Maybe they thought she was still alive when they pushed her in."

Abby swallowed. "I'm surprised no one saw, or heard the splash . . ."

"The willows will have given cover," Dee said, "but we've put a notice up on the quays asking if anyone saw or heard anything."

"Do you have any real leads?"

"No. We're running background checks on everyone but with nothing to go on we can't keep *The Potting Shed* people here indefinitely."

"Poppy is staying with Ross Mason on his boat until the end of the week."

"He has a boat moored here?"

"It belongs to a friend. The *Lucky Duck*. They've invited me out to lunch with them on Wednesday."

"You're not going?"

"Poppy thinks she owes me," Abby said. "I walked in on a row she was having with Kevin Tarr. He'd been getting directorial benefits in return for giving her career a push. Having discovered he couldn't deliver the prime spot she was about to walk out on him and the show."

"What did you do?"

"I saw the moment when she realised she'd made a mistake and waylaid her with tea and sympathy so that she could sit down and think before she did something she'd regret."

"You talked her into staying?"

"She talked herself. It took all of five minutes for her to calm down sufficiently to realise that if she walked out in a temper her television career would be over."

"So she went back to him?"

"No, she called Ross Mason and went to stay with him." Abby sighed. "He's always on hand to take care of her when she's in trouble."

"He fancies her?"

"Undoubtedly. She is very attractive."

"And so is he," Dee said. "Where are they taking you for lunch?"

"We're going to the Pike and Heron."

"Well don't leave your drink unattended. Meanwhile I'll add a note to check out Kevin Tarr in case he makes a habit of using his position to take advantage of vulnerable young women."

"If that's the case he wouldn't commit murder for them," Abby pointed out. "Not unless they threatened to expose him. In which case it would be the vulnerable young woman who ended up dead."

"What else have you got for me? Don't give me that innocent look, Abby, we both know you can't resist poking into a suspicious death."

"I wasn't about to deny anything," Abby said. "I've talked to all these people."

"And what have they said?"

"Not much," she admitted. "I saw Quentin on Sunday at May's birthday party. He was staying with the Hamiltons during the show and Katherine has asked him to design her a new border, although whether that's still on . . ."

"Why wouldn't it be?"

"She might be having second thoughts."

"Something you said?" Dee asked.

"Quentin was taking advantage and she's family."

Dee's eyebrows performed something akin to a somersault. "Family?"

"She's May's grandmother. And I think she's warming to me."

"Lucky you. Is that it?"

"No — Yes . . ."

Dee waited.

"I wondered if you'd found out anything about Fay's background."

"Not much, to be honest. She was given up for adoption as a baby, but the marriage broke up and she was collateral damage."

"That's tragic. Poor Fay."

Dee nodded. "She went into care and had quite a number of foster parents, which suggests she might have been difficult, but there's no suggestion that she went far enough off the rails to attract the attention of the police."

"So she has no family?"

Dee shook her head. "She did a business course at sixth form college and got a job working in an insurance office, where she stayed until she went to work for Daisy eleven years ago. No significant relationships although we did find evidence that she'd put her DNA on an ancestry site hoping to trace a birth parent but without result."

"We tried that in our search for Howard's mother," Abby said, "but it needs the other party to have put their DNA online to get a match."

"Which suggests that Fay's mother is either dead or doesn't want to be found," Dee concluded.

"Yes."

Dee, aware of her search for Sarah, laid a comforting hand on Abby's arm.

"Did Daisy leave any provision for Fay in her will?" Abby asked, determined not to dwell on what couldn't be changed. "I assume you've seen it."

"Fay was right about the pension. Daisy set up a generous pension fund for her. Everything else went to her cousin, but was tied up in a trust so that the husband couldn't get his hands on it."

"Daisy really didn't like him, did she? She paid for her cousin's funeral and a headstone — the invoice was eye-wateringly steep and she clearly thought the bill had been loaded. She made a note that no matter how much he whined he'd get no more money from her. How did her cousin die?"

"I've no idea. Why do you want to know?"

"Both sisters died young. You still don't how Daisy died and I wondered if there was a connection. Something genetic. If her death had been registered here it would be easy enough for you to get a copy of her death certificate."

"Why would I do that?"

"No reason. It's just that I've started on the diaries. Fay used to go to Spain for her holidays and she called in with gifts from Daisy for her cousin. Daisy was a bit of an evangelist for her herbal tea and would certainly have sent her one or more of her special blends."

"And?"

"A month after the last visit they both flew over for her funeral."

"Damn it, Abby. How do you do it?"

"Iain did ask me to mention anything that leapt out at me. It may just be a coincidence," she replied, "but it leapt."

"Okay, I'll see what I can find out. But to answer your question, in the event that her cousin predeceased her, the cottage was also to go to Fay, her London house to her agent, Tessa Anderson, and various other amounts to friends and charities."

"And after Farrell came on the scene?" Abby persisted. "Did she change it?"

"She'd drawn up a new will but it hadn't been signed. Hartford Manor was left jointly to Farrell and Tessa Anderson, presumably to protect the business, but the London house was mortgaged to finance the purchase so that will have to be sold. Fay was still to get the pension and the cottage and the bequests to friends and charities were unchanged."

"That's a huge legacy for a woman who wasn't related to her. Unless . . ." Abby's mind was whirring. "This is a bit off the wall but could Fay have been her daughter? She must be about the right age."

"Daisy's daughter?" Dee stared at her. "How did you know she'd had a child?"

"It's true?" It was Abby's turn to stare. It was one thing to speculate, quite another to have your wildest thoughts confirmed.

"The post-mortem report showed that she'd given birth. Obviously we'll need to run a DNA check," she said, "but it's a possibility." Then, raising an eyebrow, "Now I suppose you're going to totally mess with my head and name the father?"

"Well, actually . . ." Abby told her about the incident with Quentin, the gap after Daisy left her first university and how, talking to Megan, they'd speculated that she may have been pregnant.

"By Quentin?" Dee's eyebrows rose. "I wonder if he knows. Or suspected?"

Abby shook her head.

"I always thought that meeting on the train was odd," Dee said. "Could Fay have had some reason to believe Daisy was her mother and put herself in her way hoping for some instant recognition?"

"I suppose it's possible." Surely, Abby thought, a mother would sense a connection.

"Fay said that she showed a lot of interest," Dee said. "She even wanted to know her birth sign, giving Fay the chance to mention her birthday. They're both fair. Fay was leaning more towards mouse, but I imagine Daisy's streaky blonde had some expensive help."

"Daisy had run a background check on her before she offered her a job. Maybe the dates and places fitted," Abby said, excited now. "We need to find a picture of Daisy taken thirty years ago and check for any resemblance."

"A DNA test would be more accurate," Dee said, a touch dryly.

"Oh, yes." Abby frowned. "But how could Fay have found out? She tried a DNA search but without any response. And if she was Daisy's daughter, why wouldn't she acknowledge her?"

"And more to the point," Dee asked, "why would Fay keep quiet?"

CHAPTER TWENTY-NINE

"Maybe Daisy didn't want the world to know she'd given up her baby and silence was part of the deal," Abby said. "Maybe Daisy never actually admitted that she was her mother. She gave her a job, a home and even if Fay knew about the cottage, that could have been thirty years in the future. The writing was on the wall with the arrival of Patrick Farrell."

"I'd agree but for the fact that Fay herself has been murdered."

Abby humphed. People would keep pointing out the holes in her theory.

"Maybe Tessa Anderson found out that Fay had killed Daisy and lashed out." Abby shifted awkwardly. "I was going to mention it when I'd finished reading through everything, but from the diaries I suspect Daisy and Tessa may have been more than good friends."

Those descriptions of nightcaps had nothing to do with liqueurs. They had been a code for sex.

"If they were why would they keep it a secret in this day and age?" Dee asked. "Why not live together, get married? I'm sure one of the lifestyle mags would have paid good money for the photographs."

"Maybe they liked it the way it was. Meeting once every couple of weeks for good food, good wine and a good time. I'm sure Fay must have known — she had access to the diary — but unlike with Farrell, she didn't feel threatened by it. And when you think about it, it was her relationship with Patrick that Daisy was keeping a secret," Abby pointed out. "Maybe she didn't want Tessa to know. I haven't got any further in the diary but I'll check to see if the cosy nights in have continued."

"You haven't been wasting your time, have you?" Dee said, clearly amused by this revelation. "But it's not just Fay. If you're right, Daisy's defection to Patrick Farrell bumps Tessa up the suspect list for her death, too."

"I suppose. Maybe she killed both of them." One because she'd betrayed her, the other because she suspected her, maybe even accused her.

"There is a problem with that," Dee said. "If Tessa discovered that Daisy's relationship with Patrick had moved beyond business to the physical, why would she offer him refuge in her house in France?"

So he *was* there . . .

"It's business. She's still his agent," Abby said, "and it would be in her best interests to carry on as if she knew nothing. She will be getting fifteen per cent of everything he earns."

"Isn't he bankrupt?" Dee asked. "Any earnings will have been attached by his creditors."

That was a point. If he was a bankrupt he couldn't be director of a company.

"He was, but he thought he was about to inherit half of Hartford Manor. Did he believe the will had already been signed?"

"I wonder what will happen to the Manor now," Dee, who appeared to have totally given up on her dash to the supermarket, wondered.

Abby pictured the vast frontage of the manor and tried to imagine how much it would cost to bring the interior up to the kind of standard required. Not to mention the fact that as a Grade I listed building it would take years rather than months to get the necessary alterations past English Heritage.

"Frankly? I don't believe it was ever going to happen. Whoever advised Daisy to buy Hartford Manor did her no favours."

"You think it was a con from the start?"

"Probably not. I imagine Daisy got caught up in the excitement of it, but a long cool look at the place would have quickly brought Farrell back down to earth. Forget the sheer expense of the renovations with costs soaring and the staffing problems in the industry — I'm not sure it was ever going to be a viable proposition."

"So why not just tell Daisy that and put the place back on the market?"

"Maybe his ardour had cooled with his enthusiasm and the temptation to get as much out of her as possible before pulling the plug was too strong."

"And the wedding?"

"I'm sure that was the original plan. A wealthy, much older wife . . . How much would she pay to be rid of him once she realised her mistake?"

"What about Tessa Anderson? She's a smart business-woman. She brought them together."

Abby blew out a long breath. "Maybe her idea was smaller, simpler, but it got away from her. She must have been concerned."

"There are far too many people with the motive, the means and the opportunity to have slipped something lethal into Daisy's tea," Dee said. "So far it's all speculation, but we'll be seizing everyone's accounts and once we get to the bottom of the financial side of things we might have a better idea of what was going on."

"That will take time."

"That's police work. Normally." Dee glanced at Abby.

"Just trying to help," she said. "But while I can see Farrell pulling this kind of stunt on a woman caught up in what was almost certainly a romantic fantasy, how on earth did he think he'd get away with it?"

"I imagine, like most conmen, he was banking on Daisy's pride — her unwillingness to let her foolishness become public knowledge — to let him get away with it. On the other hand he does have form as a bit of hothead. If she'd caught him out, threatened to expose him . . ."

"He'd lash out," Abby said. Farrell had turned on Fay when she'd disturbed him, had barked at her, rushed off. What on earth had possessed her to go snooping around the Manor? "He'd lash out," she repeated, "but Daisy's death has all the hallmarks of careful planning."

Dee looked uncertain.

"Someone went to a lot of trouble to kill Daisy without murder being suspected. Even now you don't know how she died. The only reason you're treating it as suspicious is because someone was panicked into killing Fay, and if they'd got her into the water while she was still alive, it would have been signed off as suicide."

Dee swore. "You're messing with my head."

"You're welcome," Abby said as Dee finally made a move. "Come again — next time with news of the DNA match, background on *The Potting Shed* crew and the financial shenanigans of Farrell. Not to mention what exactly was in that tea caddy."

"Is that all?"

"I'm sure I'll think of more questions the moment you've gone."

"Then I'm out of here."

She should have asked what time Fay had died, Abby thought as Dee backed out of the drive. And what had Tessa Anderson been so anxious to find at Daisy's cottage, and did she find it? And what time had she arrived — and more importantly left — Longbourne Reach? There was no CCTV near the cottage but her car must have been picked up on traffic cameras arriving and leaving Maybridge.

Too late now.

Dee gave a toot on her horn at the end of the lane and turned not for home, but in the direction of police Headquarters.

CHAPTER THIRTY

Abby stood for a moment in her front garden. It was nowhere near as striking as Theresa Elliott's but she was glad to see how well her rose bed had recovered from the havoc wreaked upon it the previous summer, the red roses and nepeta scenting the late afternoon air.

She loved her garden and the cottage and had never imagined living anywhere else, but was Jake really happy living here? He'd been looking for a house on the river when he'd arrived in Maybridge. Something a lot grander that her cottage.

Jake had made it clear that he wanted to marry her and then he'd left the ball in her court. She had no doubt that she loved him, but did she love him enough to leave her home?

Did he love her enough to stay or had moving in been a compromise?

The children had given him their blessing and seemed happy having him around, but while they'd accepted him as her live-in partner he was still on the edge of her intimate family circle.

He'd made a friend of Lucy and Tom, talked to them, treated them like the adults they were becoming. Sophie was harder work. Still struggling with the loss of her father, she could erupt at the wrong word. Jake had seen her at her worst, but it hadn't been his responsibility to dish out the consequences.

Marriage would change that. How would Sophie react if she threw one of her tantrums and he was the one grounding her? Would she tell him that he wasn't her father and storm off?

How would he feel?

Her phoned pinged with an incoming text.

I'm catching a plane at sparrow's tomorrow to fly to Glasgow for a meeting. I'll stay at the houseboat so I won't disturb you. J x

There. That was exactly it. He wouldn't do that if they were married. She didn't want him to do that. She texted back.

Forget the houseboat. Waking up with you beside me is ample reward for getting up before dawn. Oh, and we're having a takeout tonight. You can choose. A x

It didn't take long for her to receive his reply.

Let the kids decide. Waking up with you more than compensates for whatever culinary nightmare they inflict on us. J x

She stood there, smiling to herself, but then Beattie waved from across the road.

"We saw your garden! June's planning to turn our shed into a reading nook like yours. She's all over Pinterest."

Abby laughed. "Tell her I can do her a good deal on nettles, brambles and dandelions." She crossed the lane to admire Beattie's immaculately hoed border.

"How are you, dear?" Beattie asked. "Daisy's death must have really shaken you up. I saw Dee call in. Is there any news about how she died?"

"Not yet. Did you know Daisy?" she asked.

"I knew the family. Her mother and mine were both on the committee of the WI, but Daisy was a bit younger than me."

"She seems to have left university very suddenly in her first year."

"Yes . . . It wasn't as common for girls to go to university back then and her mother made such a fuss about it, but then she was taken ill."

June had emerged and joined them. "We were talking about Daisy Dashwood," Beattie said. "Do you remember why she came home from university? Was it rheumatic fever?"

"That's what her mother told everyone," June said.

"I know she was packed off to the coast for months to recover but it can leave a weakness in the heart. Maybe it just gave up," Beattie suggested.

* * *

After a very early start, Abby spent the following morning at Beaumont Court checking that the dismantling of the quarry garden was proceeding smoothly and arrangements were in place for the transportation of the hut and the rock to their new home.

Eric, as always, was on top of that. She'd already blocked out a schedule with the client for site preparation and rebuilding and there was no more she could do for the moment.

Quentin's team were pulling apart his garden, potting up the valuable trees and shrubs. She went across and the foreman acknowledged her with nod. She'd got to know him a bit when the gardens were being built.

"Do you know if the beech hedge has been sold, Mike?"

"I don't think so, Mrs Finch. We're taking all the plants back to the yard."

"I've got a client who would like one at the rear of her garden but doesn't want to wait years for it to grow. It's quite a narrow space so I think there would be enough. I'll give her a call now."

Her client was thrilled by the possibility and urged her to get it if she could.

"Could you give Quentin a call and ask him for a price?"

"I'll give you his number—"

"I'd rather you didn't tell him that I was the one. . ." She stopped. "Forget I said that."

She took his number and made the call.

"Latimer-Blythe Designs."

"Quentin, it's Abby Finch. I'm at your show garden," she said, quickly, in case he decided to hang up. "I saw your beech hedge being potted up and it would be perfect for one of my clients. If we can agree a price it would save moving it twice."

"Damn it, Abby."

"It's business, Quentin," she replied, but thinking that with the popularity of beech hedges it would be worth buying in whips to grow on.

"Is it? Because of you Katherine has decided against the white garden."

There was nothing she could say that would change that so that's what she said. Nothing.

He sighed. "Oh, all right. I suppose it makes sense." He named his price — a touch over the odds, but she didn't haggle — and once he'd taken her card details he hung up.

She had her hedge. And the answer to one of the questions that had been bothering her.

"It's a done deal, Mike. Once they're all potted Eric will take them off your hands."

She called Kate to warn her they would be arriving and asked her to block in time for Cal to dig a trench.

"We're getting booked solid, Abby. The show has provoked a lot of interest and Cal won't be able to do it for several weeks."

"Have I got a morning anytime soon?"

"No. Your design work has backed up while you've been working on the show garden and we've had quite a few enquiries that need your attention."

"Damn."

"Anyone can dig a trench, Abby. Not everyone can design a garden. Do you want me to see if one of our freelancers is free?"

"Yes, please. Just to do the groundwork. I will somehow find the time to do the actual planting before I forget that I'm a gardener."

"That's never going to happen," Kate said, "and just in case you were short of something to do, Sarah arrived this morning."

"Sarah?" Abby froze.

"The rose you ordered?"

"Oh, yes . . ." Heart pumping, she swallowed hard, shaking off the foolish fleeting thought that Howard's long-lost mother had somehow turned up out of the blue. She took a breath. "Talking about the need for more staff," she said, "I was thinking of inviting Theresa Elliott to come and have a look around and hopefully persuade her to join us. You know her, Kate. How would you feel about that?"

"It would be brilliant if she'd do it. Have you seen her garden? It would be good to have her design talent now that we're so busy."

"I'll give her a call this evening," she said. "Keep your fingers crossed."

She returned to her office, spent a couple of hours working on a design and then, checking her messages, found one from Megan.

I've got some info. I'll be at the Buttery at one if you can make it. M x

She fired off a response to say that she'd be there, then parked in her own driveway and took the footpath into town. She was the first to arrive so took a seat in the courtyard of the Red Lion craft centre, where the Buttery had long been everyone's go-to café for a treat.

"Hi, Abby," Lola, who'd run the place since it opened, greeted her. "Are you on your own?"

"Megan's joining me any minute, Lo. How are you?"

"Well, my knees are reminding me that I'm not getting any younger, but otherwise good. Can I get you anything while you're waiting?"

"Just some water, thanks."

Megan arrived and took the seat opposite. "Posh paint-colour cards. Thinking of redecorating?" she asked.

"They're just a distraction," Abby said. "Lucy has her interview this afternoon and when I walked past that fancy new decorator shop that's opened on Market Square, it occurred to me that it's a very long time since I did anything more ambitious than buy a new cushion."

"Homemaking. Interesting." Megan laid her finger on a dusky pink. "I like that."

"I can just imagine Tom's reaction to a pink living room."

"Oh? It's the living room on your mind?"

"What else?"

Lola returned with glasses and a jug of water.

They quickly chose from the menu but when she'd gone, Megan picked up the shade card.

"I'm thinking of revamping my bedroom," she said. "I'm so tired of that pale grey that everyone seems to have at the moment."

"Cool and restful."

"And very, very dull. I looked online but according to the experts bright colours are too stimulating for the bedroom." She grinned as she turned the card for Abby to see. "I do like this dark red. It's very—"

"Keep the card." Abby was not getting into a discussion about bedroom colours with Megan, stimulating or otherwise. "Tell me what you've found out."

"Okay, well, you said the man Quentin was involved with was a lecturer. Knowing how big institutions work, I thought that if she'd made a complaint, or such a fuss that they couldn't hush it up, they would have encouraged him to seek other career opportunities."

"Invite him to resign? That sounds likely," Abby agreed.

"So the first thing to do was look for someone who was there in Quentin's first year but had disappeared by the second year."

"Yes, but—"

Megan held up a hand to indicate that she hadn't finished. "Several people left the appropriate departments that year. Two of them were women, both on maternity leave. One, in his seventies, had a heart attack. Birth announcements and an obituary in the alumni's magazine. But," she added, "someone called Nathan Peterson disappeared from the list of departmental staff."

"People leave for all kinds of reasons."

"They do but he'd been there for several years. There was nothing in the magazine to suggest he'd moved onwards and upwards. No fond farewell, no 'good luck in your new venture' message in the magazine. It's got to be him."

CHAPTER THIRTY-ONE

"How on earth did you find that out?" Abby asked. "It was nearly forty years ago. It can't be online."

"It's not, but I think I mentioned that I know someone who lives in the area. She's a researcher for a television network and has access to the university library."

"Really?"

"Yes, really." Megan's eyebrows quirked upwards. "Did you think I'd driven up there and blagged my way in?"

"No, it just seemed a bit of coincidence, that's all. Not that I doubt your ability to do just that."

"I haven't always lived in Maybridge and I can personally guarantee her discretion."

Megan never talked about her life before she moved to Maybridge, or her divorce, and despite their close friendship Abby had never pushed to know what happened. Presumably this woman had been there for Megan when she'd needed her.

"So where do we go from here?" she asked.

"Already gone." Megan sat back as their lunch arrived. "Once she'd pinpointed the most likely candidate my contact checked the local newspaper archives and found a report of police being called to a disturbance at the home of one

Nathan Peterson. His wife, it would appear, was not happy with him and had locked him out. What his children thought is not reported."

"He had children?" Abby put her hand to her mouth, horrified. "That's appalling."

"I agree, but there's nothing to indicate that he was prosecuted. We don't know whether Daisy made an official complaint—"

"Or simply made the kind of fuss that could not be ignored—"

"Or wrote to his wife to warn her—"

"Or all of the above," Abby suggested.

"But if Quentin had genuine feelings for Peterson, or felt guilty for his part in what happened, it would go a long way to explain his bitterness towards her," Megan concluded.

Abby understood but was unsympathetic. "He may have just lost his head over Quentin but no matter how willing he was he was under-age and the man was in a position of trust. I wonder what happened to him."

"Nothing good." Megan flipped open a napkin and picked up a fork. "He would appear to have lost his job, his family, maybe even access to his children in one fell swoop."

"And Quentin blamed Daisy? Hardly fair."

"No," Megan agreed. "But when has the whistleblower ever had anything but a raw deal? It would certainly seem to put him in the frame."

"Really?" Abby helped herself to a napkin, picked up her fork, then put it down again. "After forty years?"

"Why else have we been digging into his past?" She took a mouthful of her quiche. "Gosh, this is good. It would be useful to know what happened to Peterson. Dee would be the best person to instigate a search, but I'm not sure she'll be interested in ancient history without something solid to connect Quentin to the deaths."

Abby, already having food envy, toyed with a piece of beetroot. "This is absolutely confidential, Megan, but we might have that."

Megan paused, her fork halfway to her mouth. "A link with Quentin?"

"We were right about Daisy having a baby. It showed up in the post-mortem."

Megan looked momentarily floored. "Fay?"

"I'm waiting for Dee to get back to me with the DNA result, but it seems likely. She's a major beneficiary of Daisy's will."

"How major?"

"A pension and the cottage."

"That's a serious benefit," Megan said. "I could sell the cottage sight unseen for a life-changing sum of money."

"Sight unseen?"

"It's the location, Abby. Whoever bought it might demolish the cottage and build something new. But I got the impression from what you told me that she was about to be thrown out onto the street."

"That was the impression she gave me but I find it hard to believe that she didn't know."

"You're suggesting that 'poor little me' stuff was an act? Why?"

"Follow the money. If the police were involved they'd realise that she had motive. Especially as she was being pushed out by Farrell, who was draining Daisy of cash. He might be a first-class chef but let's face it, he doesn't have a great financial record."

"And the hospitality industry isn't having a particularly good time," Megan said. "I wouldn't want to invest in something that big right now."

"Exactly. If it went pear-shaped it wouldn't only be Daisy who'd lose her shirt. And Fay certainly had the time and opportunity to doctor Daisy's tea, or pretty much anything else come to that."

"But why would she think she might be a suspect? It wasn't until she was killed that the police were considering the possibility that Daisy had been murdered."

Abby buttered a piece of seeded bread and decided to take a loaf of it home with her. "If *she* knew it was murder, she'd have her story ready to go. Daisy's death wasn't a spur-of-the-moment thing, Megan. It required research and careful planning. Maybe even a test-run."

"A test-run?"

"I wonder if Daisy might have had an earlier attack. The same combination of symptoms, but somehow got over it. Fay might have remembered and mentioned it to the wrong person."

Abby and Megan stared at each other across the table.

"Okay, let's think about this. Who did Fay see or talk to?" Megan asked.

"Tessa Anderson, Daisy's solicitors." Abby thought about it for a moment. "She might not have been popular with *The Potting Shed* crew, and she may not have liked them much, but she'd been around for years. Common courtesy would suggest that someone would have called to offer their condolences, maybe take flowers."

"And no matter how reluctantly, she'd have had to invite them in."

Abby picked up her phone, but Megan, having scooped up the last mouthful of her quiche, stood and headed into the flower shop next door.

When she returned a couple of minutes later she wasn't smiling.

"Florrie had an internet order for a bouquet of pink roses from Kevin Tarr, card to read '*With condolences from* The Potting Shed *crew*'. It was delivered on Friday afternoon."

"Oh, bother, I wish I'd realised what you were doing. I've just sent Dee a text to ask if there were any fresh flowers in the cottage and another to Poppy asking if she or anyone else had gone to see her."

"Sorry, but this is the only florist in town so unless they ordered online this is where they'd have come from."

"Absolutely. Good thinking."

"I wonder who will get the cottage now?" Megan asked.

"The new will benefitting Farrell hadn't been signed, so it won't be him."

"I wonder if he knew that."

"If he's any sense he's going to swear that he did. And Tessa had already lost out on the townhouse. It was mortgaged to buy the Manor."

"So what happens to that now?"

"It will depend on how the business was set up. But going back to the test-run theory, when Fay went to Spain on holiday, which she seemed to do a couple of times year, she took gifts for Daisy's cousin. What's the betting that she included some of her special herbal teas?"

"So?"

Abby pushed her plate away. "Daisy's cousin was dead within a month of her last visit."

Megan, phone out to pay her bill, stared at her. "You're suggesting that Fay added something lethal to the cousin's tea? Because she knew that with the cousin out of the way she'd get the cottage . . ."

"It may just be a coincidence, but Dee is checking to see how the cousin died. If there was no apparent reason and the husband, having heard about what happened to Daisy, began to suspect that his wife's death wasn't natural—"

"You think he'd try and blackmail Fay?"

"Fay was at the funeral with Daisy," Abby said. "Suppose he saw her and remembered the tea, and now there's been a second death. He sounds like a man who'd go after easy money."

"No," Megan shook her head. "It's too soon. He might have got as far as thinking about it, he might even have got as far as contacting her, to offer condolences, drop a hint. But to actually do it?" Megan glanced at her watch and got out her phone. "I have to go. I've got that second viewing on Linton Lodge this afternoon."

Abby let go of the endless questions running around in her head. "Who are these people?" she asked. "Are they really likely buyers?"

"It's a woman who wants to run wedding events. She seems keen and it would be good business for Maybridge."

"If they can get the staff." Abby waved away Megan's attempt to summon Lola and pay for the lunch. "My treat."

"Thanks." Megan stowed her phone in her shoulder-bag and stood up. "I know the Lodge has been a burden, Abby, and you're worrying about Lucy. Why don't you go back to your office and distract yourself by making a list of those with the means, motive and opportunity to commit bloody murder? Maybe the answer will spring out at you."

"What a cheery thought . . ."

Lola came to clear the table. "Has Megan gone?"

"She had an appointment."

"What about you, Abby? Can I get you anything else?"

"You can." She needed to get back to the office, but the beetroot and goat cheese salad had been a mistake and she needed something to take the taste away. "I'd like a blondie, a cappuccino, a seeded loaf to go if you've got one left, and the bill."

While Lola was gone, Abby got out her notebook and dug in her bag for a pen.

It was Daisy's . . .

With a shiver, she dropped it back into her bag and found her own pen.

Until now she'd been floundering around, coming up with all kinds of reasons why anyone would want Daisy dead. It was time to make a list of credible suspects and focus on who had a serious motive to kill not just Daisy, but Fay.

"You're deep in thought." Lola had returned with her order. "Working out how you're going to top your gold medal next year?"

Abby looked up and smiled. "I don't know about that. The cost and time involved is huge and suppose I didn't get another gold? I think I'm going to stop while I'm ahead." She checked the bill, added a tip and held her phone against the card reader to pay.

"You say that now . . ." Lola laughed as she tore off the receipt and handed it to her before returning to the counter.

Abby forked up a mouthful of blondie and thought for a moment.

Patrick Farrell had to be a prime suspect. Means — Daisy would have talked about her book and what she'd found out about various plants. He had access to Daisy's kitchen and, more importantly, her tea caddy.

Motive — Follow the money. He'd been drawing down money to pay for the renovations at Hartford Manor but nothing appeared to be happening. Had Daisy found out and challenged him?

Opportunity — He had the keys to Daisy's cottage. The food in the refrigerator suggested he stayed there even when Daisy was in London. He would have had access to her notes. Was there something in the MacBook that might provide a clue as to how she'd died?

Could he have come back for it, thinking the cottage would be empty and Fay had caught him, challenged him? Could she have been running for her life when he caught up with her?

Next suspect. Quentin Latimer-Blythe. Means — He was a gardener and, assuming that it was something in the tea, he would have the knowledge. Motive — There was long-running animosity between them, but what could have happened to provoke him to murder after all these years? Could he have found out that she'd had his baby and kept it from him? Had he begged for information and she'd refused to tell him?

Opportunity — Daisy's tea caddy was part of her brand. He knew she'd have it with her and could have added something while she was at the breakfast reception with Fay.

Next. Tessa Anderson. Means — They must have talked about the book, maybe joked about some of the things that deadly poisons were used for.

Motive — Jealousy? If she'd found out about Daisy's plans to marry Farrell . . . And she stood to gain from Daisy's death.

Opportunity — The assumption was that she was working in London, but had anyone checked? It was a couple of hours on the motorway. Or, as a regular visitor, she could have added something to her tea anytime in the last few months and it was sheer bad luck that she'd died so publicly. Could Fay have seen her checking out the caddies and Tessa realised that she was a danger?

Next. Kevin Tarr. Means — He'd produced *The Potting Shed* for years and presumably had picked up some knowledge about plants, or knew where to find out. Motive — To get rid of her for Poppy. Opportunity — Anytime while Daisy was visiting the show gardens.

He'd admitted his infatuation with Poppy. And where did he go on Saturday after Poppy walked out on him?

Poppy Jensen. Means — Did she have the knowledge? Despite her claims to be a gardener, she wasn't interested in plants other than to post on her social media pages. On the other hand, there was plenty of information on poisonous plants on the internet. Motive — To get rid of Daisy to take over *The Potting Shed*. Opportunity — She had access to the green room, just a few steps away from Daisy's empty sitting room.

She was ambitious enough to sleep with the boss for favours but was she capable of murder? And what precisely was her background?

Ross Mason. Maybe someone else who wanted Daisy and Fay off the scene, but what possible motive did he have for murder? On the other hand, unlike Poppy, he had been to the cottage for filming *The Potting Shed*. Could she really add him to the list because of one intense look that probably had nothing whatever to do with Daisy or the show?

In every instance there was the unknown quantity.

She checked her messages. Lucy was on the bus, giving herself plenty of time. There was nothing from Jake but Dee had sent a text.

Pathologist reckons nothing lethal in the tea caddy, just harmless herbs from Daisy's garden. D

Seriously? Abby wondered if he'd put his money where his mouth was and actually take a sip of whatever was in it himself. Was he really that confident?

She had been sure the tests on the tea caddy would provide the answer. If the concoction was made up of 'harmless herbs', what could have killed Daisy and her cousin?

She finished the blondie, drank her coffee and gathered her belongings, then walked home, running through the poisonous plants that she knew.

Most of them had some kind of violent effect. There were none that she could think of that would just make someone keel over like that and not show up in a post-mortem. So maybe it wasn't a poison.

There were harmless things that could kill — peanuts, sesame seeds — but they caused a dramatic reaction.

She was looking for a silent killer.

CHAPTER THIRTY-TWO

Abby had cleared her diary of all but essential on-site work for the weeks during the show garden build and for the week following, imagining she'd be needed to supervise the dismantling, but Eric had it covered.

She'd had him working for her for six weeks this year already and the preparation and rebuilding the quarry would take at least another four. There was always construction work involved in new designs and it was rapidly getting to the point where she would have to consider her promise to take him on full time.

She needed more transport, and more staff during the busy summer months, but what would she do in the winter? Three months when the grass didn't grow, the ground was wet or frozen.

Why were there always more questions than answers?

Doing her best not to think about Lucy being on her way to Bath for her interview, once home she wasted no time getting back to Daisy's diaries.

The fortnightly dinners with Tessa Anderson continued but were now simply noted in the diary as an appointment with the occasional note about what they were going to discuss, business-like and missing the suggestive little liqueur notes.

How had that played out?

Had Daisy explained that the added workload of Hartford Manor meant she hadn't the time for long evenings chatting over dinner? Or had Tessa known about Patrick from the beginning and accepted it?

Questions that Fay might have been able to answer if she were alive.

She had been convinced that Daisy was murdered. Was that why she was dead? Had she said too much to the wrong person?

And why had she been so adamant that Abby shouldn't call in on the morning after Daisy died? Fay had made a big fuss about the presence of a TV van and, having her own publicity panic, she'd accepted it without question. But how likely was that? The news focus had all been on the hospital and Daisy's London house, where people had been leaving flowers.

Could Fay have been expecting someone?

While she was sitting there, running through everyone involved, trying to think of a reason for secrecy, her phone pinged.

It was a text from Dee with a photograph of a flower arrangement.

The roses came from Florrie's with condolences from The Potting Shed *crew. I checked and they were delivered to the cottage on Friday afternoon. D*

Then there was a second photograph, this time a jug full of Leucanthemum vulgare, also known as the oxeye daisy or marguerite.

You were right about Daisy's name, btw. It was Margaret and I'm told these are marguerites. There was no card but it looks more personal, maybe from Tessa Anderson? D

Thanks, Dee. Just a thought. Do you know where Kevin Tarr was on Saturday afternoon and evening? A

In his room with a bottle of whisky, accordingly to his statement. And he spent Sunday recovering from the hangover. D

Witnesses? A

The chambermaid confirmed that there was an empty bottle of whisky in his room when she finally got in there just before lunch on Sunday. D

In other words, no. He could have drunk the whisky anytime. A

But it sounded about right.

She wanted to talk to Tessa Anderson and she had the pen as an excuse. There were no telephone numbers in the diary but a quick search online gave her the Anderson Agency contact details. She decided to use her landline phone, which wouldn't give her number, not even if the person she was calling dialled 1471.

"Anderson and Partners, Bryony speaking, how may I help you?"

"Good afternoon, Bryony. I'd like to speak to Tessa Anderson if she's available."

"Who's calling?"

"Abby Finch. I was with Daisy—"

"I know who you are, Abby, but I'm sorry, Tessa isn't in the office today although she'll want to speak to you, if only to thank you for your help that morning. If you give me your number, I'll ask her to call you."

"Oh, no, of course, she was going to France," she said, hazarding a guess. "Did she manage to get away on Saturday?"

"Yes, she caught the Shuttle just after lunch. Do you want to leave a message?"

"No need to bother her while she's away. It will keep until she returns."

Abby replaced the receiver and sat back, wondering whether Bryony would take her at her word and leave it, or whether she would let Tessa Anderson know that she'd called.

She was sure that Iain wouldn't have hung around in France. His budget was probably for a day trip. This time she picked up her phone and called Dee.

"Hi, Abby." She sounded wary.

"Hi, Dee. I wondered if Iain was back."

"Back?"

"From France."

"Abby . . ."

She really was getting tired of people saying her name in that slightly exasperated way. "I'm sorry, I know you're busy but I've discovered that Tessa Anderson is there now. She caught an early afternoon Shuttle on Saturday.

"How did you discover that?" Still exasperated.

"I called her office."

"I meant—"

"I found a pen and a lipstick that belonged to Daisy," Abby interrupted, not wanting to drop Megan in it. "It was when I was picking up her things from Beaumont Court. I put them in my bag and completely forgot about it, but the pen was expensive. I was going through Daisy's diary and was about to make a note when I found it in my handbag. I was going to return it to Fay—"

"Okay, enough! I'll pick them up when I have a moment. It might have been useful to have had the lipstick earlier."

"Yes. Sorry . . ."

"The DI is home, as no doubt your partner in crime could have told you. He's spoken to both Farrell and Anderson, told them that their accounts and bank accounts have been seized for forensic examination and they must return within seven days for questioning."

"And if they don't?"

"It depends what the accountants find."

"But you suspect fraud?"

"We haven't been able to gain entry to Hartford Manor, yet, but apart from the erection of the scaffolding nothing has been done there. Until the accountants have examined the bank accounts set up in the name of the company we won't know if money was being siphoned off. What about you and the plant life that Daisy was putting in her tea?"

"I'm on it," Abby assured her. "Did you find out anything about how Daisy's cousin died?"

"I'm on it." Dee hung up.

CHAPTER THIRTY-THREE

Abby, having looked at her watch for the tenth time, reminded herself that a watched clock never chimed and did her best to concentrate on the Daisy's notes.

She'd finished the diaries and returned to Daisy's notes for the book she had been writing. The last page that she'd been looking at was about Vinca rosea . . . A plant that according to Daisy never stopped giving. It was still just notes, incomplete, and on an impulse she put it into a search engine.

Herbalists had used it as a cure for pretty much everything from piles to diabetes, and Vinca rosea produced a chemical that these days was synthesised for use in chemotherapy, especially leukaemia in children. Daisy's notes mentioned that in Jamaica she'd discovered it was used to prevent the onset of dementia, something she had been interested in for personal reasons.

There must be notes from the trip somewhere but she didn't have them. Presumably they were either on the laptop in police custody, or maybe they were in the little MacBook that had disappeared.

Had the police located that?

Deciding that it was wiser not to disturb Dee again, she put a combination of 'Vinca' and 'Jamaica' into her browser and found an online video on the uses of Vinca rosea in traditional medicine, and a mention of the tea that, among other things, was used to keep the brain alert. Possibly some chemical in the plant opened the veins?

The only caveat offered — apart from the standard 'not to be taken during pregnancy' — was that it lowered the blood pressure so should not be used if you were taking medication for high blood pressure.

Abby sat back.

A few years earlier she'd slipped on some mud and broken her arm. She'd been lying on a couch in the plastering room, the gas and air having absolutely no effect on the pain, when her eyes began to water and her vision had become blurred. She'd seen flashes of light, felt dizzy and her skin had become clammy.

The nurse keeping an eye on her had called a halt, saying that her blood pressure had dropped. She gave her water to drink, pausing everything until it returned to something nearer normal. It was unpleasant, but the water did the trick and once her blood pressure had risen, she'd quickly recovered.

That was exactly how Daisy had been when she was at her show garden. Unsteady, her eyes troubling her. She'd used her nasal spray, thinking it was hay fever, but it wasn't having any effect.

Nothing is working today . . .

But then she'd sat in her hut for a minute or two, had a long drink of water, and although she'd still been a little unsteady when she'd moved on to Quentin's garden, she had more or less recovered.

And the only medication prescribed by Daisy's doctor was for high blood pressure. She wouldn't have been foolish enough to mix the two but what she might have done was stop taking the prescribed drug and used the Vinca as a 'natural' remedy to deal with both her blood pressure and to ward off the dreaded dementia.

Who would she have told about that? Not her doctor, who would undoubtedly have disapproved, but Fay would have known. And Tessa was close enough for her to have confided her fears.

Farrell? Unlikely. She'd want to appear as youthful and fit as possible for him.

The question was, how much Vinca in her tea would it take to lower her blood pressure to dangerous levels? Or could someone, knowing what she was taking, have added blood pressure medication to her water or food?

The water she'd drunk when she'd taken a few minutes in her hut had been from an unopened bottle.

Maybe she'd remembered that it had helped. She had been clutching a water bottle when she'd staggered into the marquee, not one she'd taken from the fridge in the visitor's guest room, but a personal refillable one. She'd dropped it before she fell and it had bounced, empty, and rolled away.

Feeling unwell, possibly disorientated, her only thought would have been to find Fay . . .

Abby picked up her phone.

"I've found something," Abby said, before Dee could speak. "One of the herbs Daisy was interested in, which I think she may have been using to counteract the onset of dementia, causes a drop in blood pressure."

"And?"

"Have you ever fainted?"

"Years ago—"

"Then you'll know how that feels," Abby cut in. "That's how Daisy was that morning. Vinca rosea — tell the pathologist. There's a big pot of it in Daisy's garden. I'm sending you a picture. If Forensics have her teas, it will be in the one labelled '*Memory*', but it may have been in her water bottle."

"Was it with her things?"

"She dropped it in the marquee. I imagine it was picked up and put in the recycling."

Dee uttered a single scatological response. Then, "Is that it?"

"Ask the pathologist if her bloods showed that she'd been taking her blood pressure medication."

"Double dosing?"

"Not intentionally, Dee."

"Right." And with that Dee was gone.

Abby found the photograph on her phone and sent it to her, along with the links to the website. Then, absolutely drained, she reached for her own water bottle and took a long drink.

She sat for a while, thinking about Daisy, trying to imagine how she could have kept her daughter a secret.

Why would she do that? It was no big deal these days. She certainly wouldn't be the first celebrity to be reunited with a child she'd given up for adoption. The media was usually sympathetic, treating them as good news stories.

She tried to imagine the turmoil Fay must have been going through. To have found her mother but been kept at arm's length, unacknowledged. Presumably the job, the home, the promise of the cottage in her will, had been the price of her silence.

How did you grieve in those circumstances? Do you honour your mother's wishes and keep the relationship secret or shout it out for the whole world to know?

Poor Fay never had the chance to decide.

This felt like the day her own mother had died. She'd grabbed her spade and dug out a trench in the vegetable garden to plant sweet peas. Her mother's favourite flower. She'd dug and dug and dug until Sophie, four years old, had asked her if she was going to make the cake she'd promised.

Cake . . .

Penny, Cal's grandmother, normally kept them well supplied with her fabulous baked goods but she was away on a cruise, and with every minute of her own spare time fully absorbed in the show garden, there had been precious few homemade treats in the last couple of weeks.

Pushing herself away from her desk she went to the kitchen, washed her hands, got out her scales and began to bake.

Lemon drizzle cake, an apple pie, shortbread . . .

And as she weighed and mixed, beat and rubbed butter into flour one thought kept running through her head.

Carpe diem. Seize the day. Seize the damn fish . . .

CHAPTER THIRTY-FOUR

Abby had just taken a tray of shortbread out of the oven when her phone beeped. She picked it up with floury fingers.

> *They're going to call me tomorrow. I'm meeting Cal and we're eating in town. Lx*

No excitement, no idea of how she'd done. At least she wouldn't be kept waiting. Although it would feel like a lifetime waiting for her to get home on the back of that wretched motorcycle. Thankfully at this time of year it would still be light.

She wanted to ask a dozen questions, but texted back,

> *Take care. Don't be late. It's school tomorrow. xxx*

She took a breath. Deciding that for her own peace of mind it was time to buy that truck for Cal, she rinsed off her hands, checked the cake was rising and picked up the local paper to look at the motoring page.

One of the dealers had a couple that looked reasonable and having nursed her old Volvo through all kinds of crises and negotiated the purchase of her van, she wasn't a woman scared of used-car salesmen.

She circled them, planning to take a look at them in the morning as a text dropped in from Jake.

Any word from Lucy? J x

She hadn't bothered him, knowing that he would be in meetings all day. In meetings but still finding time to think about Lucy.

She'll know tomorrow.

About to sign off, she paused. Like the children, her business had been her territory and Jake had made a point of standing back, not interfering. Now, with that 'Seize the day' mantra still running through her head she added,

You're right about that motorbike. I'm going to buy a pick-up truck for Cal. Something beefy. Any ideas? A x

New or used? Or maybe leasing would be a better option? Check with your accountant. J x

I'm checking with you, damn it . . .

Do you know when you'll be home?

I'm booked on the 18.05 so if there are no delays or diversions it will be eightish.

Don't eat. There'll be steak and I've baked your favourite cake. A x

She was still standing there, holding her phone, thinking about the future, when it rang, startling her so that she nearly dropped it.

After a fumble she saw that it was Poppy. She pulled herself together. "Hi, Poppy. Are you having a good time?"

"It's okay, although the boat is a bit cramped. There's nowhere to get away from each other, be private," she said.

Concerned, Abby said, "You don't have to stay, Poppy. I could pick you up and run you to the station."

"No, it's fine but I'm really looking forward to lunch tomorrow."

Obviously Ross couldn't hear her. "You're alone now?"

"We needed milk and bread. Ross was cleaning things down and I didn't expect to be here for so long so I needed some things. I'm in the bookshop having a cup of coffee. I'm calling because you asked if anyone had gone to see Fay, with flowers?"

"Oh, yes. Thanks for getting back to me."

"I'm not going to be much help. I asked Ross and he said that Kevin had mentioned that someone ought to go and check on her but it couldn't have been him, because he was with me the next day." She paused, gave a little shrug. "Most of it, anyway."

But not the day after, Abby thought. Poppy had left the Queen's Head just after lunch on Saturday and Fay had been killed sometime later that same day. So where was Kevin all that afternoon and evening? Was he drowning his sorrows in his hotel room, or throwing poor Fay's body in the river?

"Did he ask Ross to go?" Abby asked.

"I asked him," Poppy replied, "but he was the last person to want to take Fay flowers or offer her sympathy."

Possibly.

"And under the circumstances he wouldn't have asked you?" Abby prompted, phrasing it as a question.

"God, no."

"So who else was there? She didn't have any friends on the set, did she? Neither did Daisy come to that."

"No. I feel bad about that. Maybe if I'd made more of an effort Daisy wouldn't have been such a cow." She stopped.

"Sorry, but she made it clear from the outset that I had no business being there."

"I imagine she saw you as a threat, Poppy, especially as Kevin was pushing you forward, but there's no point dwelling on it. As you said, it's a tough business but it's never a bad idea to make friends on the way up."

"Because you'll need them on the way down," Poppy finished. "I'll make a poster and stick it on my bedroom wall."

Abby laughed. "Good idea. And I did have an idea for you. When you and Kevin are pitching your gardening show for the younger viewers, make it clear that you consider yourself a novice," she said, going for tact, "and suggest making the show about learning together. It might just be different enough to catch the production company's interest."

Poppy was quiet for a moment. "That is so clever, Abby. I'll talk to Kevin," she said. "And I do mean talk."

"Well, good luck, but if we could get back to Fay. Could the cameraman have gone to see her?" Abby asked. "The one at the show, I mean. I noticed it was someone different yesterday."

"OB cameramen — outside broadcast, I mean — are mostly freelance," she said. "He wasn't part of the crew; he was covering all kinds of events. Honestly, I can't think there was any one of us that Fay would have wanted to see. Kevin probably asked the office to send some flowers and left it at that."

Which was exactly what he'd done.

But there were still the daisies to account for. Where had they come from?

"Have the police been to see you?" she asked.

"They came and took statements from us both this morning. They wanted to know where we were on Thursday morning and Saturday afternoon and evening. Is that when Fay was killed?"

"All I know is that she was found early on Sunday morning," Abby told her.

"It's horrible. I'd assumed she'd killed herself, but it said on the news that the police were investigating. Do they know any more about what happened?"

"Who knows? Are we still on for lunch tomorrow?"

"Totally. Fingers crossed that the weather holds."

CHAPTER THIRTY-FIVE

Abby had hoped for a peaceful evening, but when Sophie arrived home from school she picked up Princess and retreated to the den without a word.

Abby took her a slice of cake and cold drink. "Can I help?" She sat beside her, arm out for a hug.

"No one can help." And then as her daughter collapsed against her, the tears came. "Chloe's going to live in Dubai with her daddy."

"What?" Emma hadn't said anything about moving, but then again, she hadn't seen her.

All it took was a phone call to clear up that it was a visit, not a move, by which time Tom was home and, having announced that he was going to fail his Maths exam, stomped off to his bedroom. He was followed by Lucy, much earlier than expected. Cal saw her to the door, hovering at a safe distance, shook his head at Abby's offer to stay for supper and, looking tragic, left.

"Don't ask!"

Abby raised her hands, backing off, and picked up a mug.

"And I don't want tea and sympathy from you or Cal."

"Is this about the interview or have you had a row with Cal?"

"Both. I'm going to have a bath."

"Good idea. Use the lavender—" Lucy let the kitchen door slam — "bath gel," she finished. "Tea and sympathy, Patch?" she asked cat number two, who was rubbing against her legs, hoping for a treat. "Yes, please."

Treat offered and accepted, Patch allowed herself to be picked up and carried to the sofa, where they sat until Tom, driven by hunger, emerged from his room.

"What's for dinner?" he demanded.

Abby shrugged. "I don't know. What do you feel like cooking?"

"Me?"

It was an automatic reaction. Having married a man who had never had to lift a finger for himself, she'd made sure her son knew one end of a saucepan from the other.

"If you're not going to revise for your exam you might as well make yourself useful."

He thought about it for a moment, then opened the fridge door. "Sausages?" he suggested. "Jacket potatoes? Baked beans?"

"Vegetables?" Abby prompted.

"Roast vegetables?" When she didn't answer he looked at her. "Are you all right, Mum?"

"A cup of tea would help," she said.

"Make that two." Lucy wafted in in a cloud of lavender, her hair wrapped in towel, and joined Abby on the sofa. "I'm sorry about the bad temper and the door slam."

"Don't make a habit of it," she said. "Do you want to tell me what happened?"

"Nothing happened. I just saw the other candidates. They were graduates and I was there in my school uniform!"

"What?" Abby had been so caught up with Daisy and Fay that it hadn't occurred to her to suggest taking something to change into. "Lucy! I'm so sorry. I should have thought."

"No, it was down to me. I was so focused on making sure I had everything with me, what I was going to show them, that it never occurred to me to think about clothes."

"And they knew you were coming from school."

"I know but, honestly, the woman was blonde and had a sleek bob cut that had 'London salon' written all over it and she was wearing gorgeous black linen wide-leg trousers with a silky black top that slid off one shoulder."

"Really? Is that suitable for a job interview?"

"This is PR, Mum. Image is everything."

"And the other candidate?"

"Male, uber casual, designer jeans, a rock-band T-shirt and the kind of hi-tops that cost telephone numbers. You can just imagine the looks they gave me."

"Actually, I can. I imagine they were thinking that this girl, this young woman, must be really special if she's still at school and she's competing with us really cool people."

Lucy managed half a smile. "I bloody well hope so."

"What about the interview?" Abby asked, choosing to ignore the 'bloody'. "You didn't let the clothes thing put you off?"

"Oh, no. I went in first. I didn't see them until I came out."

"They were both waiting?"

"One of them must have arrived very early, although Jaz did apologise for keeping them waiting."

"Jaz?"

"Jaz Lawson. He told me to call him Jaz. He asked a lot of questions about how I'd planned to get Daisy's attention. They'd seen it on the news."

"And Cal?" Abby asked.

"Poor Cal. He was going to take me to that new vegetarian restaurant in Bath but when I saw those two and realised how stupid I must have looked I was so angry with myself." She took a breath. "I shouldn't have taken it out on him. He tried so hard to be kind but telling me that I was lovely and my clothes didn't matter just made it worse."

Poor Cal.

"Why don't you dry your hair, put on something that makes you feel good, get your apologies out of the way and then take him to the old vegetarian restaurant in Maybridge," Abby suggested.

She was gone before Tom brought over the tea. "Don't worry. I can manage two cups," she said.

There was still Jake and the way her day was going her next text would be one saying that his flight had been cancelled.

It wasn't a text. He called from a taxi.

"There's a problem with air traffic control. I'm on my way to a hotel."

"The steak will keep until tomorrow." Then, "Jake?"

"Abby?"

"Will you marry me?"

The shocked silence lasted seconds too long, then he said, "Damn it, Abby, why would you ask me that when I'm four hundred miles away?"

"Bad mistake," she admitted, "but you can give me your answer when you get home tomorrow. I'm having lunch at the Pike and Heron. I'll meet you at the houseboat just after two."

CHAPTER THIRTY-SIX

Abby might have spent the evening thinking about what kind of wedding she wanted, but she'd already had the big day, the big dress, a gazillion bridesmaids and her picture in the county magazine. She'd let Jake choose how they'd do it, assuming that he was still up for it.

Instead she called Theresa Elliott to invite her up for coffee and a chat the following morning about working for her.

She didn't hesitate.

Then Megan called. "I've found Nathan Peterson."

"Where?"

"In the 'In Memoriam' column of *The Times*. He died just over a year ago. There's an anniversary message — '*In loving memory of Nathan Peterson, after a long illness. QLB.*'"

"Oh . . . It was love then."

"So it would appear. On a brighter note, I've had an offer for the Lodge. It's a bit short of what we'd hoped, but they pointed out that the boathouse is in need of complete restoration."

"It needs pulling down and rebuilding."

"Which was allowed for in the asking price. I might be able to squeeze a little more . . ." She mentioned the sum.

"Don't squeeze, Megan. Take it."

"If you're sure?"

"Absolutely. If they think they've got a good deal then we'll all be happy."

"If they want the grounds perfect for wedding photographs they're going to need gardening services. I'll make sure they know that you're the best in the area, as well as being right on their doorstep. If you want it," she added.

"Maybe Eric and his team could restore the boathouse."

Abby sat for a while, then called Katherine Hamilton to let her know that her granddaughter would soon be getting her portion of the estate.

They chatted for a while, mostly about the garden, and then Abby called Quentin.

"Abby? Is there a problem with the beech hedge?"

"No, Quentin, no problem. I just wanted to say that I'm sorry things got a bit awkward between us."

"Oh . . . Well, that's good of you after some of the things I said. I'm afraid I'm past my sell-by date when it comes to gold medals, but I'll never get used to weeds in show gardens."

"You're not alone," she said. "And like all fads and fashions it will pass."

"No doubt, but I've decided to retire. You were quite right about the white garden. I've apologised to Katherine and she has been very gracious about it and I would like to apologise to you for my behaviour when we were filming. I read about what happened . . ."

"It was a grim for a while," she said, "but you've been going through it, too. I saw your 'In Memoriam' notice for Nathan Peterson in *The Times*—"

Quentin spluttered. "How on earth — That's private!"

She wondered if he was regretting his apology to her already.

"*The Times* isn't private."

"Nathan died a year ago. Why bring this up now?"

She took a breath. "It came up as part of the investigation into Daisy's death."

"I was a suspect?"

"You had a motive and it was you who called the cottage and asked if she was dead. I was there, Quentin."

People sound different on the phone — accents are more pronounced — and when she'd called him about the beech hedge, she'd heard a touch of the west country lilt that he had worked hard to eradicate from his voice.

"So stupid . . ." He sighed. "I regretted it the moment I did it. Have you told anyone?"

"No, and I won't. The reason for my call is that I turned the part of the garden where I found the baby's bones into a nature sanctuary. There's a memorial for him and we planted a tree for Howard. I'm going there tomorrow to plant a rose for my husband's mother and I wondered if you'd like to spend a little time there. Maybe bring something native to plant for Nathan. It's very private."

There was a moment of silence. "That's kind of you, Abby. I'd be honoured but I'm leaving quite early."

"Then let's do it at dawn."

* * *

The following morning, leaving Lucy to take care of breakfast, Abby left the cottage at sunrise, collected the rose and her tools from Earthly Designs and went across to the part of the garden that she maintained as a nature sanctuary

For a moment the birdsong ceased, but she was still, breathing in the scent of the honeysuckle and roses, and after a little while it started up again.

There were signs that the bug hotel created by the children had been in use, and the flowering shrubs and roses were alive with insects.

She knew exactly the spot for Sarah's rose and had the hole dug out by the time Quentin let himself in at the gate.

He watched her knock the plant out of its pot, loosen the roots and dust them with a fungal powder to help them grow. "Can I help?" he asked.

251

"You could hold it straight while I fill around it," Abby said.

"Sarah is a lovely rose, such a good scent," he said.

She firmed it in with her boot and watered it and then stood for a moment.

"That was the name of your late husband's mother?"

"Sarah Finch. She's been missing for forty years. I've been searching for the last year, but there comes a point when you have to accept that she isn't there to be found."

"I'm sorry." He took a breath. "I planted an oak for Nathan in my garden."

She nodded. "A good choice for a man. The children planted that one over there for their father." She indicated the oak sapling, then walked him around the garden, showing him the memorial plaque for the baby whose bones she'd found a year ago and the poetry path that Izzy had commissioned for Howard. "'Remember me when no more day by day you tell me of our future that you planned,'" she read from the inscription.

He nodded. "Rossetti . . ."

"You and Nathan found each other again," she finally said when they were sitting on the old garden bench.

"I lost him for a long time," Quentin told her, "but then one day there was a knock on the door, and when I opened it . . ." He struggled to continue for a moment, then looked at her. "It was as if he'd never been gone, Abby."

She nodded. She knew that feeling.

"He'd been living rough. Drugs, alcohol . . . but a charity had got him into rehab, he was clean, and for a while we had the life we should have had, but eventually the bad stuff caught up with him. He needed a liver transplant but he ran out of time."

"And you blamed Daisy?"

His shoulders shifted in an awkward shrug. "It's what you do. When your life gets messed up and blaming yourself is too painful."

"You weren't to blame, Quentin. You were very young."

"No one was to blame. Nathan had been living a lie too, for far longer than I had. He'd married young, had a family, but when we met . . ." He smiled at the memory. "It was the first time for both of us."

Abby, a lump in her throat, reached out and put her hand over his.

"It was easy to cast Daisy as the villain but she was shocked, hurt and she hit back with everything at her disposal. Her complaint to the college cost him his job."

"He could have been prosecuted," Abby pointed out.

"They talked her down from that, for me as much as for him. He had no choice but to resign. But Daisy felt cheated so she wrote a tear-stained letter to his wife telling her what she'd seen."

"First love is so intense."

He stared at her. "Love?"

"It had to have been love," Abby said, "to have hurt that much."

"It didn't feel like love. It felt like hate." He sighed. "They're two sides of the same coin, aren't they?"

"What happened?"

"One day Nathan was there and the next he was gone. He told me when we found each other again that that the university had warned him not to contact me. And, having tossed a hand grenade into Nathan's life, Daisy disappeared too, until I switched on the TV and there she was — sweet, sweet Daisy Dashwood, who within weeks became everyone's darling."

Anyone, Abby thought, would be bitter. She was sorely tempted to tell him about Daisy's pregnancy, about Fay, but without confirmation, she knew it was not safe.

It was the kind of sensitive information that should be passed on by someone qualified to deal with such an emotional situation.

If the DNA confirmed it was Fay then Dee would arrange for a trained counsellor to be with him while they took a DNA swab and to see him through the result.

"The weird thing is," he said, "that now she's gone I feel . . ." He shook his head. "I feel as if there's nothing left."

Abby took his hand and held it for a moment. "Stay here as long as you like, Quentin. I have to get on, but come over for coffee before you go."

"Actually, I'll get off now, Abby, but thank you for this. I couldn't bring anything today, but maybe I could come again in the autumn? I could plant some primroses for Nathan if they would be acceptable?"

"Give me a call and we can do it together."

She waved him off, gathered her tools, cleaned them off and returned them to their rightful places.

Once inside, she put the coffee machine on, made some toast and looked through the list of calls she had to return, including those from the journalists interested in doing an article. If she was taking on more staff, she needed to keep the work coming in.

Jake phoned from the airport to let her know that things were back to normal and all things being equal he'd be home mid-morning. He'd go into the office first then meet her at the boathouse.

Kate arrived, helped herself to coffee and took it across to the greenhouse. The shutters and watering were automatic, but the plants had to be turned.

Once it reached nine o'clock, Abby began her phone calls. They mostly went to voicemail and she left a message. Then, remembering her promise to Jake about Italy, she sent him a text asking him for dates.

There was no reply so presumably he was on the plane.

Theresa arrived at ten. Abby showed her around and explained that while everyone did the basics, the weekly maintenance jobs, with her dramatic flair she would be given the opportunity to take on design work.

At eleven she went home for a shower and to change for her boat trip. It was hot enough for a pair of smart longer shorts and a T-shirt. It was a bit too neat, a bit mumsy, she thought, looking at her reflection. If only she had a silky top that slid off the shoulder . . .

CHAPTER THIRTY-SEVEN

"Abby!"

Poppy waved as she saw her walking down the quay alongside the old woollen mills that were now expensive apartments with fancy restaurants and designer boutiques on the ground floor — a magnet for holidaymakers drawn by the river and the Cotswold villages within easy reach.

She stepped aboard the yellow-and-white *Lucky Duck*. "Gosh, this is bigger than it looked in the photograph."

Ross, standing at the wheel, smiled. "Welcome aboard, Abby."

"How great to have a friend who'll loan you something like this," she said, looking around. She'd half-expected one of the old, slightly battered family-owned boats that had been on the river for years, but the *Lucky Duck*, if not new, still had a shine.

"He's working in Saudi at the moment, so I take care of it while he's away," Ross said. "Will you cast off, Poppy?"

"My partner keeps talking about getting a boat," Abby said. "Can I look around?"

"Help yourself." Ross started the engine and headed out on the river. "Why don't you take Abby inside and show her around, Poppy, and then sort out some drinks?"

"This is neat." Abby took in the tiny, fitted kitchen. "Do you cook or eat out?"

"Ross is a very good cook." Poppy opened a door to her left. "There's a shower and loo in here, although it's actually called a head for some reason. This is where we sit and eat but it can be converted into sleeping quarters. And my room — cabin — is through here."

"It's all very compact," Abby said, her eyes fixed on a small laptop lying on the bed. Shiny, expensive, it was identical to the one that Abby had seen in Daisy's pantry.

"It's a nightmare for someone as untidy as me," Poppy said, picking it up and tucking it into the zipped compartment on the side of her suitcase.

It had given Abby a momentary turn to see the laptop lying there, but it couldn't be the same one. Why would Poppy have it? She wouldn't be able to exploit Daisy's recipes. It was Daisy's name on the product that was valuable, not the ingredients. The only people the computer could be of use to were Tessa Anderson and Patrick Farrell.

"Any chance of a beer?" Ross called.

"Coming," Poppy called back. "What would you like, Abby? Wine, a G&T?"

"Oh, nothing for me, thanks." She went back outside. They'd come further than she thought. "Do you still want to see Daisy's cottage?" she called down.

Poppy emerged with a glass of wine and bottle of beer, which she handed to Ross. "I do." She looked along the bank. "Where is it?"

"It's the one with the willows."

Ross slowed, drifting towards the bank so that Poppy could have a closer look just as a sudden gust shifted the trailing branches sideways to reveal a glimpse of the cottage.

"Oh, it's lovely and there's a landing stage. Can we stop, just for a minute?"

"Your wish is my command." Ross expertly lined up the boat alongside the landing stage. "Hop off and tie her up."

Because of the low rainfall, the boat was below the landing stage and Poppy had to reach up and use one of the posts to haul herself onto it and tie up.

Abby felt distinctly uncomfortable. "I'm not sure this is appropriate. It's a crime scene and—" in an attempt to put them off — "there'll be security cameras."

"No, Daisy didn't have any," Ross said.

"Oh?" Abby turned to look at him. "How do you know that?"

"We were filming here one day and Kevin asked her if she was troubled with intruders. She told him that the willows were all the privacy she needed."

He followed Poppy's example and clambered up.

"They are very large," Abby agreed. And despite what he'd told Poppy, he did remember them.

"Are you coming?" Ross hung onto a post and leaned forward to offer her a hand up.

"No, thanks. I've seen the garden."

She imagined Poppy would take her time looking around, but it seemed no time before she was grabbing hold of one of the posts and scrambling back down into the boat.

"You were right, Abby. That felt totally wrong." Poppy snatched up her wine and her teeth chattered against her glass as she took a long swallow.

"Are you okay?" Abby asked.

"No." She shuddered. "I know it's silly but I was barely into the garden when I had that thing . . ."

"Thing?"

"What my grandmother used to say was a goose walking over your grave. I just had this feeling that it was where Fay . . ." She took another gulp of wine and managed a feeble laugh. "My mother always said I had an overactive imagination but honestly, it really creeped me out."

She did look pale.

Ross returned and took his time about casting off. With a glance to the rear to make sure there was nothing coming, he headed the *Lucky Duck* back out into the river.

Abby, her arm around Poppy, thought the whole incident odd.

She couldn't understand why Poppy would want to go into a garden where someone had just been murdered or why, when he'd earlier pretended not to recognise Daisy's cottage from the river, Ross clearly remembered the two majestic willows.

And why wasn't there a police presence? She understood the reason for the lack of crime-scene tape, but even though Forensics must have been through the cottage and garden, to leave the place unattended seemed . . . strange.

Both she and Poppy were very glad to reach the Pike and Heron and walk into its cheerful garden filled with huge tubs of yellow and white daisies.

"I need the loo," Abby said. "What can I get everyone to drink?"

"A glass of white wine," Poppy said. "They have a good New Zealand Sauvignon."

"They do," Abby agreed. "Ross?"

"It's okay, I'll get the drinks," he said. "I want to look at their guest beers. What can I get you, Abby?"

Ever since the stop at Daisy's cottage the atmosphere in the boat had changed and Abby, remembering Megan's warning to keep her eye on her drink, planned to monitor hers.

Swallowing down her unease, she smiled. "I'll have a glass of water with my lunch. I have to drive out to Beaumont Court this afternoon."

"Surely it's all being pulled down?" His look suggested he knew it was just an excuse.

"It is," she said, well aware how quickly a simple lie could get complicated. "My team have been working on it since the show closed, but it's my responsibility to check that everything is left the way we found it."

"Water it is, then," he said. "Since you'll be driving."

She left him discussing the qualities of the beers on tap with the landlord and, once in the ladies, took out her phone and texted Dee.

I'm with Poppy Jensen and Ross Mason and we're having lunch at the Pike and Heron. Poppy has a laptop exactly like the one missing from Daisy's cottage and really oddly, they stopped just for a minute at Daisy's cottage. It feels a bit weird to be honest.

Dee's reply was almost instant.

We saw them. We couldn't leave a man in place full time so we installed security cameras. They didn't look at the garden. They just had what looked like an intense discussion then left.

Abby typed back:

Poppy said a goose walked over her grave. She was convinced it was where Fay was attacked.

It didn't look like that. Did you notice the way they had their hands all over those posts? Too late if they were hoping to cover up the fact that they've been there before. We'll be taking DNA from everyone today. Where are you now?

In the loo. We're just about to order. After lunch I'm walking up to the houseboat to meet Jake. Anything on Ross?

We're having trouble finding him. But on the DNA front the results are back on Fay. She is not Daisy's daughter.

What?! That was a shock.
"Are you okay, Abby?" Poppy called.
"Just coming . . ."

Aware that she'd spent rather more than a pennyworth of time, she flushed and, finding Poppy waiting for her, said, "Time of the month."

She washed her hands and followed Poppy back to the table in a secluded corner of the garden, close to the river.

"What are you going to have?" she asked. She noticed they'd left her the seat nearest the water.

Poppy looked up from the menu. "I'm tempted to try the prawn linguine."

"It's one of my favourites." Abby hadn't bothered to look at the options. "You won't regret it. Ross?"

He put down his menu. "The steak. Rare."

He started to get up, but Abby, still on her feet, said, "No, it's my treat." She retrieved the large menus before he could argue, managing to catch her glass with the corner, splashing Poppy before sending it flying onto the grass.

"Oh, lord, what a klutz! I'm so sorry, Poppy."

"It's fine." She grabbed a napkin from the holder on the table and mopped her leg. "No damage done."

"Thank goodness they use these unbreakable glasses outside." She picked it up. "I'll get a refill while I order the food." Not waiting for either of them to respond, she walked back into the bar.

"I spilled my drink, Rich," she said.

"It was just water?"

"Yes." She mentally rolled her eyes, blaming Megan and Dee for the fact that she was jumping at shadows.

Rich filled a fresh glass for her while she gave the food order to Frankie, his wife, and paid.

There was a beep on her phone. Lucy . . .

I've got it! I've got the internship!

The text was followed by a string of excited emojis.

Brilliant news. Congratulations. Tell Jake!

She managed a few emojis of her own, wishing that she was with Lucy and Jake instead of Ross and Poppy.

Duh! Have already. See you later.

"All done." She returned to their table. "And I've just had an excited text from Lucy. She's got the internship she was after with a PR company."

"Oh, that's exciting," Poppy said.

"There'll be celebrations tonight," she agreed. They were sitting in the sun and, mouth dry, she took a drink of water. "Now you both know all about me," she said, working to the script she'd prepared in her head to find out more about them, "what about you two? How did you end up working in television?"

"Why? Do you fancy it?" Ross asked, his apparent amusement just short of a sneer.

"Doesn't everyone?" She made an effort to sound astonished that he'd even asked.

"There's nothing glamorous about it, not when you're an assistant director." He went on to tell her a long and complicated story about the production companies he'd worked for, most of whom appeared to have gone broke.

Frankie arrived with their food and they sorted themselves out with a flutter of napkins, unwrapping cutlery, finding mustard for Ross, and once they'd started eating he carried on with his boring life history until he got to *The Potting Shed*.

Frankie returned to check that their food was okay and ask if they wanted any more drinks. Abby, who was finding the heat oppressive, asked for a jug of tap water.

She took off her hat and, as she fanned herself, she noticed that the tub of daisies nearest to them had a patch of bare stalks. As if someone had cut themselves off a bunch.

She had a feeling that could be important, but she was feeling a little dizzy and as she attempted to spear a prawn she discovered that the fork was too heavy to hold. Everything was too heavy.

"Are you okay?" Poppy asked.

"I think there's going to be a storm." *The daisies* . . . "I hope you'll be okay on the boat."

"We're leaving this afternoon."

"Oh, right. Good timing." She forced a smile. "So you've told me all about your job, and Poppy told me that she's from an army family in Warminster, but what about you, Ross? Where's your home, your fam—"

"You are always asking questions, Abby," he said, cutting her off. "You're quite a celebrity in Maybridge."

"Hardly." The smile was still there but Abby sensed something off in his manner. She had to make herself smile back as she shrugged and said, "Just the statutory fifteen minutes of fame for my gold medal."

"I'm sure they'll put that in your obituary."

"Obit—" Her eyes began to water and the last thing she wanted was the food in front of her.

"But there's a lot more to you than gold medals," Ross insisted. "I checked you out online and discovered that people seem to die around you. Your husband, a couple of old people last Christmas." He paused. "Daisy and Fay."

"That's not . . ." Abby began, but her throat was suddenly dry. Where was that water? "I don't—"

"Oh, I know you didn't kill them," Ross said.

"No . . ." That's not what she was going to say . . .

"I'm not suggesting that you killed them, but you have quite a reputation for digging out who did. You've been asking questions all around *The Potting Shed* ever since dear Daisy took a dive into the grass. And now you're asking about my family."

Abby looked at Poppy, but she was staring at her nails.

"Just making conversation," she managed.

"The truth is there's not much to tell. My mother didn't want me and I don't know who my father is. I was adopted, handed over to strangers."

And in that moment, despite the fuzzy head, the fact that her eyes were watering and she was finding it a struggle to remain sitting upright, Abby realised what had been staring her in the face for a week.

That while they'd all been thinking that Daisy must have had a daughter, they were wrong.

She'd had a son.

Tall, fair, good-looking . . . Not like Quentin. Quentin had been beautiful, a 'golden lad', Megan had called him.

She tried to reach for her glass but it was empty and it hit her like a sledgehammer that while she'd been keeping an eye on Ross, it was Poppy's glass that was very close to her own. Poppy, who'd been flapping napkins, covering up what she was doing with her hands. Poppy, who was sitting there with an odd little smile on her face . . .

"It was both of you." She fumbled in her pocket for her phone but before she could do anything with it Poppy grabbed her wrist.

Abby's head was telling her to shake her off, but her eyes were doing weird things and her hand wasn't getting the signals.

"Be careful," Poppy said. "You might drop it."

And she watched, helpless, as a blurry Poppy took her phone and tossed it into the river. "Oops."

"You killed your mother because she gave you up," she said, a slur in her voice. "Poppy . . . ?"

"I helped because I love him."

Oh, sugar . . . Poppy had a degree in drama. She was an actress and she'd been acting all along. In front of the camera, with Kevin — with her.

And she was sitting far too close to the river. All it would take was for Ross to stick out his foot and give her chair a push and she'd fall in, probably banging her head on the wooden piles before sinking down to where her phone was lying with that last message.

See you later.

Where the hell was Frankie? Tables were filling up but the nearest couple were engrossed in their menu and the message to move wasn't getting through to her legs.

"Ross told me all about Daisy," Poppy said. "Someone who'd been there at the mother and baby home got in touch to tell him who his mother was. She'd seen her on the television, all sweetness, and that made her so angry. She told him that sweet Daisy wouldn't even hold him after he'd been born, wouldn't even look at him."

"Too painful," Abby managed. "How did you kill her?"

"She was always on about a herbal tea she drank to lower her blood pressure. We just added a few drops of a beta blocker in her water bottle to help her out. After that her blood pressure dropped like a stone. Just the way yours is dropping now."

CHAPTER THIRTY-EIGHT

"I'm sorry I was so long," Frankie said arriving with a jug of water. "Rich was in the cellar putting on another barrel." She paused when she realised that no one was eating. "Is there a problem?"

Water . . . Abby said the word in her head but no sound emerged.

"Abby isn't feeling very well," Poppy said, standing up. "We need to get her back in the boat so that she can lie down."

"Abby?" Frankie bent closer. "What's wrong? Do you want me to call Jake?"

"We're taking her to Jake," Poppy said. "At the houseboat."

I didn't—

I didn't tell them about the houseboat! She was screaming but no sound was making it out. How did they know about the houseboat?

Because while she'd been making enquiries about them, they'd been checking up on her.

"That's the best thing," Frankie said. "He'll take good care of her."

No! No! Frankie!

But Frankie, with a pub full of customers, was already hurrying back to the bar as Ross took her arm and hauled her to her feet. "Come on, Abby, it's time for a little boat ride."

No . . .

She stumbled over feet that didn't know what they were doing.

Poppy grabbed her other arm and held her up.

"She's had one too many in this heat," Ross said to a man who'd looked up from his menu and was staring at them.

She tried to open her mouth, tell him that they were lying, that they were going to kill her, but her throat seemed to have seized up. They half-carried her to the dock and she felt them tense as they prepared to lift her onto the boat.

Once they had her on board they were going to dump her in the river and they wouldn't make the same mistake they had with Fay. They'd take her downstream, where the current would carry her far away . . .

"I've got her," Ross said and, as Poppy stepped back, he bent and caught her behind the knees.

She was nearly six foot — it was her curves that had got her the hot date for the school prom with Howard all those years ago — and she was a dead weight.

He staggered, took a step back and then a voice said, "She's mine. Put her down."

Poppy gave a shriek of alarm and leapt into the boat. Ross dropped her and jumped in after her followed by a couple of familiar figures in uniform.

Abby landed on the dock with a grunt and then Jake was there, lifting her head so that she could drink from the water bottle he was holding. It was cool, sweet, and she drank it down, feeling it her giving her back her life.

"Jake . . ."

"Dee rang and suggested I join you for lunch. And she said that if you weren't feeling too good, I should give you water," he said.

Always there when she needed him . . .

"Am I really yours?" she said.

"You'd better believe it."

* * *

266

"You cut that fine," Abby said the following morning. She'd been given a clean bill of health and discharged from the hospital. "I thought I was going to have to dive into the river and drink that."

"Too fine." Having seen her into his car, Jake climbed behind the wheel. "Next time I might be too late. "

"No," she said. "The superpower is in full working order."

"Wrong answer. There isn't going to be a next time. Damn it, Abby, when I saw you — You were so white, looked so out of it that I thought—"

She took his hand. "I'm sorry."

"I know. You always are." He sighed. "I thought we'd agreed that you weren't going to do this again."

"I didn't go charging in. I wasn't poking a hornet's nest. I told everyone where I was going," she pointed out, "and who I would be with. And Dee acted the minute she discovered that Ross Mason wasn't his real name. Full blues-and-twos response," she said. "But I'm glad you got there first."

"Only because I'd already decided to collect you from the pub. Iain Glover knows exactly how I feel about the way he involved you in this."

"He only asked me to look at Daisy's paperwork."

"But he knows you. You will get involved . . . What on earth were you thinking, going off on a boat with those two?"

"How was I to know he was Daisy's son? Or that he and Poppy had known each other for ever and spent years planning his revenge?" She stopped. None of that was important. "Will you still marry me if I ask you?"

"Will you give up hunting down murderers?" he asked.

"How many murderers is one person likely to come into contact with in a lifetime?"

"That's a no, isn't it?"

"Would it be a deal breaker?"

"Why don't you ask me?"

"Will you marry me, Jake Sullivan?"

"I thought you'd never ask."

"I'm sorry it's taken me so long. Let's go home."

* * *

267

"I can't believe that Ross was Daisy's son," Megan said later that day.

Abby and Jake had a full house. Megan, June and Beattie were all there to make sure that she was fully recovered, Dee and Iain to explain what they'd found out.

Dee cleared her throat. "Ross wasn't Daisy's son. Our inquiries have confirmed that the child Daisy was carrying was premature and did not survive."

"Then what on earth . . . ?"

"He was a fantasist," Abby suggested.

"That would appear to be it," Iain agreed. "He told us that a woman who worked in a mother and baby home told him about Daisy being there, then said, probably as joke, that he looked like her and suggested he write to her."

"That's awful . . ."

"He became obsessed with the idea that she was his mother. He must have written to her because we found a letter from her in his flat. Daisy was sympathetic," Dee said, "but she explained that it was not possible and even wished him well in the search for his real mother. But she didn't explain that her baby had died, so he didn't believe her."

"He would have felt rejected all over again," Jake said.

Abby quietly took his hand beneath the table.

"He continued to send letters insisting that she was his mother. Her solicitor confirmed that they warned him that if he wrote again they would seek an injunction," Iain said. "The letters stopped after that."

"The letters, but not the obsession."

They were sitting at the dining table, the bifold doors open to let in the scent of the roses. Lucy carried over a pot of tea, a cafetière and a tin containing the shortbread Abby had made.

"But how did Poppy get involved?" Megan asked.

"They met at a party at university. He told her his tragic story and according to him it was her idea to kill Daisy and then come forward as her long-lost son to claim his inheritance."

"That's ridiculous," Jake said. "A DNA test would disprove it in a minute."

"What does Poppy say?" Megan asked.

"She's going for the 'innocent who was fooled by a brilliant sociopath'. But Kevin Tarr told us that she knew about Daisy's blood pressure. He'd been warned that his was on the high side and she was there when Daisy told him all about her wonder tea and offered to give him some."

"Poppy stole some of Kevin's blood pressure medication and added that to Daisy's water bottle, which Ross picked up in the marquee after the show and discarded in a bin in town."

"So he's admitting it all?" Jake asked.

"He's still convinced he's Daisy son and he believes the truth will come out during the trial. He's planning to sell his story to one of the tabloids."

"I still don't understand why Poppy got involved," Abby said.

"It happens," Iain said. "She's not the first to be drawn in by an obsessive."

"But how did Ross get on the television show?" June asked.

"He got a place as a mature student at Bath," Dee explained, "and then managed to get an internship at the production company, which is based in Swindon. Once he got into the team working on *The Potting Shed*, he introduced Kevin to Poppy."

"They were setting him up as the patsy should Daisy's death come under suspicion?" Megan suggested.

"I think Fay was in line for that role." Abby said. "Her 'suicide' was supposed to put an end to any inquiries. Unfortunately Poppy hit her too hard."

"Poppy?"

"I don't suppose there's any physical proof, but that little scene when we pulled up at Daisy's garden . . . She knew I'd spotted the laptop and needed to tell Ross. She should have stuck to acting. She was very good at it." Abby shivered at the memory. "She took Fay the daisies they cut from one of the tubs at the Pike and Heron, killed her and stole the little laptop for Ross. Maybe she thought there would some proof on there."

"Poor Daisy. Poor Fay," Megan said.

"I have one final piece of information for you, Abby." Dee said. "You'll be relieved to hear that Daisy's cousin wasn't murdered by Fay. She died from an aggressive form of breast cancer."

"What about Anderson and Farrell?" Megan asked. "What's going to happen to them?"

"They sound like a double act," Beattie said.

"And that's what they are. Tessa Anderson is in dire financial trouble, while Daisy was raking it in. She got together with Farrell, who also has money problems, and they devised a scheme to part Daisy from a large chunk of her assets. They are currently under investigation for fraudulent conversion."

* * *

Later that evening, after everyone had left, they'd raised a toast to Lucy, eaten yet another takeaway and the children were about to make a getaway before they were asked to clear up when Jake, very serious, said, "Don't rush off."

"It's okay, I'll clear up," Sophie said, with a weary sigh.

"Thank you, Sophie, but that's not it."

"He got you!" Tom said and Sophie scowled at him.

"Shut up, you two," Lucy said. "What is it, Jake?"

"First I want to thank you for saying yes when I asked if it was okay to date your mother," he said. "I want to sincerely thank you for sabotaging the pull-out bed at Christmas and then for insisting that I stay in case I froze to death in the houseboat."

"You're welcome," Tom said.

"Now I have another question to ask you. It's the big one. Is it okay with all of you if I marry your mother?"

"Shouldn't you ask her that?" Lucy said.

"Well, she's the one doing the asking . . ." He let out a yelp as Abby elbowed him in the ribs. "Okay, I asked first, but it involves all of you, so what do you say?"

"It's about time," Tom said.

Lucy smiled. "I second that."

"Sophie?" Jake prompted.

She shrugged. "Okay, and I'll be a bridesmaid, but no frilly dresses."

Jake turned to her. "Abby?"

"No frilly dresses," Abby promised. "You can wear whatever you like."

"Okay, then."

"Where will you get married?" Lucy asked.

"Jake can decide." She turned to him. "Church, register office, Melchester Castle." She grinned. "That fancy hotel where we had the school prom?"

"I vote for the houseboat," Tom said before Jake could answer.

Lucy rolled her eyes. "Don't be ridiculous. They can't get married on the houseboat. It hasn't got a licence."

"Red tape," he muttered. "I suppose they'll have to do the official bit at the register office but then they can do the soppy stuff at the houseboat and we can have a party on the riverbank."

"It's Jake's decision," Abby insisted.

"I'll go with the houseboat," he said, taking her hand.

"Great. We can decorate it." Lucy reached for her notebook and called up Pinterest. "But it'll have to be soon, while it's still summer."

"Soon as you like."

"Where will you go for your honeymoon?"

"Well, Paulo's offered us his villa for the summer but it's too big for two so I thought we could all go," Jake said. "Abby?"

"That sounds perfect."

THE END

THE JOFFE BOOKS STORY

We began in 2014 when Jasper agreed to publish his mum's much-rejected romance novel and it became a bestseller.

Since then we've grown into the largest independent publisher in the UK. We're extremely proud to publish some of the very best writers in the world, including Joy Ellis, Faith Martin, Caro Ramsay, Helen Forrester, Simon Brett and Robert Goddard. Everyone at Joffe Books loves reading and we never forget that it all begins with the magic of an author telling a story.

We are proud to publish talented first-time authors, as well as established writers whose books we love introducing to a new generation of readers.

We won Trade Publisher of the Year at the Independent Publishing Awards in 2023. We have been shortlisted for Independent Publisher of the Year at the British Book Awards for the last four years, and were shortlisted for the Diversity and Inclusivity Award at the 2022 Independent Publishing Awards. In 2023 we were shortlisted for Publisher of the Year at the RNA Industry Awards.

We built this company with your help, and we love to hear from you, so please email us about absolutely anything bookish at feedback@joffebooks.com

If you want to receive free books every Friday and hear about all our new releases, join our mailing list: www.joffebooks.com/contact

And when you tell your friends about us, just remember: it's pronounced Joffe as in coffee or toffee!

Milton Keynes UK
Ingram Content Group UK Ltd.
UKHW030959080824
446563UK00004B/244